BY JANET EVANOVICH

TOP SECRET
TWENTY-ONE

TOP SECRET TWENTY-ONE

A STEPHANIE PLUM NOVEL

Janet Evanovich

BANTAM BOOKS NEW YORK

Copyright © 2014 by Evanovich, Inc.
Pros and Cons copyright © 2013 by The Gus Group LLC

All rights reserved.

Published in the United States by Bantam Books, an imprint of Random House, a division of Random House LLC, a Penguin Random House Company, New York.

Bantam Books and the House colophon are registered trademarks of Random House LLC.

Pros and Cons by Janet Evanovich and Lee Goldberg was originally published separately in a digital edition by Bantam Books, an imprint of Random House, a division of Random House LLC in 2013.

ISBN 978-0-345-54292-2
eBook ISBN 978-0-345-54294-6

Printed in the United States of America on acid-free paper

www.bantamdell.com

2   4   6   8   9   7   5   3   1

First Edition

TOP SECRET
TWENTY-ONE

ONE

I WAS PERCHED on a barstool in a dark, noisy, overpriced restaurant in Princeton, New Jersey. I was wearing a red dress that was too tight, too short, and cut way too low. And I was wearing an earbud that connected me to a guy named Ricardo Carlos Manoso, aka Ranger.

My name is Stephanie Plum. I usually work as a bond enforcement agent for my cousin Vinnie, but tonight I was moonlighting as a lookout for Ranger. Ranger was stalking Emilio Gardi, a man many considered to be untouchable. Gardi had friends in high places, an army of thugs guarding his body, and money to burn, and his enemies tended to disappear without a trace. He was currently facing a racketeering charge in Miami, but he'd decided to keep his dinner date in Jersey rather than attend his court hearing in Dade County. This meant that the idiot who'd been dumb enough to post a bond for Gardi was out big money unless Gardi was dragged back to jail. The idiot happened to be Ranger's cousin.

Ranger owns Rangeman, a small high-tech, high-end security firm. Ordinarily Ranger doesn't do bond enforcement, but tonight he was making an exception. He was standing off to the side at the entrance to the dining room, and he was watching Gardi.

Gardi was wearing a tan sports jacket over a shirt with red and yellow flowers printed on it—the South Beach–meets–JCPenney look. He was in his fifties. He was balding. He was built like a fireplug. He was drinking red wine and eating rack of lamb, having a good time, entertaining three other men who were laughing too hard at his jokes.

Ranger was in his usual black—a perfectly tailored black suit, and a black dress shirt open at the neck. The Glock at the small of his back was also black. Ranger's body is perfect. His hair is very dark brown. Cut short. His eyes are dark brown and intense. His skin is the color of hot chocolate, the lucky result of his Latino ancestry. His earbud matched his skin tone and was barely detectable.

Standing beside Ranger was a guy named Tank. Tank is big and solid and lethal. He'd been with Ranger's unit in Special Forces, and now he's second in command at Rangeman and watches Ranger's back.

I didn't see any of Gardi's henchmen. They'd waited for him to take his table and then left the room.

"The room is clean," I said to Ranger via the earbud.

Ranger moved forward, his gaze never wavering from his quarry. Eye of the tiger. I've seen him focus like this on other takedowns, and it always raises the hair on my arms and at the nape of my neck.

Tank was steps behind him, surveying the rest of the room. Ranger unbuttoned his jacket to get better access to his gun and handcuffs. He stopped behind Gardi, put his hand on Gardi's shoulder, and said something to him, close to his ear.

Gardi shrugged Ranger away, said something I couldn't hear, and everyone at the table laughed.

Ranger didn't laugh, and even at a distance I knew things were about to get ugly. Ranger made another civil attempt, Gardi got angry and brushed him off, and in one swift move Ranger snatched Gardi out of his chair like a wolverine rooting out a groundhog.

In a heartbeat Gardi's head was smashed onto the table, everyone grabbed their drinks, and Ranger cuffed Gardi behind his back and handed him over to Tank. Ranger told the table he was sorry for the intrusion and followed Tank and Gardi out of the room. The whole episode had taken maybe a minute.

A Rangeman vehicle idled in front of the restaurant, ready to take Tank and Gardi back to Rangeman headquarters in center city Trenton. In the morning Gardi would be escorted onto a plane and extradited to Miami.

My job done, I turned back to my black sambuca. Okay, I know they put food coloring in the sambuca to make it black. Don't care. It's sexy. And I swear the black tastes better. I guess

I could also say that about Ranger. Not that he's my boyfriend or anything, but we have had a moment.

I downed the sambuca, paid my tab, and went outside to meet up with Ranger. The Rangeman SUV was pulling away, and Ranger was waiting for me beside his black Porsche 911 Turbo.

"Babe," he said.

"Babe" covers a lot of ground for Ranger. It can be a simple greeting, or a warning that a tarantula is sitting on my shoulder. Tonight it came on the heels of a full body scan, and I was pretty sure it suggested he liked my dress.

Ranger slipped an arm around me, leaned close, and kissed me. The kiss was a further indicator that he liked the dress. In fact, the kiss suggested that while he liked the dress a lot, he wouldn't mind getting me out of the dress as soon as possible. And I was thinking that was a great idea. Fortunately we were in Princeton, and my apartment was at least a half hour away if the traffic was moving. I was going to need that time to talk myself out of sleeping with Ranger.

Ranger keeps me safe from everyone but himself. He's the panther stalking the gazelle, keeping all other predators away. He enjoys the hunt. And I enjoy being the gazelle, although truth is I'm more prairie chicken than gazelle.

Ranger's reflexes are quicker, his brain engages faster, his instincts are far superior than the average man's. My skin heats under his touch, and his kiss sets delicious things in motion in my body. I know from past experience he's magic in bed. I also know he has dark secrets that take precedence over personal relationships. And I know it's in my best interests to keep him at arm's length.

Plus, I sort of have a boyfriend.

Ranger pulled out of the restaurant lot, stopped for a light, and his hand went to my knee and traveled north.

"Um," I said.

He cut his eyes to me. "Is there a problem?"

"Your hand is moving up my leg."

"And?"

"We've talked about this."

"Not lately," Ranger said.

"Has anything changed?"

"No."

"Well, then."

"Is that a definite 'Well, then'?"

"Afraid it is."

"Too bad," Ranger said.

Thirty minutes later, Ranger parked behind my apartment building and walked me to my door.

"Call me if you get lonely," he said.

"I have you on speed dial," I told him.

A barely perceptible smile twitched at the corners of his mouth, he gave me a light kiss, and he left.

Truth is, I would have liked to invite him in, but that wouldn't have been the smart thing to do. Not that I always do the smart thing, but tonight I'd managed to keep from grabbing him and ripping his clothes off. Two points for Plum.

I let myself into my apartment and went to the kitchen to

say hello to my hamster, Rex. Rex lives in an aquarium on my kitchen counter and sleeps in a soup can. He was running on his wheel when I looked in on him.

"Hey," I said. "How's it going?"

Rex blinked his round black eyes at me and twitched his whiskers. That's about as complicated as our conversations ever get. I dropped a peanut into his cage and he jumped off his wheel, shoved the peanut into his cheek, and scurried into his soup can with it.

· · ·

My cousin Vinnie's bail bonds office is on Hamilton Avenue. It's a one-story storefront building with some parking spots by the back door. Vinnie has an inner office where he hides from people he's stiffed, pissed off, infected with herpes, or previously incarcerated. Vinnie looks like a weasel in a pimp suit. His wife, Lucille, is a saint. His father-in-law, Harry the Hammer, owns the agency and didn't get his nickname because he was a carpenter.

Connie Rosolli, the office manager and guard dog, was at her desk when I walked in.

"How'd it go last night?" she asked.

"It was good. Ranger walked up to Gardi, yanked him out of his chair, and cuffed him. Very smooth."

"And?"

"That was it."

"No naked Ranger in your bed?"

"Nope."

"Disappointing," Connie said.

Tell me about it. "Anything new come in for me?"

"I have a failure-to-appear. High money bond. Jimmy Poletti."

"He owns all those car dealerships, right? He shoots his own commercials. 'Make a deal with Jimmy!'"

"Yeah, turned out some of the deals were taking place in the back room and involved underage girls imported from Mexico."

I took the file from Connie and paged through it, stopping to look at Poletti's mugshot. Very respectable. Sixty-two years old. Face a little doughy. Thinning gray hair. Crisp white dress shirt and striped tie. Nice dark blue suit jacket. Looked more like a banker than a car dealer.

"Boy," I said, "you never know from looking at someone."

The front door banged open, and Lula stomped in. At 5' 5", Lula is a couple inches too short for her weight. She's a black woman who changes her hair color like other women change their underwear, and her fashion preferences run to tiny spandex skirts and tops. Almost always she overflows out of the skirts and tops, but it seems to work for her.

"I just got a traffic ticket," Lula said. "Do you believe it? What's this world coming to when a woman can't even drive to work without this harassment?"

"What's the ticket for?" Connie asked.

"Speeding," Lula said.

I looked over at her. "Were you speeding?"

"Hell, yeah. I was doing forty-three miles an hour in a thirty-mile-an-hour zone and Officer Picky pulled me over. There should be a law against thirty-mile-an-hour zones. My car don't want to go that slow. It's painful to drive thirty miles an hour."

"I've got donuts," Connie said, gesturing to the white bakery box on her desk. "Help yourself."

Lula's face brightened. "That helps perk up my mood. I'm taking one with sprinkles. And maybe one with chocolate icing. And look at this one with the pink gooey stuff oozing out of it."

Lula bit into the one with the sprinkles. "What happened last night with you and Mr. Tall, Dark, Handsome as Hell, and Hot?"

"He captured Gardi. No shots fired."

"And?"

"There's no 'and.' "

"Say what? There's no 'and he got naked and waved his magic wand'?"

"Nope," Connie said. "No magic wand. She didn't get to see the wand."

"Well, you know he got one," Lula said. "How come he didn't wave it and make her a happy princess?"

Connie and Lula looked at me, eyebrows raised, waiting for an explanation.

"It was a job," I said. "It didn't involve his . . . wand."

Lula shook her head. "That is so sad. Opportunities wasted. What did you wear? Did you wear some dumpy business suit?"

"I wore the little red dress."

"I know that dress," Lula said. "It's definitely wand-worthy."

Vinnie stuck his head out of his office. "What's with all the yammering? I can't hear myself think in here. And why aren't you out catching some scumbag? I'm out big money for Jimmy Poletti. Go drag his butt back to jail."

Vinnie slammed his door shut, and Lula stuck her tongue out at him.

"I saw that," Vinnie yelled from inside his office. "Have some respect."

"How'd he see that?" Lula asked.

Connie pointed to a camera newly installed over Vinnie's office door. "He's got security cameras all over the place."

Lula gave the camera the finger.

"I saw that too," Vinnie yelled.

I shoved Poletti's file into my messenger bag and hiked the bag up onto my shoulder. "I'm heading out. It shouldn't be hard to find Poletti. It's not like he's a gangbanger."

"He's sort of a TV star," Lula said. "I wouldn't mind going with you to see what he looks like up close."

We went out the back door and stood looking at our two cars. Lula was driving a red Firebird, and I was driving a rusted-out Ford Explorer.

"Probably," Lula said, "we should take your car in case we have to shoot him. It won't matter if he bleeds out in *your* car."

"We're *not* going to shoot him."

"You don't know that for sure," Lula said.

"He's a businessman. He was wearing a suit for his mugshot.

He's not going to go nuts on us. And besides, we don't shoot people . . . hardly ever."

Lula buckled herself into the passenger seat. "I'm just saying."

It was nine o'clock Monday morning. It was August. It was hot. It was humid. The air had a brown tinge to it and sort of stuck to your eyeballs and the back of your throat. It was summer in Jersey.

I had my shoulder-length curly brown hair pulled up into a ponytail, and I was wearing jeans and a red tanktop. Lula was wearing a black satin bustier from her Wild West 'Ho House collection, and a poison green skirt that came just a couple inches below her doo-dah. Lula is shorter than me, but there's a lot more of her. I could be naked standing next to Lula, and no one would give me a second glance.

TWO

JIMMY POLETTI LIVED in an upper-end neighborhood on the western edge of the city. According to the bio Connie had given me, he was on his third wife, had two adult sons, and owned a second home on Long Beach Island.

I took Hamilton to Broad and then cut onto State Street. I turned off State and wound around until I found the large brick colonial that belonged to Poletti and his wife, Trudy. I pulled into the drive court, and Lula and I got out and took it all in. Professional landscaping. Four-car garage. Two stories. Oversize mahogany front door. Dog barking somewhere inside. Sounded like a small dog.

I rang the bell, and a woman answered. She was slim. In the vicinity of forty. Long brown hair. Dressed in black Pilates pants and an orange fitted short-sleeve tee.

"I'm looking for Jimmy Poletti," I said.

"Take a ticket," she told me. "We're *all* looking for him."

"Does that mean he isn't here?"

"Last I saw him was at breakfast on Friday. I went to my Pilates class, and he was gone when I came back."

"Did you report it to the police?"

"No. I didn't see much point to it. It's not like he was kidnapped."

"How do you know he wasn't kidnapped?"

"He left me a note telling me to remember to take the garbage out on Monday and Thursday."

"That was it? Nothing else in the note?"

"That was it."

"No sign of struggle or forced entry here?"

"Nope."

"Did he take anything with him?"

"Some clothes. One of the cars. He took the Mustang."

"And you haven't heard from him?"

"Not a word."

"You don't seem too upset."

"The house is paid off, and it's in my name. And he left the dog and the Mercedes." She checked her watch. "I need to run. I'm late for Pilates."

"Guess it was one of them love matches with you and him," Lula said.

"Yeah," Trudy said. "I loved his money, and he loved himself."

I gave her my card. "I represent his bail bonds agent. I'd appreciate a call if you hear from him."

"Sure," she said, and slammed the door shut.

Lula and I got back into my Explorer.

"I don't think she's gonna call you," Lula said.

I dialed Connie.

"Did you check on his dealerships?" I asked her. "Has he been going to work?"

"One of them was shut down. I spoke to the managers of the remaining two, and no one's seen him since his arrest. I guess he talked to them on the phone a few times. But not since he disappeared."

"Do you have addresses for his kids?"

"One is in North Trenton, the other's in Hamilton Township. I'll text Lula the street addresses and also places of business."

I returned to State Street and headed for North Trenton.

"His one kid lives on Cherry Street," Lula said, reading Connie's text message. "And it looks like he works at the button factory."

Twenty minutes later I parked in front of Aaron Poletti's house. It was a narrow two-story row house, similar to my parents' home in the Burg. Postage-stamp front yard with a small statue of the Virgin Mary in the middle of it. American flag hanging from a flagpole jutting out from the tiny front porch.

"It's a pretty Virgin," Lula said. "I like when they got a blue dress like this one. It looks real heavenly and peaceful except for the chip in her head. She must have gotten beaned by a baseball or something."

Lula and I went to the front door, I rang the bell, and a young woman with a toddler on her hip answered.

I introduced myself and told her I was looking for her father-in-law.

"I do *not* know where he is," she said. "And he certainly isn't welcome here. He's a horrible person. I mean, *honestly,* I have a little girl, and what he was doing was *so awful.*"

"Has he been in contact with your husband?"

"No! Well, at least not that I know. I can't imagine Aaron even talking to him."

"Aaron works at the button factory?"

"He's on the line. His father wanted him to be part of the business, but Aaron declined. They've never gotten along."

I gave her my card and asked her to call if she learned anything new about her father-in-law.

"Okay, so she's not gonna call either," Lula said when we were back in the Explorer. "Jimmy Poletti's not gonna hide out there."

Probably true, but you never know for sure.

"We gonna go to kid number two now?" Lula asked.

"Might as well."

Kid number two lived in an apartment in Hamilton Township. According to Connie's information he was twenty-two, single, and worked as a fry cook at Fran's Fish House on Route 31.

The apartment complex consisted of three unimaginative redbrick chunks of building hunkered down around a blacktop parking lot. Each building was two stories with a single door in its middle. Landscaping was nonexistent. This was not a high-rent deal.

I parked, and Lula and I entered the center building and took the stairs to the second floor. The building was utilitarian. The hall was dimly lit. Probably that was a good thing, because the carpet didn't look wonderful. We found 2C and rang the bell.

The door got wrenched open, and a skinny guy peered out at us. He was around 5' 10", with bloodshot eyes, bed-head hair, reeking of weed, and his arms were decorated with burn scars, which I supposed were from working the fry station. He was wearing pink boxers with red hearts on them.

"Oswald Poletti?" I asked.

"Yeah. You Girl Scouts selling cookies?"

"Nice shorts," Lula said.

He stared down at them as if he was seeing them for the first time.

"Some girl gave them to me."

"She must hate you," Lula said.

I introduced myself and told him I was looking for his dad.

"Haven't seen him," he said. "We aren't close. He's an even bigger dick than me. I mean, dude, he named me Oswald."

"Do you know where I might find him?" I asked.

"Mexico?"

I gave him my card and told him to call me if anything turned up.

"We're batting zero," Lula said when we got back into the car. "You're not gonna get a call from him 'less he needs cookies."

"So Jimmy Poletti's kids don't like him. And his wife doesn't like him. Who do you suppose likes him?"

"His mama?"

I called Connie. "Do you have an address for Jimmy Poletti's mother?"

Two minutes later, the address appeared in a text on my phone.

"She lives in the Burg," I told Lula. "Elmer Street."

"This is getting boring. No one wants to talk to us. No one knows nothing. This keeps up and I'm gonna need lunch."

I turned off Hamilton at Spring Street and two blocks later turned onto Elmer. I drove one block and pulled to the curb behind a hearse. The hearse was parked in front of the Poletti house, and the front door to the house was open.

"That don't look good," Lula said. "That looks like someone else who isn't gonna talk to us. Unless it's Jimmy. Then hooray, case closed."

I got out and walked to the house and stepped inside. A bunch of people were milling around inside. Two guys who looked like they were from the funeral home, an old man who was dabbing at his nose with a tissue, a man in his fifties who was more stoic, and two women. I knew one of the women, Mary Klotz.

"What's happening?" I asked Mary.

"It sounds like it was her heart," Mary said. "She's been sick for a long time. I live across the street, and the paramedics were always here. I'd see the lights flashing once a week."

"The two men . . ."

"Her husband and a relative. I think he's a nephew or something."

"No sign of her son?"

"He didn't come around much. I imagine you're looking for him."

"He didn't show for his court date." I gave her my card. "I'd appreciate a call if you see him."

Lula was waiting for me in the car. Lula didn't like dead people.

"Well?" Lula said.

"Poletti's mother. Sounds like a natural death. His father is still alive, but I didn't get to talk to him. I didn't want to intrude."

"Did you see her?"

"No."

Lula gave a whole-body shiver. "Gives me the creeps just being here. You know there's spirits swirling all around the house. I could practically hear them howling."

"Howling?"

"That's what they do! They come to get the dead person's soul. Don't you ever go to the movies? You ever see any of them Harry Potter films? Anyways, I'm getting hungry. I could use a Clucky Burger with special sauce and bacon and some cheese fries."

I took Lula to the drive-thru at Cluck-in-a-Bucket, then dropped her off at the office and headed for my parents' house. They live a short distance away, in the heart of the Burg, in a duplex house that shares a common wall with a very nice widow who is older than dirt. She lives a frugal existence off her husband's pension, has her television going every waking minute, and bakes coffee cakes all day long.

My Grandma Mazur was at the door when I parked in front
of the house. Grandma came to live with my parents when my
grandfather went to the big reality TV show in the sky. We
hid my father's shotgun a month after Grandma moved in.
There are times at the dinner table when his face turns red, his
knuckles turn white, and we know we did the right thing by
removing temptation. My mother has found her own way to
cope. She drinks. Personally, I think my grandmother is a hoot.
Of course, I don't have to live with her.

"Just in time for lunch," Grandma said, opening the screen
door. "We're having leftover meatloaf sandwiches."

I followed Grandma into the kitchen. My parents don't
have central air. They have freestanding fans in all the rooms,
an air conditioner hanging out of a living room window, and
similar air conditioners in two of the bedrooms. The kitchen
is an inferno. My mother accepts this with quiet resignation,
her face flushed, occasionally dripping sweat into the soup pot.
My grandmother doesn't seem to be affected by the heat. She
says her sweat glands stopped working when her ovaries went
south.

I took a seat at the small kitchen table and dropped my bag
onto the floor.

"Are you after Jimmy Poletti?" Grandma asked. "I heard he
skipped out on his bail bond."

"I talked to his wife and both his sons, and no one seems to
like him or know where he's hiding."

"Yeah, he's a real stinker. His own mother didn't even like
him."

"I tried to talk to her too, but she's dead."

"I heard," Grandma said. "Rose Krabchek called an hour ago. Mrs. Poletti is going to be laid out at the funeral home on Hamilton. It's going to be a good viewing. She's high-profile now that her son is a fugitive."

The Burg doesn't have a movie theater, so everyone goes to viewings at the funeral parlor on Hamilton Avenue.

"Any gossip going around about Jimmy?" I asked Grandma.

"Haven't heard anything that would be useful. He had a house at the shore, but I'm told it washed away with that last hurricane. I saw pictures, and the beach isn't even there. What happens with that? Does he own part of the ocean?"

My mother put plates and paper napkins on the kitchen table. "Who wants a meatloaf sandwich?"

I raised my hand. "With lots of ketchup."

"And chips," Grandma said. "I want one with chips and a pickle."

My mother is an older version of me with shorter brown hair and a thicker waist. My grandmother used to resemble my mother, but gravity's taken its toll and now Grandma has slack skin the color and texture of a soup chicken and steel gray hair permed into tight curls. She's of an age where she's fearless and has enough energy to light up Cleveland.

"Jimmy Poletti wasn't real popular with his family," Grandma said, "but he sure could sell cars. He was one of them personable people on television. If I was in the market, I'd buy a car from him. He was always dressed up in a nice suit, and you could see he had a good package."

"He was selling girls out of the back room in his car dealership," my mother said. "He's a disgusting human being."

"I didn't say he was a good person," Grandma said. "I just said he had an impressive package. 'Course, maybe he faked it. Like he could have put tennis balls in his Calvins. Or he could have padded them with toilet paper. Do you think men do that?"

I had two men in my life, and neither of them needed tennis balls.

My mother brought the meatloaf sandwiches to the table and took a seat. "I'd see his second wife at mass sometimes. Sometimes she'd have bruises. Just terrible. She'd be praying and crying, poor woman. We were all relieved when she left him."

"I met his *third* wife," I said. "I don't think she's going to be in church crying and praying."

"You just never know," my mother said. "A man like that doesn't value life. He would do anything."

"This is good meatloaf," my grandmother said, taking a bite of her sandwich. "I like that you put barbecue sauce on top of it."

"I saw it on the Food Network," my mother said.

"And it's real moist."

My mother chewed and swallowed. "I soaked it in bourbon."

THREE

I LEFT MY parents' house and returned to my apartment. I have some search programs on my computer, and I thought I'd do some snooping around on Poletti. I live in a perfectly okay but not fantastic apartment building on the north edge of Trenton. The building has a fancy door that fronts the street but is never used. Everyone parks in the large lot at the rear. Eighty percent of the residents are senior citizens who wear their handicapped status as a badge of honor and judge the quality of their day by how close they're able to park to the building's back door.

My apartment has one bedroom, one bathroom, a small kitchen, and a combined living-and-dining room. My furniture is sparse and mostly secondhand from relatives who made their initial purchases in 1950.

I'd just plugged Jimmy Poletti into a background search program when someone pounded on my door. I went to the door, looked out the security peephole, and saw nothing. I turned to go back to my computer and there was more pounding. I did another look out the peephole.

"Down here," someone yelled. "Look down, you moron."

I knew the voice. Randy Briggs. Not one of my favorite people. He was my age, with sandy blond hair. He was about three feet tall. And he was cranky.

I opened the door. "What?"

"How is that for a greeting?" he said, pushing past me into my apartment. "It's because I'm short, right? You hate me because I'm short."

"I don't care that you're short. I like lots of things that are short. Little dogs and daffodils. I hate you because you're mean as a snake. Would it kill you to be nice?"

He looked up at me. "Why do you say that? Did you hear something?"

"About what?"

"About killing. Like that someone wants to kill me."

"So far as I know, everyone who meets you wants to kill you."

"I'm serious. Did you hear about a contract?"

"On you?"

"Yeah. I'm in trouble." He went into my kitchen and looked around. "You got anything to drink? I could use a drink. Vodka rocks would be good."

"I haven't got any vodka."

"How about wine? You got a nice pinot noir?"

"I think I have a beer."

"I'll take it."

I opened the beer and handed it to him. He chugged it down, wiped his mouth with the back of his hand, and gave me the empty bottle.

"I suppose you want to know about the contract," he said.

"No."

"How could you not want to know?"

"Easy. Not my business."

"Yeah, but we're friends."

"I don't think so."

"Boy, that's harsh. After all we've been through together." He went back out into the hall and returned with a duffel bag.

"What's that?" I asked, staring down at the bag.

"My stuff. I need a place to stay."

"Not here."

"Why not?"

"I don't like you."

"Yeah, but my apartment got blown up. I need to stay with someone who's got a gun."

"Oh no. No, no, no, no."

"I won't be any trouble. Look at me. I'm little. You won't even know I'm here."

"I know you're here because I have a sharp burning pain behind my left eyeball."

I grabbed his duffel bag and ran for the door with it. He grabbed my leg, and I went down to one knee a couple feet short of the door.

I tried to shake him loose. "Let go!"

"Not until you say I can stay."

"Never."

"Please, please, please. I'll be nice. You gotta help me. I don't want to die. Jimmy Poletti is trying to kill me."

"Jimmy Poletti?"

"Yeah, he looks nice on television but he's a nasty bugger."

"Why does he want to kill you?"

"I did his bookkeeping. I know all his secrets. The money laundering, the payoffs, the offshore accounts."

"He obviously hired you because he knew you were a slime bucket, so why does he suddenly think you're a threat?"

"When he got arrested, the cops were climbing all over everything. We managed to get rid of the paperwork, but I'm left swinging in the wind."

"He's worried you'd rat him out?"

"Yeah."

"Would you?"

"Hell, yes."

"Have you gone to the police?"

"No. I'm sort of implicated in the cooked books. At first, my choice was to die or try a plea deal, but then I thought of you. If you can bring Poletti in, he'll get locked up for a hundred years and he won't kill me. And I won't have to talk to the police."

"Okay, I'll buy all that. But why do you have to stay *here*?"

"No one else will let me in."

"I'd buy that too."

"You gotta help me," Briggs said. "I'm a dead man without you. You know what's left of my apartment? It's in that duffel bag. Good thing I was in the basement doing laundry when he rocketed the firebomb through my living room window. The guy's nuts!"

And he wanted Randy Briggs. And I had Randy Briggs. So maybe I could somehow use Briggs as bait to capture Jimmy Poletti.

"What?" Briggs said. "You've got that look. The scary look that means you're thinking."

"I might let you stay if you'll help me find Poletti."

"Anything." He released my leg. "What do you want to know?"

I took my hands off the duffel bag and stood. "Do you have any idea where he's hiding?"

"Not exactly," Briggs said, "but I know where he owns property, and I know some of his mob friends."

"Would his mob friends hide him?"

"Depends if they thought they could get their hands on his money. He's got a *load* of money stashed away."

"Do you know where the money is stashed?"

"Who, me? No."

"You do! That's why he wants to kill you."

"It's not like I have access to it. I just might know where he keeps it."

Oh boy. "What else?"

"That's it. I swear."

I spread a map of Trenton out on my dining room table. "Where are his properties?"

"There's the three dealerships," Briggs said. "You know

about them. Then there's a parking garage where he keeps his inventory. It's by the government buildings. He rents part of it out. It's at the corner of State Street and Norton. So far as I know there aren't any offices in it. It's just parking. He has the house in West Trenton. I'm sure you've already been there and met Poletti's soulmate." Briggs gave an involuntary shiver. "She scares the crap out of me. They had a house at the shore, but it floated out to sea. He owns a slum on Stark Street that operates as a rooming house. And he owns houses in North Trenton that he rents out."

Briggs used my red Sharpie to put dots on the map, showing the property locations.

"And his friends?" I asked.

"He doesn't exactly have friends. He has *associates*. They all played poker together, and they hung out in the back room of the dealership on Route 41. It was like a social club. Bernie Scootch, Ron Siglowski, Buster Poletti, who's a cousin, Silvio Pepper, and Tommy Ritt. I'm told two of them have disappeared. Bernie Scootch and Ron Siglowski. They could be with Jimmy or they could be dead."

"Do you think Jimmy's cleaning house?"

Briggs shrugged. "He tried to get me while I was crossing a street yesterday. Tried to run me over, but I got out of the way in time. He took a shot at me and missed. And then this morning someone sent a firebomb through my window."

"Are you sure it was Jimmy?"

"It was Jimmy yesterday. I got a good look at him. I guess I don't know about this morning, but I know he's got rocket launchers and flamethrowers. He has a place in the Pine Barrens where he goes with the guys to shoot and blow stuff up. I don't exactly know where it is."

"What was he driving yesterday?"

"The Mustang. I rode in it once. It's all tricked out. Black and silver. Real sweet ride."

"So where do you think I should start looking for Jimmy?"

"If all he wanted to do was hide, I'd say the Pine Barrens until he could get out of the country. Since he seems to want to kill me, I'd have to go more local. Maybe the slum on Stark Street. Or maybe you want to look in the parking garage. See if there's an RV with the air-conditioning running."

I folded up the map and tucked it into my messenger bag. "Let's go."

"Are you sure you want to take me? I've got a big bull's-eye painted on my back."

This was true. And it was the only reason I was even talking to him. Still, I didn't want to hang him out there unless I absolutely had no other choice. No point putting myself in harm's way of stray bullets, right? On the other hand, I didn't feel comfortable leaving him alone in my apartment.

"You can stay in the office while I go look for Poletti. I'll drop you off and pick Lula up."

• • •

"No," Connie said. "No way. No how. You can't leave him here."

"I can't take him with me," I told her. "People will shoot at us."

"Why can't you leave him in your apartment?"

"He'll buy pay-per-view porn and go through my underwear drawer."

We all looked at Briggs.

"He can't even *reach* your underwear drawer," Lula said.

"I can stand on a chair," Briggs said.

"How about we take my Firebird and lock him in the trunk," Lula said.

"How about we auction you off by the pound for a pig roast," Briggs said.

Lula shoved her hand into her purse and started rummaging around. "I got a gun in here somewhere."

"You can't shoot him," I said.

"Why not?"

"I need him to get Poletti. Anyway, you know you can't just go around shooting people. It isn't nice."

"Yeah, but he insulted me."

"You insulted me first," Briggs said. "How'd *you* like to get locked in a trunk?"

"People wouldn't want to lock me in a trunk on account of I got a pleasing personality," Lula said.

"Maybe for a rhinoceros," Briggs said.

I stepped in front of Briggs to keep Lula from hurling herself across the room at him. "I haven't got time for this. I need to get Poletti. We'll take Randy with us, and we'll disguise him somehow. A hat or something, and he can scrunch down in the backseat."

Ten minutes later Randy was in the backseat of my Explorer. He was wearing a platinum blond wig and large black-rimmed glasses. He looked like Andy Warhol if Andy Warhol was only three feet tall.

Lula, looking like a 'ho all dressed up for *Let's Make a Deal,* was riding shotgun. And weird as it might seem, she made it look pretty good. When I'm with Lula, I always feel like she's chocolate cake with a lot of fancy frosting and I'm more in the ballpark of a bagel.

FOUR

I TOOK STATE Street to the parking garage and idled at the entrance. There was a lot of police activity on the second level. I leaned out my window, took a ticket from the machine, and rolled into a ground-level spot.

"Stay here," I said to Lula and Briggs. "I'll go investigate and report back."

I took the stairs and walked to the back of the garage, where cop cars were angle-parked and yellow crime scene tape was already in place. I spotted Joe Morelli standing inside the taped-off area. He's part of the Crimes Against Persons unit, mostly working homicide cases, so someone was probably dead on the cement floor.

Morelli also happens to sort of be my boyfriend. He's six feet tall and all lean muscle. He has a lot of wavy black hair, his brown eyes can be soft and sexy or hard and assessing, he's got a dog and a toaster, and his grandmother is even crazier than mine. Today he was wearing a blue dress shirt with the sleeves rolled to his elbows, jeans, and running shoes. He had his Glock clipped to his belt, and his hands were on his hips as he stared down at the guy sprawled on the pavement.

I ducked under the crime scene tape and moved next to him. The guy on the ground was facedown in a pool of dried blood. He had a hole in the back of his head the size of a potato.

"Holy crap," I said to Morelli, "he looks like he's been shot with a cannon."

"It's the exit wound," Morelli said. "Whoever killed him flipped him over. Half his brain is splattered on the silver Honda over there."

A wave of nausea rolled through me, and I felt myself break out in a cold sweat.

"You're kind of white," Morelli said. "You're not going to do the girl thing and faint, are you?"

"'The girl thing'? Excuse me?"

Morelli grinned. "You're such a cupcake."

I sucked in some air and made an effort to settle my stomach. So big deal if I *am* a cupcake. Seemed to me it was a lot better than being a bagel.

"Who is he?" I asked.

"Tommy Ritt."

"Oh boy. He's one of Poletti's poker buddies."

"And you're after Poletti," Morelli said.

"Yes. That's why I'm here. Poletti owns this property. I was hoping to find him holed up here in a Winnebago."

"Sorry, I haven't seen any Winnebagos." He turned his attention to me. "Mike Kelly said he saw you with Ranger last night."

"It was business."

Morelli continued to look at me with what I call his cop eyes. They're hard and unwavering. An emotionless stare he uses to extract confessions from killers in the interrogation room.

"Not going to work," I told him. "I have nothing to confess."

That got another grin. "You know all my tricks."

I raised an eyebrow, and his grin widened.

"Randy Briggs showed up on my doorstep this morning," I said. "He claims Poletti tried to run him down with his Mustang and took a shot at him. And then someone shot a firebomb into his apartment."

"I heard about the apartment. I didn't know it belonged to Briggs. What's his connection to Poletti?"

"He was Poletti's accountant."

"Ow. Not a healthy job choice. Did Briggs stop by to tell you he was on his way to Argentina?"

"Something like that. I don't suppose you have any idea where I might find Poletti?"

"Not at the moment," Morelli said, "but I'll let you know if something turns up. We'll be looking for him too. He's a person of interest in this shooting."

"He's driving a tricked-out black and silver Mustang. And he's probably packing a rocket launcher."

Morelli ducked under the tape with me and walked me to the stairs. "Bob misses you," he said.

Bob is Morelli's big orange, floppy-eared, shaggy-haired dog.

"I miss him too."

Morelli pulled me behind a van and wrapped his arms around me. "How about me? Do you miss me?"

"Maybe a little."

"The Yankees are playing Boston tonight. You could come over, catch the game, and spend the night."

"No can do."

"Okay, I'll throw in a pizza."

"Tempting, but no."

"Working?"

"If only it was that simple. Briggs is staying with me."

"You hate Briggs."

I blew out a sigh. "I don't *hate* him. I just find him enormously annoying. Poletti exploded his apartment. He needed a place to stay."

The cop part of Morelli's brain put the pieces together. "You're using Briggs as bait to get Poletti."

"I'd rather think of my generosity as a charitable act."

"So why is this charitable act keeping you from spending the night with me?"

"I don't trust him alone in my apartment. He'll drink milk directly out of the carton and sleep in my bed."

"Maybe I can arrest him for something, or you can get

Ranger to shoot him. Nothing serious. A flesh wound that would send him to the hospital for a day or two."

"Boy, you must *really* miss me."

"It's Bob," Morelli said. "Bob's desperate."

Morelli slid his hand under my shirt, kissed me with some tongue action, and I felt heat rush through my stomach and head south. A cop on the other side of the garage yelled for Morelli, and Morelli broke from the kiss.

"Think about it," Morelli said, stepping away, turning toward the crime scene. "Ranger would probably like the opportunity to shoot someone."

I took the stairs to the ground level and returned to my Explorer.

"What's going on up there?" Lula asked.

I put the car in gear and drove out of the garage. "Tommy Ritt is facedown on the cement, and his head has a big hole in it."

"How bad is it?" Briggs asked.

"All the king's horses and all the king's men aren't going to put Tommy Ritt back together again."

"It's Poletti," Briggs said. "He's freaking nuts."

"Where we going now?" Lula asked. "I'm tired of sitting in this car with short stuff here. He's kind of creeping me out in that wig."

"I could take it off," Briggs said, "but then Poletti might put a bazooka up your butt."

Lula glared at him. "Is that a dig at my former profession?

Because I wasn't that kind of 'ho. That's a specialty 'ho what does that."

"Cripes," Briggs said.

I took State Street to Stark Street and counted off blocks. The lower part of Stark wasn't so bad, with legitimate bars, tenement-style apartment buildings, and mom-and-pop businesses. As the street went on it got progressively worse until it resembled a bombed-out war zone where only the rats and the crazies lived.

Poletti's rooming house was on the fourth block of Stark. Not the worst part of Stark, but not the best either. Gang graffiti covered the buildings, and the stoop sitters were blank-faced druggies. I parked across the street from the rooming house, and we stared out at it. Three stories of grime-coated red brick missing a front door. One window on the third floor was painted black, and two windows on the second floor were cracked. Black soot around one of the third-floor windows suggested there'd been a fire. A rat ran out of the open doorway and scurried down the sidewalk.

"We should take a look," I said. "And someone needs to stay with the car to make sure it's not stolen."

We all sat still as statues. Hard to tell if it was worse to stay with the car or go into the building.

"Okay, I'm going in," I said. "And I'll take Briggs with me."

"Hunh," Lula said. "How come I have to be the one to stay behind?"

"You're the one with the gun."

Lula looked at Briggs. "He don't have a gun?"

"It got blown up in my apartment," Briggs said.

I got out of the Explorer, and Briggs hopped out after me. We crossed the street and went into the small entrance hall of Poletti's building.

"I knew it was a slum, but this is worse than I imagined," Briggs said. "It smells like a warthog died in here."

There were two doors on the ground floor. One had MANAGER written on it. I knocked on that door, and it was answered by a small Hispanic woman who was somewhere between fifty and ninety.

"What?" she asked.

"I'm looking for Jimmy Poletti."

"Don't know him."

"He owns this building."

"Good for him. Tell him my toilet don't work."

She attempted to close the door, but I shoved my messenger bag between the door and the frame.

"I'm legal," she said. "I got a driver's license."

"Are you the building manager?" I asked her.

"The what?"

"It says 'manager' on your door."

"No manager here. It must be wrong." And she slammed the door shut.

I turned and hammered on the door across the hall. I heard a lot of scrambling going on in the apartment, and finally a crazy-eyed, emaciated woman answered the door. "There's no butterflies here," she said. "You got the wrong place."

"I'm not looking for butterflies," I told her. "I'm looking for Jimmy Poletti."

"Poletti confetti," she said. "Poletti confetti." She spied Briggs standing behind me and leaned forward for a closer look. "Nice doggy," she said, patting him on the head.

Briggs growled at her, and she jumped back into the apartment and slammed the door shut.

There were four doors at the next level. Two of them were open, and the apartments were trashed. Soiled, lumpy mattresses on the floor. Garbage everywhere. Used drug paraphernalia. A bunch of giant roaches lying sneakers up. Probably overdosed. It looked like someone had had a bonfire in one of the units.

"They weren't cooking hotdogs and marshmallows here," Briggs said.

I knocked on one of the closed doors, and a moment later a shotgun blast blew the top half of the door apart.

"Holy crap," Briggs said, diving to the floor.

The door opened and a totally tattooed guy looked out. Hard to tell his age. Somewhere in his twenties, maybe. I was flattened against the wall with my heart beating hard in my throat.

"Did Jiggy send you?" he asked.

I shook my head no.

"Fuck," he said. "Fucking Jiggy."

I inched my way toward the stairs. "I might have knocked on the wrong door."

Briggs got to his feet and straightened his wig. "You could have killed us, asshole," he said to the tattooed guy.

"I would have been doing you a favor," the guy said. "That's the worst wig I ever saw."

"I'm in disguise," Briggs said. "Do you know Jimmy Poletti?"

"What's he look like?"

"He looks like a fat middle-aged car salesman and slum owner," Briggs said.

The guy shook his head. "Don't think I know him."

"Who lives in the apartment next to you?" I asked.

"About forty Guatemalans," the guy said. "They make noise all night long. They're almost as bad as the damn dogs."

"You got a dog problem?" Briggs asked.

"Feral Chihuahuas. There's a whole pack of them. They'll eat you alive."

I trudged up the stairs with Briggs several steps behind me. Four more units here, but three of them were charred, gutted, and closed off with boards hammered across their doorways. The fourth unit's door was ajar. I stepped in and looked around. One room plus bath. A fridge like you might find in a dorm. Fridge door open. Not plugged in. A double mattress that had been ripped to shreds. A single sneaker about a size 12 and mostly chewed. This was the room with the window painted black.

"Looks like the Chihuahuas were here," Briggs said.

We took the stairs to the street, and we gasped when we saw the Explorer. It was up on cinderblocks, missing all four wheels and some of its innards. No one was around. Just the picked-clean car sitting at the curb all by itself.

Lula was inside, slumped behind the wheel, head back, eyes

closed, mouth open. I didn't see any blood. She wasn't moving. I wrenched the driver's side door open, and Lula snorted and opened her eyes.

"Are you okay?" I asked her.

"Yep. It's like a ghost town here. Nothing going on." She looked straight ahead, out the windshield, and saw that the hood was up. "What's with that?" she asked.

"Someone stripped the car while you were asleep," Briggs said. "Boy, are you stupid."

Lula got out and stared at what was left of the Explorer. "That's just rude. I rest my eyes for a minute, and Mr. Sneaky Thief comes along. These people have no respect. They took our wheels. What's with that? Anyone could see I was in the car and needed those wheels to get home. How am I supposed to get home without wheels?"

Briggs stood on tiptoes and looked under the hood. "They took more than wheels."

I called Connie and asked her to come rescue us.

"Can't," Connie said. "Vinnie isn't here, and I can't leave the office."

I couldn't ask Joe. He was working. I didn't want to ask my father. My mother would have a cow if she knew I was on Stark Street. That left Ranger. He was also working, but he had a lot of flexibility. And if he couldn't personally rescue me, he could send one of his men.

"Babe," he said when I called him.

"Someone took my wheels."

"Your car is on the fourth block of Stark Street."

41

Ranger has the annoying but sometimes life-saving habit of hacking into my cellphone and placing tracking devices on my car. So Ranger knows where I am 24/7.

"Yes, and I'm with my car, but my wheels are apparently someplace else."

There was a moment of silence, and I knew he was smiling. Ranger finds me amusing.

"I'm with Lula and Randy Briggs," I said. "And I could use a ride to my parents' house so I can get Big Blue."

"I'm in the middle of something, but I can send Hal. He's in the neighborhood."

"Is Gardi back in Miami?"

"He's got a nine o'clock flight tonight."

FIVE

BIG BLUE IS a 1953 powder blue and white Buick Road-master that's been retrofitted with seat belts and power brakes. It gets three miles to the gallon, and it does nothing for my self-esteem, as I aspire to be a slick Porsche person. My budget sees me more as a broken-down-junker-car person. My Great Uncle Sandor bequeathed the Buick to my Grandma Mazur, and it now lives in my parents' garage in anticipation of automotive emergencies. Unfortunately, I have these on a regular basis.

Ranger's guy met us on Stark, removed my plates from the Explorer carcass, and drove us to the Burg. I got the car keys from Grandma and backed the Buick out of the garage. Lula and Briggs got in, and we drove to North Trenton to scope out Poletti's rental properties.

"It's the white house coming up on the right," Briggs said.

"Personally, I can't see him in any of these rentals. They're leased through a management company. Strictly investment deals. I'm not sure he even knows he has them."

"No stone unturned," I said. "We'll just do a drive-by unless we see the Mustang or some other sign of Poletti."

An hour later I dropped Lula off at the office and returned to my apartment.

Briggs followed me in and pulled the wig off his head. "I'm hungry. What's for dinner?"

"I was going to have a peanut butter sandwich."

"That's not dinner. That's lunch if you're seven years old."

"What did you have in mind?"

"Steak."

"Are you buying?"

"My money and my credit cards got blown up."

"Then I guess you're not having steak."

Briggs looked in my fridge. "There's nothing in here."

"Not true. I have olives. I put them on my peanut butter sandwich."

"That's sick."

I pulled a box of Froot Loops out of the overhead cabinet. "How about cereal?"

"You don't have any milk."

"And?"

"You're supposed to have cereal with milk."

"These are Froot Loops. They're perfect right out of the box. They're pretty, they don't stick to your fingers, and the box says they're filled with vitamins and minerals."

"Maybe I should rethink this. I'd get better food in prison."

I made myself a peanut butter and olive sandwich and ate it while I leaned against the kitchen counter.

"Where do we go from here?" I asked Briggs.

"We could check out the poker players. Of course, one's dead and two are missing, but last I heard, Buster was still around."

"The cousin."

"Yeah. He was tight with Jimmy. He was the guy Jimmy trusted to go to Mexico to solve labor issues."

"You mean with the cars?"

Briggs ate a handful of Froot Loops. "I don't know. I didn't ask questions. I just tapped in Buster's travel expenses. Hotels and planes and stuff. I came to the dealership on Broad twice a week and cooked the books. It didn't seem like such a big deal. Everyone hates the IRS, right?"

"Do you know where Buster lives?"

"Downtown Trenton. I don't know exactly where. His wife kicked him out of the house and took out a restraining order, so now he lives in an apartment over a pizza place. I think he owns the building."

I went to my computer and ran Buster through a search program.

"He's on the third block of Stark," I said. "So far as I can see, he hasn't got a job."

"He had some kind of deal with Jimmy. He got money under the table. And there's a holding company called Bust Inc. that I think is his."

I gave the last chunk of my sandwich to Rex and grabbed my messenger bag. "Let's take a look at Buster."

"Great, but I'm not wearing the wig. It itches. And it's a stupid disguise. I'm four feet tall if I wear lifts and lie. People figure it out."

"If those people who figure it out start shooting at you, I'd appreciate it if you'd step away from me."

. . .

I rolled down the third block on Stark and slowed as we approached the pizza place. A bunch of guys were hanging in front of it, smoking whatever, trying hard to look bad. Heck, what do I know . . . probably they *were* bad. Probably they were the ones who'd taken my wheels.

"This pizza place is a dump," Briggs said, "but it's full of people."

"Dinnertime," I told him. "It's easy food."

Briggs was sitting on his knees, his nose pressed to the window. "I swear I can smell it! Oh man, would I love a piece of pizza! We should check it out. You want to talk to Buster anyway, right?"

"Right."

I found a parking place across the street from Buster's building.

"I'm going to sit here and watch the second-floor windows," I said to Briggs. "You can run across and get a slice of pizza."

"I'll get trampled. You have to come with me."

"You won't get trampled. I've seen you in action. You've destroyed more knees than pro football."

"Yeah, but then there's usually a riot."

This was true.

"Okay, I'll come with you, but you have to promise not to bite anyone or whack anyone with your iPhone."

The pizza place was just counter service. Strictly takeout. No tables. The room was packed. A single fan spun overhead. No air. We squeezed in and inched along with the rest of the people who were making their way to the counter.

"Do you see the pizza?" Briggs asked. "What have they got?"

"I can't see the pizza. I can't see anything."

"I want extra cheese and pepperoni."

"I'm on it."

"Are we almost there?"

"Yeah. I think so."

I like pizza, but I was finding it hard to believe the pizza here was *that* good. There were other options on Stark. There were a bunch of fast-food pizza places, plus you could dial a pizza and have it delivered. Either this pizza was super cheap or it came with a side of weed.

Five minutes later we had our pizza and were out the door. We crossed the street and leaned against the Buick while we ate.

"This is good," Briggs said. "Greasy, with just the right amount of cheese. Real Jersey pizza."

I finished my pizza, wiped my hands on my jeans, and

looked across the street. The pizza place took up the entire first floor of Buster's building, with the exception of a door at the end. I assumed this door led to the apartment on the second floor. There were five second-floor windows looking out at the street. None had shades drawn. So far, I hadn't seen any shadows pass in front of the windows.

"What's the plan?" Briggs asked.

"We go to the door and ring the bell."

"Suppose no one answers?"

"I call his phone."

"What if he doesn't answer his phone?"

"I write him a letter."

I had the car keys in one pocket, pepper spray in another, and cuffs tucked into my jeans at the small of my back. Just in case.

"Let's go," I said to Briggs. "Let's see if Buster wants to talk to us."

We crossed the street, went to the door, and I was about to ring the bell when I heard someone inside thundering down the stairs. The door was yanked open, and a guy rushed out and slammed into me. He looked at me, then he looked down at Briggs and his face flushed.

"You son of a bitch," Briggs yelled at him. "You blew up my apartment. What the fuck is the matter with you?"

"Jimmy Poletti?" I asked, already knowing the answer.

"Yeah," he said. "What are you doing here with the runt?"

"Runt?" Briggs said, his voice an octave higher than normal, a vein popping out in his forehead.

I grabbed my cuffs and clapped one onto Poletti's wrist. "I represent your bail bondsman."

"Of all the crap luck," Poletti said. Then he gave me a hard shove into Briggs. Briggs went flat on his back, I tumbled on top of him, and Poletti turned and ran. I scrambled to my feet and chased Poletti down Stark. He had a good lead, but I was faster. We ran to the end of the block and around the corner. He cut down an alley, and I was almost at arm's length when he slipped into a building, slammed the door shut, and threw the bolt. It was, I realized, the rear entrance to the pizza place.

Briggs pulled up behind me.

"Stay here in case he tries to sneak back out," I told him. "I'm going around to the front."

"What if he shoots at me?"

"Yell for help."

"I could be dead."

"Deal with it," I said, and I raced back to Stark.

Just as I rounded the corner, Poletti jumped into a car and roared away. The car wasn't the Mustang. It was a small silver sedan. It all happened too fast for me to get the plate or the make of the car.

I took a moment to catch my breath, then I texted Briggs and told him to come around to the front. I rang the bell while I waited. No answer. I called the phone number I had for Buster, but no one picked up, and I couldn't hear the phone ringing upstairs.

"Where is he?" Briggs asked when he reached me. "What happened?"

"He got away."

"Now what?"

I looked at the door that led to the second-floor apartment. It was still open. "We go upstairs and look around," I said.

"Is that legal?"

"Yes. I have reason to believe there's a felon up there."

"Who?"

"Poletti."

Briggs's eyebrows shot up. "Really?"

"No. Not really. Not even *maybe*."

We stepped inside and closed and locked the door behind us. I paused at the top of the stairs and announced myself. "Bond enforcement. Anyone home?"

Silence.

"This is a pretty nice apartment," Briggs said, looking around. "He's got a flat-screen television and a leather recliner. And he's got a real kitchen."

The refrigerator was stocked with food. Dirty dishes in the half-filled dishwasher. An iPhone charger on the kitchen counter. No iPhone. We moved into the bedroom and found a guy stretched out on the floor, staring up at the ceiling.

"Is this Buster?" I asked Briggs.

"No. It's Bernie Scootch. He doesn't look so good. Is he okay?"

Bernie was definitely not okay. He was lying in a pool of blood, and his chest had a bunch of bullet holes in it. For that matter, I wasn't doing so great either. I was clammy with cold sweat and the horror of Bernie Scootch leaking his bodily fluids all over the carpet.

I bit into my lower lip. "I'm pretty sure he's dead."

"Oh jeez," Briggs said. "That's bad. That sucks."

I dialed 911 and gave the dispatcher the address and the big picture. Five minutes later a uniform arrived, with Morelli following. I was on the sidewalk when they angle-parked at the curb.

"I was on my way home from my mom's house when I heard the call come in," Morelli said. "What's the deal here?"

"There's a dead guy upstairs. Randy identified him as Bernie Scootch. He's been shot . . . a lot."

Morelli went upstairs to take a look and returned after a couple minutes. "You're right," he said. "He's been shot a lot. What were you doing in the apartment?"

"I was looking for Jimmy Poletti."

"You had reason to believe he was there?"

"It's sort of a gray area."

Morelli looked like he needed a Rolaid. "You didn't shoot Scootch, did you?"

"No!"

I gave Morelli the long version while more people showed up—the coroner, a crime photographer, a couple more uniforms, the crime lab techs, and Bryan Kreider.

Kreider is another plainclothes cop in the Crimes Against Persons unit. He nodded and smiled at me. "Hey, Steph, how's it going?"

"It's going good except for the dead guy upstairs."

Kreider looked at Morelli. "Have you seen him?"

"Yeah. Multiple bullet wounds. Looks recent."

Kreider trudged upstairs, and Morelli turned back to me.

"So this is Buster's apartment," he said, "but there's no Buster."

"Haven't seen him," I said. "I also haven't seen the murder weapon. It wasn't near the body, and Poletti didn't have it on him."

"You're sure he wasn't carrying?"

"He was wearing a shirt tucked into slacks and there was no gun. Plus he didn't try to shoot Briggs."

The line of Morelli's mouth tightened a little. "Opportunities missed."

The sun was low on the horizon, hidden by the urban landscape. Stark Street was in deep shade. Lights blinked on in Buster's apartment. The customers were beginning to thin out at the pizza place. A few people were standing around, gawking at the police activity, but a murder on Stark doesn't draw much of a crowd.

"I'll pass the information on to Kreider," Morelli said, "and then I'm heading home. I've got Bob in the car."

"I'm heading home too," I said, looking across the street at the Buick. "I've got Briggs in the car."

Briggs was on the edge of his seat when I slid behind the wheel.

"Did you hear them?" he asked, eyes wide, hands braced on the dash.

"Who?"

"The dogs. The Chihuahua pack. I heard them yipping. Like tiny coyotes. And at the end of the block I saw a tiny shadow with glowing red eyes. It was eerie. It gave me goosebumps."

"I didn't hear them. Are you sure you didn't imagine it?"

"I got it on my phone."

Briggs passed me his phone, and I looked at a dark screen with two little red dots.

"This could be anything," I said. "It's just dots."

"Those are the eyes of a wild demon Chihuahua," Briggs said.

SIX

IT WAS A little after nine A.M. when I got to the office with Briggs in tow.

"You look like crap," Lula said to me. "You either had a really good night or a really bad night."

"I had a *horrible* night. Randy and I checked out Buster Poletti's apartment and found Bernie Scootch stretched out on the floor with a bunch of holes drilled into him. That's two dead men in one day! I couldn't sleep. I kept seeing the bodies. And then when I finally fell asleep I had nightmares."

"Sounds like the only one having a worse night was Ranger," Connie said.

I helped myself to coffee. "What's with Ranger?"

Connie's eyebrows went up. "You didn't hear? His building is sealed off. I don't know all the details, but they had to evacuate.

Gardi and one of the Rangeman guys are in the hospital. It's all a big secret. No one's saying anything."

"I bet it's anthrax," Briggs said. "It's always anthrax when they seal off a building."

I tapped Ranger's number into my phone.

"What happened at Rangeman last night?" I asked him.

"There was an incident with Gardi."

"Was it anthrax?"

"No. It wasn't anthrax. I'll catch you later." And he disconnected.

"It wasn't anthrax," I told everyone.

"He's supposed to be a real hotshot in bed," Lula said, "but he sure don't waste any time explaining things."

I made an effort not to smile too wide. "He has his moments."

Lula fanned herself with her copy of *Star* magazine, and Connie did an eye roll.

"Jeez," Briggs said. "Does anybody know I'm standing here? This is an embarrassing conversation. And just to set the record straight, there are some ladies who think *I'm* hot."

"That's a disturbing announcement," Lula said. "I don't want to meet those ladies."

I stepped outside and called Morelli.

"What happened at Rangeman last night?" I asked him.

"I don't know. I haven't been briefed on it, but it must be serious because the building is sealed and the feds are in charge. And Gardi is in St. Francis in isolation with a security guard in front of his door."

"Ranger said it wasn't anthrax."

"Ranger should know."

"Anything new on the two murders? Did Buster ever turn up?"

"Buster came home at ten o'clock. He said he'd been in Atlantic City all day. One of those package deals with a bus trip included. He went with his girlfriend. It checked out."

"How did Jimmy get into his apartment?"

"Jimmy had a key. Buster gave it to him years ago when he first bought the building. He said they were using the apartment like a storeroom, but I'm guessing it was used to house the girls they imported."

"Did you find the murder weapon?"

"No. Not yet."

I've seen enough violent death to know that Bernie hadn't been dead long and that he'd been killed in the bedroom. So it bothered me that the police couldn't find the gun and that Poletti didn't have it on him when he rushed out of the apartment. Of course he might have killed Bernie earlier, left the apartment, and then returned without the gun for some reason. Still, it felt off.

"Have you talked to the remaining poker players?"

"Kreider questioned Silvio Pepper. He said Pepper was nervous. We can't find Ron Siglowski. Kreider interviewed his neighbors and got nothing. Ditto his relatives."

"I get that Pepper is nervous. I'd be nervous too. Poletti is cleaning house. Most likely Siglowski is already dead, and just hasn't turned up yet. That leaves Pepper and Briggs."

"Is Briggs still hiding out in your apartment?"

"Yes. And it's not fun."

"Maybe we should tie him to a parking meter downtown and see if Poletti takes the bait."

"Tempting, but I can't see Poletti being that stupid."

"I have to run," Morelli said. "Let me know if you come up with something better than the parking meter."

I went back inside and asked Connie to run checks on Silvio Pepper and Ron Siglowski. Five minutes later I had more information than I needed on both men. I had photos, ages, street addresses, second-grade spelling scores, sock sizes, cheese preferences, and colonoscopy reports.

"First up is Silvio Pepper," I said to Lula. "Do you want to ride shotgun?"

"Is short stuff going?"

I looked at Connie.

"Yeah," Connie said, "he's going."

"I guess I'll go anyway," Lula said. "If someone takes a potshot at him, I don't want to miss it."

Silvio Pepper lived in a small two-story house on the northern edge of the Burg. He was sixty-three years old, married, and the owner of a long-haul trucking company with offices on Broad Street.

I took Hamilton Avenue to Broad Street and turned left. Pepper Trucking was a relatively small operation several blocks down Broad. The single-story redbrick building had a small parking lot attached to it. Not big enough for an eighteen-wheeler, so the trucks were obviously kept elsewhere. I parked in the lot and told Lula and Briggs to wait in the car.

"Why do I have to wait in the car?" Lula asked. "Waiting in the car is boring."

"I don't want to drag everyone in there with me," I said. "Two people are partners. Three people make a parade."

"So why can't we leave Briggs here? We can crack a window for him."

"Jeez," Briggs said. "What do I look like, a golden retriever?"

"I want Poletti, and Briggs is my bait. I don't want to come back and find Briggs gunned down or missing and Poletti long gone."

"I guess I could see that," Lula said, "but how do you expect me to pull off this Briggs rescue?"

"I guess you could shoot Poletti in a nonvital area."

"Like his knee?"

"Yeah."

"Okay, I'm cool with that," Lula said.

I slung my messenger bag over my shoulder, crossed the lot, and pushed my way through the front door of Pepper Trucking. The woman at the front desk was in her forties and looked overworked, overfed, and underpaid.

"I'd like to talk to Silvio," I told her.

Looking like she could care less, she punched a button on her multiline phone.

"There's a woman here to see you," she said. She rolled her eyes and looked over at me. "Who are you?"

"Stephanie Plum."

"Stephanie Plum," she repeated into the phone. She hung up and looked down the hall. "Second door on the right."

Silvio looked like his photo but more wrinkled.

"You're the bounty hunter, right?" he said. "I know you from around. I guess you're looking for Jimmy."

"Do you know where he is?"

"No, but I know where he should be. He should be in the nuthouse. He was always this smart guy. Businessman. Good poker player. Okay, maybe he had a weakness for the ladies, but who doesn't? And so he made some bad business decisions, but hey, that's no reason to go off the deep end and kill people."

"So you think he's the one who killed Bernie and Tommy?"

"Who else would kill them?"

I shrugged.

"I think it's Jimmy," Silvio said. "I think he's afraid he'll get ratted out. We were all pretty close. Not that we were involved, but we knew stuff."

"What about Buster? Was he in business with Jimmy?"

"I don't know exactly. Jimmy would send him on trips, and we figured it was business, but it could have been just to get cars."

"I guess you're worried."

"Damn right I'm worried. Two of my best friends are dead. It's terrible. How does stuff like this happen?"

"Maybe you should disappear for a while, like Ron."

"Ron's retired. He can go wherever he wants. I got a company to run. I've got people depending on me."

"I don't suppose you know where Ron is?"

He shook his head. "He just took off. No goodbye or anything. I hate to say it out loud, but he could be dead somewhere. He could have been the first one Jimmy took out."

I gave him my card. "Let me know if you hear anything."

He took the card and stared at it, blank-faced. "Sure."

I went back to the Buick and got behind the wheel.

"Well?" Lula asked. "How'd it go?"

"As expected," I said. "He knows nothing. He wasn't involved. He thinks Jimmy's gone postal."

"Do you think all that's true?" Lula asked.

"I don't think *any* of it is true," I said.

"I think the part about Jimmy going postal is true," Briggs said.

I called Connie and asked her to do some snooping on Pepper Trucking. Was Silvio Pepper the sole owner? Where were the trucks kept when they were in town? What did the trucks haul?

I disconnected, then scanned Ron Siglowski's background report. He was seventy years old and widowed. No children. He'd sold his insurance business five years ago and moved into a golf course community in Cranbury. His credit check didn't turn up any recent airline tickets. No new withdrawals from his bank account. No new action on his credit cards. So either he was being smart and not leaving a trail, or else he was dead. I had no gut feeling either way.

The next stop was Pepper's house. I knew a lot of people in the Burg, but I didn't know Miriam Pepper. I left Lula and

Briggs in the car and went to the door. Miriam answered the bell in a fuzzy pink bathrobe. She was in her sixties. She had short brown hair streaked with gray. She was chubby and rosy-cheeked. And the drink in her hand looked like Coke but smelled like hundred proof.

"You must be Stephanie Plum," she said. "Silvio called and said you might be stopping by. He said I shouldn't talk to you because goodness knows what I might say."

It was eleven o'clock and the woman was in her bathrobe, getting cozy with Jim Beam. How lucky was this?

"You seem like an intelligent woman," I said. "I'm sure you wouldn't say anything inappropriate."

"Thank you. I'm very discreet."

"And that's a lovely pink bathrobe."

"Pink is my favorite color. It's a happy color."

"That's so true. And I can see that you're a happy person."

"Especially when I have a little nip of something." She leaned forward and whispered at me. "Actually, I'm an alcoholic. Would you like a Manhattan? I make an excellent Manhattan."

"Thanks, but no. It's early for me."

"I like to get a head start on the day."

"I wanted to ask you about Jimmy Poletti."

Miriam knocked back some Manhattan. "He's a pig."

"In what way?"

"He's a man. Isn't that enough?"

"I was hoping you could be more specific."

"Well, there's his wife."

"Yes?"

"She's thin."

"I know," I said. "I've met her."

"How am I supposed to compete with that?"

"I'm sure Silvio loves you just the way you are."

"Who?"

"Silvio. Your husband."

She did a major eye roll. "*Him!* All he thinks about is that trucking company. I've had it up to here with that trucking company."

"What sort of stuff does he haul?"

"He has a contract with a plant in Mexico that makes salsa and a plant in Newark that makes the containers. He carts the containers to Mexico and comes back with them full of salsa."

Okay, now I'm getting somewhere. Another Mexican tie-in.

"Does he ever haul anything other than salsa?" I asked.

"I only know about the salsa. I've got a garage filled with five-gallon cans of the stuff. What the heck am I supposed to do with it all? I mean, do they pay him in salsa?"

"Did he ever haul anything for Jimmy?"

She stared into her whiskey glass. "It's empty," she said. "I hate when that happens."

"About Jimmy."

"Boy, I could use a cigarette," she said. "Do you have any cigarettes on you?"

"No. Sorry. I don't smoke."

"Xanax?"

"No."

"Cupcakes?"

Standing just inside the front door, I saw a car pull into the driveway. Silvio.

I gave Miriam my card. "Call me if you want to talk."

"Sure," she said, "but you have to bring cupcakes."

I passed Silvio on the sidewalk.

"Your wife is lovely," I said. "You're a lucky man."

"Yeah," he said. "Lucky me."

SEVEN

"THIS ISN'T WORKING for me," Lula said when I got back to the Buick. "I don't want to be locked in the car with short stuff anymore."

"Hey, what about me?" Briggs said. "You aren't exactly my dream date."

"You'd be lucky if I'm your dream date," Lula said. "You never had a dream as good as me."

"You're not a dream," Briggs said. "You're a nightmare."

"Oh yeah? How'd you like me to nightmare you a broken nose?"

"There's not going to be any broken noses," I said. "Jeez Louise, can we have some civility here?"

"We need a fun activity," Lula said. "I think we should ride by Rangeman and see what's going on. Maybe there's guys in hazmat suits. Or maybe they got the building covered by one of them big yellow tents they use when you got termites."

I headed out of the Burg and took Broad Street to downtown Trenton. Rangeman was located on a quiet side street, in a seven-story building that had secure underground parking. Ranger's private apartment was on the top floor. Other floors were used for temporary housing of employees and detainees, a command center, offices, a gym, and an apartment for the building manager. A small plaque by the front door announced the name of the business. Windows were impact glass. All floors with the exception of the seventh were under constant surveillance.

I turned right off Broad and was stopped from making another turn by orange cones and yellow crime scene tape. The entire Rangeman block was cordoned off. An eighteen-wheeler crime scene lab was parked in front of the building, plus a bunch of cop cars, an EMT truck, a fire truck, and a hazmat unit truck.

A uniformed cop from the sheriff's office was manning the barricade.

"What's going on?" I asked him.

"There's a contaminant in one of the buildings here," he said. "No one's allowed on the street until the building checks out."

"How long is that going to be?" Lula asked.

The cop didn't know.

A news service helicopter hovered over the building.

Rangeman would be on the evening news. Ranger would hate that.

"I don't get how something could contaminate this building," Lula said. "This building is scary secure."

I called Morelli.

"I'm idling at a barricade to Ranger's street," I said. "The whole street is blocked off, and there's an eighteen-wheeler crime scene lab parked here. I've never *seen* an eighteen-wheeler crime scene lab. What's going on?"

"I can't talk now," Morelli said. "I'll meet you for lunch at Pino's. Twelve o'clock." And he disconnected.

Lula looked over at me. "Well? What's going on?"

"He couldn't talk."

"Did he say if it was terrorists?"

"No, but I think it's unlikely terrorists would target Ranger's building."

"This is killing me," Lula said. "I hate when I don't know stuff."

It was killing me too. I had a sick feeling in my stomach. Something really bad had happened here. I was worried about Ranger. And I was worried about his men.

I drove away from the crime scene, turned at the next corner, and cut across town to Stark. As long as I was sort of in the neighborhood it wouldn't hurt to check on Buster, and it would take my mind off Ranger. It was midmorning and the pizza place was filled with people. The area around it looked normal. No sign of police activity. I parked half a block away, on the opposite side of the street, and I watched the building while Lula and Briggs went to get pizza.

I tapped in Buster's number, and he answered on the second ring. I introduced myself, and he hung up. I tried again, and he didn't pick up. I ran across the street and banged on his door. Nothing. The door was locked.

Lula and Briggs joined me. Lula was carrying a large pizza box.

"We got a whole pie," Lula said. "They were having a half-price sale."

We backed up on the sidewalk and looked at the second-floor windows. No moving shadows. No television sounds drifting down to us.

"Did you try knocking on the door?" Lula asked.

"Yep."

"Then I'm guessing nobody is home, and we should go eat our pizza."

· · ·

I didn't want to drag Lula and Briggs along on my lunch date, so I dropped Lula at the office and took Briggs to my parents' house.

"Just in time for lunch," Grandma said, opening the front door.

"I can't stay," I told her, "but I was hoping I could leave Randy here."

"I suppose that would be okay," Grandma said. "How long do we have to keep him?"

"An hour or two."

"As long as you pick him up by three o'clock. Your mother has a dentist appointment, and I'm getting my hair done for the viewing tonight. It's going to be a good viewing what with all the scandal. The place will be packed. And people are going to be hoping to get a showing from Jimmy."

Grandma and her lady friends went to viewings four days out of seven, whether they knew the deceased or not. The funeral home served cookies, was filled with flowers, and was the Burg's premier place to be seen and swap gossip.

"I doubt Jimmy will make an appearance," I said to Grandma. "And I can't see him going to the funeral either. He'd be instantly arrested."

"Well, I'm going anyway," she said. "There's nothing on television but reruns."

"I'm going too. Even if Jimmy isn't there, the place will be filled with friends and relatives. Do you need a ride?"

"Sure, I could use a ride. You could come for dinner, and we could go together. Your mother is making pot roast tonight, with chocolate cake for dessert."

"I *love* pot roast and chocolate cake," Briggs said.

"I guess he could eat here too," Grandma said.

"You have to behave yourself," I said to Briggs. "No growling, biting, or kicking."

"Yeah, we don't give out chocolate cake to biters," Grandma said.

"Jeez," Briggs said. "You make me sound like an animal."

I set my hands on my hips and looked down at him.

"Okay," he said. "I might have done some of those things in the past, but they were justified. I gotta compensate for my size. It's not like I can punch a guy in the nose."

"That's true," Grandma said. "He has a point."

"Thanks," Briggs said. "You're all right for an old lady."

"I'm not so old," Grandma said. "I got some good years left."

I had my hand on the door handle. "I have to go," I said to Grandma. "Put the television on for him. Cartoons or something. And don't give him the remote or he'll sign up for porn."

"Those porn films have the best titles," Grandma said. "I wouldn't mind seeing some of them. I bought one once, but it was all naked girls and I wanted to see naked men."

$\cdots$

Morelli was already seated at a table when I walked into Pino's. Pino's is the restaurant of choice for most of the cops. It's got a good bar, a small side room with a handful of tables, and a menu heavy on pizza and Italian American comfort food.

I sat across from him and glanced at the menu. It was a formality, because I knew the menu by heart. I'd been eating at Pino's for years, and the menu never changed.

"Meatball sub," I told the waitress. "And a Coke."

"Same for me," Morelli said.

He was wearing jeans, a black T-shirt, and a plaid shirt with the sleeves rolled to his elbows. His hair was about four weeks overdue for a cut, curling over his ears and at the nape of his neck. His brown eyes were serious, but there was a sensual softness to his mouth. He looked like the movie star version of an undercover cop.

"Did you leave Briggs locked in the car?" he asked.

"No. I dropped him off at my parents' house."

"I was afraid I'd be eating lunch with him."

"I wouldn't do that to you."

Morelli grinned. "What *would* you do to me?"

"All sorts of good things," I said.

"And what can I do to you?" he asked.

"I have a list."

"Am I going to get to walk my fingers down that list anytime soon?"

"As soon as I capture Poletti and get rid of Briggs."

Morelli ate part of a breadstick. "I'm working on it. I have my own reasons for wanting to talk to Poletti."

"Any leads?"

He shook his head. "No leads, but his wife invited me to come back anytime."

"So it wasn't a total loss?"

Another grin. "I'm saving myself for you."

I mostly believed him, but truth is, Morelli just about leaks excess testosterone from his pores. We have a tense relationship that skirts permanent commitment but acknowledges the "L" word. I'm careful not to question him too closely on his sex life beyond our relationship, because if I ever found out he was sleeping with someone else I'd have to kill her. Okay, maybe I wouldn't kill her, but I'd certainly buy out the candy aisle at 7-Eleven, eat it all, and throw up.

"Let's change the subject," I said. "Tell me about Ranger."

"Ranger had Emilio Gardi in custody, waiting for extradition to Miami. Gardi apparently had some very bad stuff with him that he was going to use to take out Ranger and his whole operation. Something went wrong, and Gardi accidentally took the hit. One of the Rangeman guys is also pretty sick, but everyone else got out in time."

"Gardi was a setup?"

"Looks that way. I don't know all the details. The feds aren't releasing any information on the contaminant, but Gardi and the Rangeman guy are in isolation and being treated for radiation poisoning. And the first responders said Gardi was screaming about polonium, begging for medical help."

"What's polonium?"

"I don't know exactly. I didn't have time to Google it, but I'm told it's the stuff some speculate killed Yasser Arafat. Supposedly it's not a nice death."

"That's creepy."

"Yeah. Probably you're going to be too creeped out to sleep tonight and you're going to need a big strong guy like me to keep you safe."

I narrowed my eyes at him. "Did you make all this up just so I'd sleep with you?"

"No. I'm not that clever, but I *am* getting desperate, so let me know if it's working."

"I have Briggs to protect me."

"I hear some sarcasm there, but I know Briggs, and he's a mean little bastard. I wouldn't underestimate him in a bar fight."

Our food arrived, and we dug in.

"This doesn't add up for me," I finally said. "I was under the impression that Ranger and Gardi hadn't met prior to Gardi's arrest. Why was Gardi trying to take down Rangeman?"

"I imagine Gardi was working for someone. When it all went down, someone at Rangeman hit the big red button and the call simultaneously brought in the feds, the hazmat team, and Trenton first responders. The feds immediately took over and put a lid on any information coming from Gardi. I'm surprised you don't know more from Ranger."

"I spoke to him briefly, but he couldn't talk."

"I'm sure he's scrambling, trying to keep his business running without his control room."

And knowing Ranger, he was on the hunt for whoever'd sent Gardi.

"How long do you think he'll be out of the building?" I asked Morelli.

"No one's saying. This is the tightest security I've ever seen. Everyone's walking around with their ass clenched."

Welcome to my world. My sphincter isn't exactly relaxed. Ranger has lots of enemies, and he sits with his back to the wall, so I've become used to a certain element of danger that always surrounds him. This was a whole other deal. This was stone cold scary.

"What are you doing this afternoon?" I asked.

"Paperwork. And I want to walk around Buster's backyard. We still haven't found the murder weapon."

"I have my theory."

Morelli finished his Coke and sat back in his chair. "I bet we both have the same theory."

"I'm thinking Poletti isn't the killer."

"Yeah, it's worth throwing into the mix. He could have let himself into the apartment for whatever reason, found another dead poker player, left in a panic, and ran into you on the way out."

"Buster was in Atlantic City, so who else has a key?"

Morelli signaled for the check. "Turns out lots of people had keys, including Scootch."

"Did you talk to Miriam Pepper?" I asked Morelli.

"I did. She was completely hammered at one in the afternoon. And I got a better offer from her than I did from Poletti's wife."

"Let me guess. She offered you a Manhattan."

Morelli pushed back from the table. "I was inches from taking it."

EIGHT

I LEFT MORELLI, drove back to my parents' house, and retrieved Briggs.

"I got to take a look at tonight's cake," he said. "It's awesome. Chocolate cake and chocolate frosting. And the frosting is real thick."

"I'm surprised you didn't carve off a chunk when no one was watching."

"Someone was always watching. What are we doing now?"

"I don't know. I'm at a dead end with Poletti."

"If you haven't got anything special to do, maybe we could drive past my apartment. The last time I saw it, fire trucks were all over the place and it was still smoking."

I rolled out of the Burg and followed Hamilton to Grand Avenue. I parked across the street from Briggs's building, and we looked over at it in silence. It was an ugly redbrick building built in the fifties. Three stories. Briggs lived on the second floor, and it was clear which apartment was his. The windows had been blown out in the explosion and were now patched with plywood. Thick black soot stained the brick on the second and third floors. The building's front door was open, and hoses snaked out and dumped grimy gray water into the gutter. Two fire restoration vans were parked at the curb.

"Do you want to go in?" I asked him.

He shook his head. "I just wanted to take a look at the building. No point going in. I got a call from the insurance adjuster, and he said there was nothing left. He said the explosion blew a hole in the ceiling, and the fire spread to the third floor. Lucky no one was home there, either. No one got hurt."

"Sorry about your apartment," I said. "It's hard to lose all your stuff like that."

"You've had your place blown up a couple times," Briggs said. "It must have been bad for you too."

"The first time it happened was the worst. I was really rattled. Nothing like that had ever happened to me before."

"Hard to believe," Briggs said. "You're a magnet for disaster. I figured you were one of those kids who had their bike run over by the garbage truck."

"Only once," I said. "But it was never blown up."

"Yeah, there's something about getting your shit blown up that takes it to a whole new level."

"I've pretty much gone through my bag of tricks for tracking down Poletti," I said. "I think it's time to hang you out there as bait."

"*What?* Are you nuts? He wants to kill me."

"I'll take precautions."

"Such as?"

"I'll be watching."

"And?"

"And I'll catch him before he kills you."

"How are you going to catch him?"

"I'll rush him," I said. "And give him a faceful of pepper spray."

"I'm not completely comfortable with that."

"I'll use my stun gun."

"What if you can't get close enough to him?"

"Okay, how about if I put bullets in my .45, and then I can shoot him?"

Briggs nodded. "Bullets are good. That's a good start. How's your aim?"

"I'm a crack shot at ten feet."

"You're making me nervous. I might be getting diarrhea. I'm not well. I got IBS."

"This won't be a big deal. All you have to do is walk up and down Stark Street in front of Buster's building."

"What if I get diarrhea? I can feel it coming on just thinking about it."

"Go into the pizza place and use their bathroom."

"They might not have a public bathroom," Briggs said.

"Then go out the back door and hide behind the dumpster."

"Boy, that's cold," Briggs said.

"It's Stark Street. People probably go behind the dumpster all the time."

"All right. I guess I could try it, but I want to see your gun."

"I don't actually have my gun with me," I said.

Briggs crossed his arms over his chest. "I'm not doing it unless you have a gun."

"Okay, great, fine, whatever. I'll go get Lula. She always has a gun."

· · ·

"Damn right I got a gun," Lula said, taking the front passenger seat. "I don't mind using it either if it's for a good cause. Or in this case to get Poletti before he rids the world of Mr. Poopie Pants."

"It's a legitimate medical condition," Briggs said.

"So where are we gonna show him off?" Lula asked.

I put the Buick in gear and pulled into traffic. "I thought we'd start on Stark Street. We can stand him in front of Buster's building."

"Yeah, that's a good idea," Lula said. "Buster could look out his window, and see Briggs, and call Poletti to come off him."

"Cripes," Briggs said. "Could you phrase it some other way?"

"Your problem is you don't know how to relax," Lula said to Briggs. "You take everything so serious."

"You're talking about people killing me," Briggs said. "That's serious!"

"Do you have your cellphone?" I asked Briggs.

"Yeah. I got my cellphone."

"When we get to Stark Street I'm going to drop you off in front of the pizza place, and then I'm going to park, and Lula and I will take up surveillance somewhere. Keep your cellphone handy, because I'll call you if I think you're in danger."

"You're going to be close, right? I mean, you're only accurate to ten feet."

"No problem," I said. "We'll make sure you're covered."

"And if you have to poop," Lula said, "you tell us so we know we can take a break. I might need a piece of pizza or a donut or something."

"Sure. How long do I have to do this?"

"I'm thinking until someone shoots at you, or runs you over with a car," Lula said.

I stopped in front of the pizza place, and Briggs got out. He had his cellphone in his hand, and his face was white.

"Don't worry," I said. "You'll be fine."

He nodded and shuffled around a little.

"There's a parking place on the other side of the street," Lula said. "Go around the block and come back the other way."

I drove around the block and parked two doors down and across the street from Briggs. He was still clutching his cellphone, and he was pacing the length of Buster's building. Back and forth. Back and forth.

"He don't look natural," Lula said. "Nobody's gonna shoot him with him looking like that."

"We don't want him shot," I said. "We just want to drag Poletti out into the open."

"I guess that's one way to go."

A half hour later a black SUV cruised down the street and stopped in front of Briggs and the pizza place.

"I can't see Briggs anymore," Lula said. "That big-ass black car is in my way."

"Give me your gun."

"What?"

"Your gun!"

Lula stuck her hand into her purse and rooted around. "It's in here somewhere."

I was out of the Buick, running across the street, when the SUV took off. No Briggs on the sidewalk. I ran back to the Buick, jumped behind the wheel, and roared after the SUV.

"They've got him," I said to Lula. "Have you found your gun yet?"

"I might have left it in my other purse. At the last minute I decided to wear these purple shoes, and you know how important it is to coordinate properly."

I have two purses. One is a messenger bag I use every day. The other is a little evening bag I use three times a year. They're both black.

The Buick has no pickup, but once it gets rolling it's a tank. I was half a block behind the SUV when it stopped for a light. I rammed the Buick into the back of the SUV, bouncing it halfway into the intersection. One of the doors opened on the passenger side, and Briggs was tossed out. The light changed, and the crumpled SUV drove off.

Lula and I got out and picked Briggs up off the road.

"Are you okay?" I asked him.

"No thanks to you. I just got kidnapped."

"Was it Poletti?"

"No. It was two whacked-out guys who said they always wanted to kidnap a midget. I mean, what the heck is wrong with this world? What has it come to?"

"Did you explain to them you aren't a midget no more?" Lula asked. "That you are a very short person now?"

"No. I punched one of them in the nuts, and he threw me out of the car. I thought you were supposed to be protecting me. Suppose that was Poletti?"

"Hey, she crashed into that car for you," Lula said. "She didn't even care about damaging her own personal property."

We all looked at the Buick. Not a scratch on it. The Buick is invincible.

Cars were pulling around us, beeping their horns. Briggs was giving them the finger.

"We should get in the car," Lula said. "Not a good idea for a little white man to be giving the finger to people in this neighborhood."

I drove us the length of Stark and turned left at State Street. I cut through town and took a small detour to check out Ranger's building. The street was still cordoned off and filled with emergency vehicles. My heart stuttered in my chest, and a chill ripped through me. I circled the block and continued on to the bail bonds office. I dropped Lula off and brought Briggs back to my apartment.

"I thought we were going to your parents' house for dinner," he said. "Why are we here?"

"I have to change my clothes. I'm going to Mrs. Poletti's viewing after dinner, and I can't go in jeans and a T-shirt."

"Why not?"

"It would be disrespectful. And my mother would hear about it, and she'd yell at me and get out the ironing. She irons when she's upset. You want to stay away from her when she's ironing."

"If you ask me, your whole family is goofy."

"I like to think we're normally dysfunctional."

I set Briggs in front of the television, then changed into a tailored black suit and a stretchy white tanktop with a scoop neck. I stuffed my feet into black heels, brushed my hair out and pulled it up into a new ponytail, added an extra swipe of mascara to my lashes, and I was good to go.

"Well, la-di-da," Briggs said when he saw me. "Look at you all dressed up. If Poletti comes after me, you can spear him with the heel on your shoe."

NINE

GRANDMA WAS WEARING shocking pink lipstick, a shocking pink dress, and white tennis shoes.

"You're right on time," she said, opening the front door and motioning us inside. "We're having beer with the meal, but you could have a snort now if you need it."

"Sounds good," Briggs said. "I wouldn't mind a cocktail. What have you got?"

"We got whiskey," Grandma said. "I could fancy it up with ice, or you could take it like a man."

"Whatever," Briggs said.

Grandma ran off to get the whiskey, and I wandered into the living room with Briggs. My father was in his chair, watching television and doing the Jumble.

"Oh jeez," he said when he looked up and saw Briggs. "You again."

"It's always a delight to see you, sir," Briggs said.

"Boy, you really want that chocolate cake bad," I said to Briggs.

"Fuckin' A," Briggs said.

Grandma trotted in with a tumbler of whiskey for Briggs. Briggs looked at the glass, looked at my father, and belted back half the whiskey. He gasped, and choked, and his eyes watered.

"Good," Briggs said. "Smooth."

Grandma and I helped my mother get the food to the table, and we all took our seats.

"God bless," my father said, offloading half a cow onto his plate. He added a mound of mashed potatoes and four green beans, then poured gravy over everything. My father never got the memo about red meat, colonoscopies, or heart disease. His philosophy was that if you never went to the doctor, you never found out there was something wrong with you. So far it was working for him.

"This is delicious," Briggs said to my mother, taking the pot roast for a test drive. "How do you get the gravy to look black like this?"

"She burns the meat," Grandma said. "That's the secret to good gravy. It's got to be full of them carcinogens."

Briggs gulped down the rest of his whiskey, looked at me, and mouthed "Help."

"Just keep thinking about the cake," I told him.

"This is going to be a real good viewing," Grandma said. "There's going to be lots of people there. We have to go early to get a good seat up front."

My father kept his head down, working on his pot roast. And Briggs scraped the gravy off his potatoes.

"I hear they had to scramble to get a good casket for poor Mrs. Poletti," Grandma said. "Nobody made arrangements ahead of time. Can you imagine? I got my casket all picked out. I've got it on the layaway plan. It's a beauty. It's got a white silk lining and everything."

My father kept eating, but his knuckles were turning white holding his fork.

"No, sir," Grandma said, "I'm not going to be caught short. I'm even working on my bucket list."

Everyone stopped eating and turned to Grandma.

"What's on your bucket list?" I asked.

"I got six things so far," Grandma said. "First off, I want new breasts. These ones I got are a mess. They got all flattened and droopy. Second, I want to see Ranger naked. If I can't see him naked, I'll settle for almost naked. Except, I sure would like to see his privates. I bet they're a sight, and I don't get to see a lot of privates these days."

My mother's face flushed, Briggs squirmed in his seat, and a piece of pot roast fell out of my father's mouth.

"And then I want to get Joe's Grandma Bella," Grandma said. "She don't scare me with her evil eye baloney. I don't know how I'm going to get her, but I'm going to get her good. The fourth thing is I want to march in a parade. The fifth thing is I want to take down a bad guy. And the last thing is a secret." Grandma looked over at Briggs. "How about you? Do you have a bucket list?"

"Nothing formal," Briggs said. "Mostly I'd like to stay out of prison and not die anytime soon."

"That's a good start," Grandma said.

With the exception of the boob job, my bucket list was about the same as Grandma's. It might be fun to march in a parade, and I'd already seen Ranger naked but he was worth another look . . . or two or three or many. And that thought gave me a small anxiety attack. I sent him a text message that said *Talk to me*, and he texted back *Patience*.

Briggs washed his pot roast down with two beers, and I thought he looked a little glassy-eyed.

"Are you okay?" I asked him.

"Mmmm," he said. "Mmmmarvelous." And his eyes drooped closed.

"Maybe he needs some cake to perk him up," Grandma said.

"He's trashed," my father said.

Grandma looked at him. "Guess he's not so good with liquor."

Considering he was only about three feet tall and had just chugged down a water glass of hooch plus two beers, I thought he'd done okay. If I drank all that, I'd be under the table.

I helped Grandma clear the dishes, and my mom brought the cake to the table. Briggs opened his eyes and tried to focus.

"Cake," he said. "Cake good."

He plowed through his piece of cake and slumped in his seat. His eyes slid closed, and a little chocolate drool oozed from the side of his mouth.

"Maybe we should get him to the couch and let him sleep it off," I said.

"There's no way in hell I'm sharing my living room with him," my father said. "If you want him to keep breathing, you'll dump him someplace far away from my television."

"We could lay him out on the kitchen floor," Grandma said. "That way he won't mess anything up with his drooling. And if we put him behind the table, no one will step on him."

My mother took one foot, Grandma took the other, I got Briggs under the armpits, and we lugged him into the kitchen. We stretched him out behind the table, and Grandma put a kitchen towel under his head.

"He looks real peaceful there," Grandma said.

I thought about handcuffing him to the stove so he wouldn't wake up and wander away, but I only had one pair of handcuffs with me, and I might need them if I found Poletti.

• • •

I was lucky enough to get the last spot in the small parking lot attached to the funeral home. A few people were gathered on the big front porch, and more people were milling around in the lobby. Mrs. Poletti was in Slumber Room No. 1, which was a spot of honor reserved for the deceased who were expected to draw larger than usual crowds—mob bosses, victims of violent deaths, minor celebrities, and Grand Poobahs of the Knights of Columbus.

Grandma marched straight to the viewing room without so

much as a nod to the cookie table. Her eyes narrowed and her lips compressed when she saw that the first row in front of the casket was already taken by the Poletti family. She would have to settle for a seat in the second row.

"Some of them family members should be standing at the head of the casket with the husband of the deceased," Grandma said. "This new generation don't know much."

I recognized the two grandsons, Oswald and Aaron, Aaron's wife, and Buster. "Who's the man sitting next to Buster?" I asked Grandma. "He was at the house the day Mrs. Poletti died."

"He's some out-of-state relative who was visiting while he was on a job interview," Grandma said.

"And the three older women next to him?"

"Sisters of the deceased. All of them spinsters. There was rumors of them always being a little off."

"In what way?"

"I heard they liked each other too much, if you know what I mean."

People were pouring in after us, filling all the seats, forming a line to give condolences and check out Mrs. Poletti's hair and makeup.

Grandma knew everyone.

"Who's that man?" I asked her.

"Buster's father," Grandma said. "He was a construction expeditor. The woman behind him knows Mrs. Poletti from Bingo."

After an hour, the river of mourners dwindled to a small trickle, and I left my seat to eavesdrop and ask questions.

Everyone had some connection to the Poletti family, whether it was blood or Bingo. Except for Grandma, who was just plain nosy.

Jimmy Poletti's wife, Trudy, was noticeably absent. Silvio and Miriam Pepper arrived late, gave their condolences to the family, and left through a side door before I had a chance to talk to them. Aaron and his wife also left early. Oswald Poletti ambled out of the Slumber Room fifteen minutes before the viewing ended and pushed through the crowd to the cookie table. He was shoving Oreos into his rumpled jacket pocket when I cornered him.

"Sorry about your grandmother," I said.

"She was, like, old," he said.

"I don't suppose you've heard from your father."

"Dear old Dad don't call much."

"I don't mean to be judgmental, but is there ever a moment in the day when you aren't stoned?"

"What?"

Buster moved into my line of vision on his way to the door, and I ran after him.

"Stephanie Plum," I said, extending my hand. "I've been wanting to talk to you."

"You're the bounty hunter who broke into my apartment and found Bernie."

"I didn't break in. The door was open."

"I heard you were with Jimmy's bookkeeper. For a little guy, he gets around."

"He's helping me find Jimmy."

"Whatever." He focused on my breasts in the stretchy white tanktop. "You're cuter than I expected. I bet you're good with handcuffs."

"I'm even better with a stun gun," I said. "And I've been known to shoot people on occasion."

"Stop. You're getting me excited. I'm getting a boner."

"I guess that's an accomplishment at your age," I said.

Buster grimaced. "Jeez, you really know how to ruin a moment."

"About Jimmy . . ."

"I don't know anything about Jimmy. Personally, I think he was framed. And I don't know where he is now. End of story."

"He was in your apartment."

"Yeah, but I wasn't there. He has a key. Lots of people have keys. I'm that kind of guy. I never took the keys back when I moved in."

"You don't talk to Jimmy?"

"Who, me? He's a felon. Do I look like the kind of guy who would talk to a felon?"

"Yes."

"Boy, that hurts. I'm a law-abiding citizen."

"Did you get the blood out of the carpet?"

"No. I tossed it. Some people have no consideration for other people's property. Somebody had a lot of nerve popping Bernie in my apartment."

"So you have no idea who killed Bernie?"

"If I knew who killed Bernie, I'd send him a bill for my carpet."

"Everybody thinks it was Jimmy."

"That's jumping to conclusions. I don't see Jimmy killing someone."

"He tried to kill his bookkeeper."

"Yeah, but everyone wants to kill Briggs. He's annoying. Anyway, Jimmy only *tried* to run him over. Briggs pissed Jimmy off when he boinked the missus."

"Excuse me?"

"You didn't know?"

"Randy Briggs and Trudy Poletti?"

Buster grinned. "Yeah, Briggs is an animal. He probably humped the dog when he was done with Trudy."

I felt my upper lip curl back. "Ewwwww."

"We all knew Trudy fooled around, and Jimmy mostly looked the other way, but doing the bookkeeper was insulting. Briggs was a fucking employee. Not to mention people were making unflattering comparisons between Briggs and Jimmy. And just between you and me, I've seen Jimmy, and Briggs might be bigger in the old shlongarooni department." Buster rocked back on his heels. "I guess you would know more about that than me."

"I know nothing! Briggs had a firebomb shot into his apartment. He asked me for protection, and in return he's helping me find Jimmy. Are you sure you don't know where Jimmy is hiding?"

"Maybe I'll remember if you show me your tits."

"That's disgusting. This is a viewing. There's a dead woman in there."

"How about if I ask to see them in a bar?"

"No."

"Suppose I bought you dinner?"

"No."

"What if I was in the hospital with a heart attack?"

"No."

"Boy, you're tough. Most women would go for the heart attack."

TEN

BRIGGS WAS STILL asleep on the kitchen floor when I brought Grandma home. I nudged him with my foot, and he mumbled something, but he didn't wake up.

"Is it okay if I leave him here?" I asked my mom. "I'll come get him first thing in the morning."

"As long as it's first thing."

I drove home, parked in my lot, and noticed that the lights were on in my apartment. Morelli had a key, but his green SUV wasn't in the lot. Ranger's black Porsche wasn't there either, but that didn't mean much. Ranger has a lot of cars available to him.

My cellphone rang and Ranger said, "Babe."

"Are you in my apartment?" I asked him.

"Are you alone?"

"Yes."

"Then I'm in your apartment."

He was in my kitchen with a bottle of water in his hand. He was wearing jeans and a black T-shirt, a Glock, and an unzipped flak vest. Not his usual all black perfectly tailored uniform. No Rangeman logo.

"This must be casual Tuesday," I said to him.

"They won't let anything leave the building. Ella had to do some fast shopping."

Ella is half of a housekeeping couple that maintains Ranger's building. She makes sure everyone is appropriately dressed and well fed, she supervises the cleaning crew, and she personally tends to Ranger's private apartment.

"Are you okay?" I asked him.

"Yes. I wasn't onsite when the poison was released. Bruce McCready discovered Gardi with the canister. There was a struggle, the canister was activated, and McCready and Gardi were contaminated. Gardi panicked and told McCready everything he knew, hoping he could get treatment in time to save himself. Fortunately, McCready was able to evacuate the building before the poison spread."

"Is McCready going to be okay?"

"No one is saying, but from the limited information I have, I suspect McCready and Gardi received a lethal dose. This stuff takes a while to kill. McCready is a good man. He's a team player. Everyone likes him. There are a lot of prayers being said at Rangeman."

"That's horrible. How did this happen?"

"We didn't do a body cavity check. Technically, we're not empowered. Gardi obviously knew this, because he had a delayed-action aerosol cartridge of polonium-210 hidden in him. The plan was for him to release it into the air-conditioning system just before he left for Miami. At least that's what he told McCready, and what McCready passed on to us before he was hospitalized. I haven't been able to talk to either McCready or Gardi since they were admitted. They're both in isolation under heavy guard."

"I've never heard of polonium."

"It's produced in nuclear reactors. It's rare, and it's difficult to detect. If it enters the body through an open wound, if it's eaten, if a person breathes contaminated air, it's deadly. It causes multiple organ failure.

"McCready was watching the cell video feed when Gardi pulled the canister out, and McCready went to investigate. If the poison had gone undetected into the building ventilation system, it would have infected everyone in the building."

"Morelli said he thought Gardi was working for someone who had a vendetta against you."

Ranger was leaning against my kitchen counter, looking relaxed, his brown eyes mostly black in the dim light. "I've made some enemies."

"That's it? That's all you've got? Some enemies?"

The corners of his mouth turned up into the smallest of smiles. "Are you worried about me?"

"Of course I'm worried about you."

"Nice." He looked at his watch. "I have to go."

"What? Are you serious? You didn't tell me anything."

"This is why I'm not married," Ranger said. "Women ask questions."

"Unh!" I said, smacking my forehead with the heel of my hand. "That's not why you're not married. You're not married because you're . . . impossible."

He dragged me to him and kissed me, and I felt the kiss travel like lava to my doo-dah.

"I have some issues to resolve," he said.

No kidding.

He gave my ponytail a playful tug and left.

• • •

It was almost eight A.M. when I got to my parents' house. Grandma was looking out the front door with her arms crossed over her chest, and Briggs was pacing on the sidewalk. His hair was a mess, and his shirt was stained and disheveled.

"Why are you out here?" I asked. "And what have you got all over your shirt?"

Grandma leaned out the open door. "It's chocolate," she said. "He woke up and snarfed down the cake. All of it. Your father went after him with a baseball bat. Lucky for Briggs it was your father's duty time. You know how your father has to keep on schedule with his morning duties. Good thing you got here before he was done in the bathroom."

"Somebody had to eat it," Briggs said. "It was just sitting there."

"The funeral is tomorrow morning," Grandma said to me. "Are you going?"

"Maybe."

"I hear there's going to be undercover cops there in case Jimmy shows up. There might even be a shootout. I'm thinking I might wear my flak vest just in case."

"You have a flak vest?"

"I got it a while ago from one of them home shopping shows on television. I thought you never know when you might need one. It's navy, and it would look good with my navy pantsuit."

I loaded Briggs into the Buick and drove him back to my apartment.

"Honestly," I said. "Did you have to eat *all* the cake?"

"I got carried away. I was hungry."

"I have things to do at the office. I'm going to drop you off so you can get cleaned up, and I'm going to pick you up later. I'm going to trust you to behave yourself."

"I might take a nap. The cake made me sort of sick."

"Do *not* take a nap in my bed."

"I'll take a shower first."

"No! You can sleep on the couch. If I find any evidence, a single new wrinkle in my sheets, you'll be sleeping in the parking lot."

"Boy, you'd think I had cooties or something."

"I'm *sure* you have cooties."

I watched Briggs amble through the back door of my apartment building, gave a shudder, and headed for the office.

"Where's half pint?" Lula asked when I walked in.

"I left him home. He was tired this morning."

"I thought you didn't trust him alone in your apartment."

"I don't, but I can't keep babysitting him every minute."

Connie waved a file at me. "I just got a new FTA. It's not worth a lot of money, but it should be easy to clear. It's Stanley Kulicky."

"I know Stanley," I said. "I went to school with him. What's his problem?"

"He broke into the Sunshine Diner and stole a couple five-gallon jugs of rice pudding. I guess he was high and he got the munchies for rice pudding. The diner was closed so he helped himself."

"That don't sound like much of a crime," Lula said.

"After he got the rice pudding strapped into his backseat, he went back in and tried to make himself a burger and fries and ended up setting the kitchen on fire. He panicked and took off, and on the way out of the parking lot he rammed a cop car. No one was hurt, but the cop car was trashed. Kulicky said he didn't see it. Said it jumped out at him from nowhere."

I looked at the file. "Unemployed and living with his parents." I flipped the page to his photo. "Whoa! What happened to him?"

Lula looked over my shoulder. "He's fat," Lula said. "I don't use that term a lot on account of it could be derogatory, but there's no other way to describe him. He's all swelled up."

"He was a skinny guy in high school," I said.

"Maybe he got a glandular thing going," Lula said.

I thought it was more likely a rice pudding thing.

I dropped the file into my messenger bag and took a donut from the box on Connie's desk. "I'm on it," I said.

"Me too," Lula said. "You might need help."

"I called him earlier," Connie said. "His parents are at work, but he's at home. He sounded cooperative. He said he forgot about the court date."

"They all say that," Lula said. "Then they shoot at you."

Stanley's parents lived just outside the Burg on Cobb Street. The house was a small bungalow with a long narrow backyard and a detached single-car garage at the back of the property. Stanley was sitting on the garage roof. And he was naked.

"This might not be a good time," Lula said, looking the length of the driveway.

"At least we know he's not armed."

We walked back to the garage and stood, hands on hips, staring up at Stanley.

"How's it going?" I said to him.

"Pretty good. How's with you?"

"Not bad. What are you doing on the roof?"

"I like it up here. It's peaceful. I have a nice view of the yard. And I can look in Mrs. Zahn's bedroom window. Sometimes she's naked."

"Is that why *you're* naked?"

"No. I'm doing the laundry, and I didn't have anything to wear."

"Do you have any of that rice pudding left?" Lula asked.

"No," he said. "I didn't get to keep it. The cops took it."

"Case closed," Lula said. "I'm thinking we're out of here."

Fortunately, I had the keys to the car. And I wasn't ready to leave just yet. I wasn't leaving without Stanley.

"I need to take you downtown to get your court date rescheduled," I said to Stanley.

"I don't want to do that. They'll put me in jail again."

"Only for a little while, until you get rebonded."

"No."

"You told Connie you'd cooperate."

"I changed my mind."

"One of us is going to have to go up there and get him," I said to Lula.

"I'm only the assistant bounty hunter," Lula said. "You're the real bounty hunter. You're the one what does that shit."

Stanley had to be close to three hundred pounds. He was a giant, immovable blob. I had no clue how I'd get him down and into my car. If I stun-gunned him he'd roll off the roof and crash to the ground. God knows what would happen when he hit. He could burst apart like a water balloon.

"Listen up, Humpty Dumpty," Lula said. "It's not like you're an attractive sight up there. If you don't come down I'm gonna take your picture and put it on YouTube. And then I'm gonna put the hose on you."

"I've already been on YouTube," he said. "I took a leak on YouTube."

"That's disgusting," Lula said. "I'm glad I didn't see that."

"Does your mother know you're out here with no clothes on?" I asked him. "I'm calling her."

"That's low," he said. "I'll make you a deal. I'll give you some weed if you don't call her. I got really good stuff."

"I'll make you a better deal," I said. "I won't call her if you get some clothes on and come downtown with me."

"I told you, my clothes are all getting washed."

"How about we cut a hole in your bedspread and punch your head through it," Lula said. "That should be about your size."

"You should talk," Stanley said. "You're fat!"

Lula's eyes bugged out. *"What?"*

"You're fatter than I am."

"I am not nearly as fat as you. I'm a big and beautiful woman, and I am *not* fat. There's a difference between being *big* and being *fat*."

"Well, you look fat to me."

"That does it," Lula said. "I'm coming up there, and I'm kicking your lard ass off that roof."

A ladder was propped against one side of the garage, and Lula climbed it like she was on fire. She got onto the roof, and Stanley shrieked and tried to scramble away, lost his footing, and fell off the garage.

WHUMMMP!

Humpty Dumpty had a great fall. He was spread-eagle on his back with a massive hydrangea bush squashed flat as a pancake under him.

"Are you okay?" I asked.

"Do I look okay?"

"That's sort of a trick question."

"I might have broken my back."

"Try wiggling your toes."

Lula came down the ladder. "Can he wiggle his toes?"

"Yep."

"Too bad he can't see them. You know what else he can't see?"

"Focus," I said to Lula. "We need to get him into the car."

"You gonna put him in your car naked? I don't think that's a good idea. He's gonna have them little blue hydrangea flowers all stuck up his ass. You'll get them all over your seat covers."

"I might need an ambulance," Stanley said.

"Hard to believe he could have broken something with all that padding he's got," Lula said.

"His face is kind of white," I said to Lula. "Maybe he hit his head."

"Yeah, I'm feeling faint," Stanley said. "I'm not feeling good. I'm having a hard time breathing."

I called 911 and asked for an EMT truck.

Lula looked down at him. "You should have told them to send one with a forklift."

"He isn't *that* big," I said. "And he probably looks better with clothes on."

"I'm cute with clothes on," Stanley said. "I've been told I look cuddly."

"I could see that," Lula said, "now that you mention it. You do have that cuddly stuffed bear look to you."

"Maybe we could get together when I get out of the hospital," Stanley said.

I checked my watch. It was midmorning. This wasn't the way I'd planned out my day. It was one thing to walk a simple skip through the process and collect my body receipt. It was a whole other deal to protect my property while it was left on a gurney in the emergency room. It could take hours. And then I had the further complication of either signing him into the lockdown ward at the hospital or shuttling him over to the police station. I'd be going through menopause by the time this was finalized.

"I don't suppose you'd want to stay with him at the hospital," I said to Lula.

"No way. Hospitals creep me out."

The EMT truck backed up the driveway. The two guys got out and grimaced when they saw Stanley.

"He's naked," the one guy said. "How'd he get out here naked? Is he nuts?"

"Sort of," I said. "He was sitting up on the roof, and he fell onto the hydrangea bush."

"Can he wiggle his toes?"

"Yeah."

"Can he wiggle anything else?"

"Are you gonna load him up or what?" Lula said. "On account of we haven't got all day to be standing here."

Ten minutes later, Stanley was in the truck.

"Are you going with him?" the EMT asked me.

"No," I said. "I'll call his mother and let her know."

"Not my mother," Stanley yelled from the truck.

I looked at Lula.

"Okay," she said. "I'll go with him, but you owe me. I want one of them five-gallon jugs of rice pudding when I come out of that hospital."

I gave her my paperwork and told her to call if there was a problem. The EMT truck pulled away with Stanley and Lula, I got into the Buick, and my phone rang.

"There's sort of a problem with your apartment," Briggs said. "I've got it mostly straightened out, but you might want to come see for yourself."

"Is it the toilet?"

"No."

"The television?"

"You have insurance, right?" Briggs asked.

ELEVEN

MY BUILDING'S PARKING lot was filled with people standing in clumps around the fire trucks, police cars, and EMT trucks. There were black smudges around my apartment windows and a hole punched into the brick in the general vicinity of my living room. I immediately spotted Briggs. He was standing in the middle of the lot, holding Rex's aquarium, his clothes in tatters, his hair and face sooty. And one of his shoes was missing. He was talking to a uniformed cop, who was taking notes.

I parked the Buick, ran to Briggs, and grabbed the aquarium from him. I looked inside and saw that Rex was in his soup can. He peeked out at me and blinked his shiny black eyes.

"He's good," Briggs said. "I got him out before it got too smoky."

My eyes filled with tears.

"Sorry about your apartment," Briggs said.

"As long as Rex is okay," I said. "The rest is just stuff."

"It's not as bad as it looks," Briggs said. "The rocket missed the window and hit the building, so the fire wasn't as bad as mine. It was mostly put out by your superintendent. He said he's getting good at putting out fires in your apartment."

"This must have happened right after I left."

"Pretty much. I figure Jimmy knew I was staying here, and he was watching to get me alone."

I turned to the uniform. "Did anyone see the rocket get shot off?"

"I don't know," he said. "We're canvassing the building and the neighborhood. Hopefully we'll find a witness."

I saw Morelli making his way around the fire hoses and responders. He was wearing his stoic cop face. He got to me and looked in at Rex.

"Is he okay?"

I nodded. "Yes. Briggs got him out in time. I was making a capture in the Burg when it happened."

Morelli looked up at my apartment. "Rocket?"

"Looks like it," I said. "I haven't had a chance to talk to anyone other than Briggs and the cop."

"I was in the living room when it happened," Briggs said. "I was going from the kitchen to the bathroom. I was going to take a shower. And all of a sudden there was this big *bang* that shook the building, and I was knocked on my keister. And there was a fireball on one side of the living room, by the window. And the fire ran up the curtains and there was a lot of black smoke, and the smoke detectors went off, and I got to my feet, ran to the kitchen and got the rat, and ran down the stairs with him and out of the building."

"He's a hamster," I said.

Morelli looked around. "I assume your car is here somewhere?"

"It's back by the dumpster," I said. "I couldn't find a place to park."

He gave me the keys to his SUV. "I'm behind the EMT truck. Wait there while I poke around. I'll get back to you." He looked at Briggs. "Do you need medical help?"

Briggs shook his head, and some small chunks of plaster fell out of his hair. "I'm okay, but I wouldn't mind you looking around for my shoe if you get into the apartment."

Morelli left, and Ranger called.

"I'm fine," I told him. "Briggs was in the apartment when it happened, and he carried Rex out."

"I've got Hal on the scene if you need him. He said Morelli's there so he's hanging back."

"How do you know all this without your control room?"

"We're functioning offsite."

An hour later the fire trucks and EMTs started pulling out of my lot. The fire marshal was on the scene. The gawkers were dribbling away, going back to their houses, and most of the people in my building were allowed to return to their apartments.

Morelli returned to the SUV and handed Briggs his shoe.

"How bad is it?" I asked.

"I've seen worse," Morelli said. "You were lucky it missed

the window and hit the wall. Your living room is destroyed, but the rest of the apartment is intact. Mostly what you've got is smoke damage and water damage. Your super went in immediately with commercial fire extinguishers and minimized the fire. He said he keeps them in the utility closet next to your apartment."

"How soon can I get in?"

"If the investigators don't find any structural damage, you should be able to get in this afternoon, but you're not going to be living here for at least a week or two. Maybe longer."

So my plan to use Briggs as bait had worked . . . but not in a good way.

"I'm staying here," Morelli said. "This is part of the Poletti investigation. If you want to take off, I'll call you when you can go in."

Briggs put his shoe on, and we walked to the edge of the lot, where the Buick was parked. My plan was to go to my parents' house and drop Rex off. If my father wasn't home, Grandma and my mother might let Briggs into the house long enough for us to regroup.

· · ·

"Holy Hannah," Grandma said when she saw Briggs. "What happened to him? Did your father catch up to him?"

"Someone shot a rocket-propelled firebomb into my apartment," I said.

"Again?" Grandma asked.

"Yeah, I was hoping I could leave Rex here." I peeked into the house. "Is my father home?"

"He's in the kitchen, finishing up lunch. And he's still complaining about the cake. You might not want to go in there with the little guy."

I handed Rex over and went back to the car with Briggs.

"You're going to have to find a place to live," I told him. "I'm going to move home with my parents until my apartment gets fixed, and you can't stay there."

"Where am I supposed to go?"

"Go anywhere. Mooch off friends or relatives. Move into a motel."

"Poletti will find me."

I put the car in gear and drove away from the curb. "He found you in my apartment, and now it's got a big hole in it!"

"What about using me as bait?"

"Been there and done that."

"Boy, this is the thanks I get for saving your rat."

"*Hamster*. And he wouldn't have been in danger in the first place if it wasn't for you."

"I'm thinking I should see some gratitude. I could have just run out and left him there, but I took the time to save his life."

I turned onto Hamilton Avenue. "You have a lot of nerve pulling the gratitude card on me after all I've done for you."

"You got me drunk, kidnapped, and almost blown up!"

"And you want more?"

Briggs slumped in his seat. "I don't know what I want. I'm depressed."

My phone rang, and I saw from the display that it was Lula. "I need you to come pick me up," she said. "I'm done here."

"What about Stanley?"

"He's with me. They discharged him. He just had a panic attack, but he's okay now. You can pick us up at the emergency entrance."

It took me three minutes to get to the hospital. Lula was standing at the curb, and Stanley was alongside her, wearing a hospital gown and handcuffs.

"You don't have to worry about anything," Lula said to me, helping to get Stanley into the backseat. "I put him in two gowns so his rear door don't flap open. And I got extra big gowns, too."

"I'm hungry," Stanley said. "I didn't get any lunch."

"Yeah, I'm hungry too," Briggs said. "I had an upsetting morning."

Lula looked over at Briggs. "What the heck happened to *him*?"

I steered the Buick into traffic and pointed us in the direction of Cluck-in-a-Bucket. "He was in my apartment when it got torched. Someone rocketed a firebomb into it."

"Say what?"

"He's out to get me," Briggs said. "He's not going to stop until he gets me."

"Maybe you shouldn't have done his wife," I said.

"Everyone's done his wife," Briggs said. "I was last in line. There was no one left to do her. I thought I was doing everyone a favor."

"Hold on here," Lula said. "Are we talking a rocket like *ZOOM BANG!* and everything's blown all to hell?"

"It was more like *BANG WHOOSH*," Briggs said. "It punched a hole in the brick instead of sailing through the window, and Steph's living room got cremated. And at great personal risk to myself I rescued the *hamster*."

"No shit?" Lula said. "Is that true?"

I swung into the parking lot to Cluck-in-a-Bucket. "Looks like it. I haven't been allowed into my apartment yet. What do you all want here?"

"I want a double Clucky Burger with large fries, onion rings, and a Diet Coke," Stanley said. "And I want an apple pie for dessert."

"I'll second that," Lula said.

"Yeah, me too," Briggs said.

"Who's going in for this?" I asked.

"Not me," Briggs said. "I can't see over the counter."

"I'd go," Stanley said, "but I don't have any money, and I can't carry all the drinks with these handcuffs."

"One of us gotta keep an eye on the prisoner," Lula said to me. "Pick your poison."

"Hey!" Briggs said. "Look at that guy who just got out of the black SUV and is going into Cluck-in-a-Bucket. That's Jimmy Poletti. That's the son of a bitch who blew up my apartment." Briggs was out of his seat belt and out of the car. "You son of a bitch!" he yelled at Poletti.

Poletti turned, saw Briggs and company, and took off at a run.

Lula and I bolted out of the car and ran after Poletti, chasing him around the building and across the street. I was in sneakers and jeans, and Lula was in five-inch stiletto heels and a skirt that came just two inches below her ass. I was gaining on Poletti. Lula was pounding the pavement behind me. And Briggs was running third, yelling obscenities and threats at Poletti.

The black SUV careened around the corner and slid to a stop, Poletti jumped in, and the car sped away.

"Shit!" Briggs said. "Shit, shit, shit, shit!"

Lula tugged her skirt down. "That Poletti has no luck at all. He's shot off two rockets so far, and neither of them's put a dent in Mr. Short, Pale, and Creepy here. And not only that but he got no guts. He obviously don't want to kill Briggs in front of witnesses. What's with that?"

We walked back to Cluck-in-a-Bucket, got our order, and carried it to the Buick. No Stanley.

"Somebody stole Stanley," Lula said.

"Yeah," Briggs said. "There's high demand for a fat guy wearing handcuffs and a hospital gown."

I drove the route from Cluck-in-a-Bucket to Stanley's parents' house, but we didn't see Stanley.

"Call me crazy," I said, "but I don't feel like putting any more effort into capturing Stanley today."

"It's no problem anyway," Lula said. "I got a date with him for Sunday night. I'll let you know when we get out of the movies, and you can come get him."

TWELVE

I **WAS AT** the office, finishing my lunch, when Morelli texted to tell me I could return to my apartment. I left Briggs with Lula and Connie, trudged out to the Buick, and slowly drove down Hamilton. I drove slowly because I didn't want to go home. I didn't want to see the destruction. It was depressing. I'd done this drill too many times. I was tired of it. At least this time there would be no blood spatters, I told myself. That was good, right? And honestly, why was I so upset? It's not like I was in love with the couch that got cooked. And it's not like the rocket was personally directed at me. I was a victim, but I wasn't the *targeted* victim. That would be Briggs.

Morelli was leaning against his car, waiting for me, when I pulled into the lot.

"You're talking to yourself," he said when I got out. "I don't know if that's a good sign or a bad sign."

"I was trying to talk myself out of being morbidly depressed."

"Did you succeed?"

My eyes filled with tears.

Morelli wrapped his arms around me and held me close. "It's not so bad," he said. "A coat of paint and it'll be like new. And you never liked that couch anyway."

"Yes, but the apartment was just painted after that guy blew himself up in my foyer. I liked the new color."

Morelli took my hand and tugged me toward the building. "We'll paint it the same color."

We took the stairs to the second floor and ran into Dillan Ruddick, the building super. He had a wet vac going, sucking up water from the soggy hall carpet.

"Thanks for saving my apartment," I said to him.

"No problemo," Dillan said. "I've got it down to a science. The alarm goes off and I run straight to your apartment and grab the fire extinguishers."

"Nice to know," I said to Dillan. "I'm a disaster!" I whispered to Morelli.

"Yeah, you keep life interesting," Morelli said, unlocking my apartment. "Be careful where you walk. The carpets are soaked. We'll get a restoration team in here tomorrow. As you can see, most of the damage is confined to the living room."

"There's a hole in my wall! I can see daylight through it."

"Dillan's going to board it up as soon as he gets rid of some of the water. I thought you'd want to get some clothes. Probably everything's going to have to be cleaned and aired to get rid of the smoke smell."

I filled my laundry basket and two garbage bags with clothes. I added food for Rex and some basic toiletries, grabbed the things that belonged to Briggs, and we left the apartment.

Morelli stuffed everything into the Buick. "Where are you going now? Are you moving in with your parents?"

"Probably, but I don't know what to do with Briggs. They won't take Briggs."

"He's an adult," Morelli said. "He can take care of himself."

"Everything in his apartment was destroyed. And Poletti is trying to kill him."

"It's not like he's blameless. He helped Poletti cheat on his taxes, and he boinked his wife."

"You know about the wife?"

"Everybody knows about the wife."

"And he saved Rex."

"Now we're getting somewhere," Morelli said.

"I can't just walk away from him."

Morelli looked like he was trying not to grimace. "You're such a cupcake."

My eyes filled with tears again.

"Oh crap," Morelli said, cuddling me into him. "You can stay with me. And you can bring Briggs with you."

. . .

I brought my clothes to my parents' house and filled the washer with the first load.

"I'll take your black suit and hang it outside to air," Grandma said. "You'll need it for the funeral tomorrow."

Oh joy, the funeral. The only thing I hate more than a viewing is a funeral. I grabbed some chocolate chip cookies from my mom's cookie jar, told Grandma I'd be back, and chugged off to the office in the Buick.

"I'm surprised you haven't gotten a new car by now," Lula said when I walked in.

"No time to look, and no money to buy," I said. "I need to capture Poletti." I handed Briggs the duffel bag filled with his clothes. "It was lucky you were keeping your clothes in this heavy-duty bag. They might not smell too smoky, and they shouldn't have any water or foam damage."

Briggs took his clothes bag to the bathroom to change, and Connie sprayed the office with air freshener.

"You have to get him out of here," she said. "Even with clean clothes he's still going to smell like charbroiled goat."

"Have you heard any news about the Rangeman building?" I asked Connie. "Is it still under quarantine?"

"So far as I know," Connie said. "My cousin Loretta called about a half hour ago. She's a nurse at St. Francis, and she said Emilio Gardi isn't doing well. He's in kidney failure."

A sick feeling swirled through my stomach.

"What about Ranger's man McCready?"

"I haven't heard anything about him."

I called Ranger. "How's McCready doing?"

"He's managing. They're trying something new with him."

"And you?"

"I'm not running at full capacity, so be careful. I can't always see you."

He disconnected, and I took a moment to calm myself. There've been times when I'd welcomed the news that Ranger wasn't following my every move, but this wasn't one of them.

"You're whiter than usual," Lula said to me. "Are you okay?"

I sat in the chair by Connie's desk and hung my head between my legs. "I'm a little freaked out."

"You know what helps me when I get freaked out?" Lula said. "Donuts. You probably need donuts. And I wouldn't mind having some donuts either."

Briggs came out of the bathroom. "I'd like a donut."

He'd washed the smudges off his face, combed his hair, and put on clean clothes. He still smelled like smoke, but it wasn't at the charred goat level anymore.

"I don't need a donut," I said. "I need some sanity to my life. Some normality."

"Yeah, but a donut's a good start," Lula said. "I always think better when I got a donut in my hand."

"Where do you suppose Ranger is hiding out?" I asked Connie.

"I don't know," Connie said, "but I'm guessing he's not too far away from Rangeman. He's a cautious guy. He probably has a small satellite office with his account information duplicated offsite somewhere safe. I can't see him trusting the cloud."

I knew he owned several properties in Trenton. All under different holding companies. I didn't know any of the addresses.

"Okay," I said, "I'm going for donuts. Who's going with me?"

"I am," Lula said.

"Me too," Briggs said.

I drove Lula and Briggs to Tasty Pastry, gave them a twenty, and told them I wanted two chocolate-covered donuts. As soon as they were in the bakery, I took off. It was a sneaky thing to do, but I needed some personal space. I wanted to find Ranger, and I couldn't do it with Lula and Briggs tagging along.

My phone rang two minutes later.

"What the heck?" Lula said.

"I had to get away from Briggs so I could talk to Ranger," I told her.

. . .

I started at the Rangeman building and methodically explored a six-block area. I was looking for a building with secure parking and reflective glass windows. Ranger was all about privacy. I enlarged the grid and found a building on Bender Street that had promise. It was about a half mile from the Rangeman building. It was a three-story townhouse with tinted windows. An alley ran along the back of the townhouse, the backyard was enclosed by a nine-foot cement wall with an automated security gate, and security cameras looked down at the alley from the roof.

I got out of the Buick and waved at one of the cameras. Thirty seconds later my phone chirped.

"Babe," Ranger said.

I smiled at the camera. "Howdy."

The gate opened. I got back into the Buick and drove into the paved parking area. There were three black SUVs parked and three more spaces. The back door to the townhouse opened, and Tank looked out. He didn't look happy to see me. I stepped past him into a hallway that led to the front of the house and a six-man elevator.

"Third floor," Tank said, holding the elevator for me.

The elevator opened onto a third-floor loft and Ranger. He didn't look that happy either, but then it's hard to tell with Ranger. He doesn't usually show a lot of emotion.

The walls were white. The furniture was sleek black leather. The floors were cement. There was a small ultramodern galley kitchen, a dining room table and six chairs, a corner set aside as an office, a couch and a coffee table in front of a flat-screen television, and a section partitioned off that I imagined was a bedroom and bathroom.

"Is this the Batcave?" I asked him.

"It was a safe house until you discovered it."

"And now it's not safe?"

"Now it's a home," Ranger said.

"Wow!"

The corners of his mouth twitched into the beginnings of a smile. "Don't read too much into that."

"It was a profound revelation. And I don't know how to tell you this, but your safe house wasn't that hard to find."

"Only because you know me so well. And it's more satellite office than safe house. Was there a specific reason for this visit?"

"I have two problems. The first is Jimmy Poletti. I know Poletti is in the area because he just shot a firebomb into my living room. Unfortunately, I'm not having any luck capturing him. I thought you might be able to help me."

"Do you have a plan?"

"I have some ideas."

"And your second problem?"

"It's you. I don't like the thought that some freakazoid polonium assassin will have better luck the second time around and you'll end up glowing in the dark. It's causing me stress, so I wish you'd find the guy and eliminate him."

"I'm working on it."

"Do you have any leads?"

"I think this person is probably Russian. Either mob or military. I've apprehended some members of the Russian mob. And it wouldn't be hard to imagine Gardi moving in those circles."

"Why Russian?"

"The polonium-210 that was in Gardi's possession is a relatively obscure radioactive poison that has limited production. To my knowledge it's currently being produced only in Russia and is available only to well-connected Russians."

"And you think some Russian mob guy hates you enough to do this?"

"It would require a certain level of insanity, but it's possible."

"So how do you find this guy?"

"It's hard without access to Gardi."

"Morelli said even the police don't have access."

"He's been charged with nuclear terrorism. He's guarded by an army of FBI agents, and no one at the federal level is sharing information."

"I bet I can get you in."

One eyebrow raised a fraction of an inch.

"I've got Randy Briggs," I said. "He was briefly head of security at Central Hospital, and while he was at Central he filled in weekends at St. Francis. I'm sure he knows everyone's schedule and all the ways to get onto a floor."

THIRTEEN

THERE WAS A single donut left in the box when I got back to the office. I helped myself to the donut and turned to Briggs.

"Ranger needs to talk to Gardi," I said. "Can you get him into St. Francis?"

"That could be tough. From what I hear the floor is crawling with FBI. They won't even let hospital security in."

"Someone must be getting in," I said. "Doctors, nurses, housekeeping, food service. What would be our best shot?"

"Housekeeping. I'm sure everyone going into that room is gowned and masked, so that's an advantage. I can get you suited up, and then all you have to do is go in with a stack of towels and sheets. Late afternoon is best. Unless Gardi's having an emergency, he should be alone. Doctors do rounds in the morning, and nurses do paperwork around four o'clock. Usually, security doesn't stay in the room. They hang outside the door. The problem is with Ranger. Housekeeping's all women. They work in pairs, pushing a cart filled with supplies."

"I could be a pair with Stephanie," Lula said. "Ordinarily I don't like being in a hospital, but this would be different. This would be like one of them doctor shows where I'd have a chance to give an award-winning performance. I could perform the snot out of this role."

"Are you sure you can't get Ranger in?" I asked Briggs. "He needs some specific information."

"I can suit him up," Briggs said. "And I can tell him how to get on the floor. I don't know if he can bluff his way past the FBI. If I was protecting Gardi, I'd be reluctant to let a big guy I didn't know get into the room."

"But being we're ladies we wouldn't have those problems," Lula said. "We could go about our business like we were invisible."

"Maybe," Briggs said. "I think it's a crapshoot."

"Do you know what Ranger needs to get out of Gardi?" Lula asked me.

"He wants to know who gave Gardi the polonium."

"If you need information from Gardi you want to try to get it sooner rather than later," Connie said. "He's not doing well."

St. Francis is walking distance from the bail bonds office, but we had Connie drive us. I called Ranger on the way and told him the plan.

"This wasn't what I had in mind," he said.

"If I get caught you'll be my one phone call."

This was met by silence on Ranger's side, so I disconnected.

Briggs took us to a back entrance that was used for maintenance purposes. The door had a four-digit thumb lock. He tapped in the combination, and the door opened.

"They never change the combination," he said. "This isn't exactly the world's most secure hospital."

We followed him down an empty corridor to a supply room. We pulled scrubs on over our clothes, grabbed sterile gowns and masks, and Briggs rolled a laundry cart over to us.

"Connie said he's in isolation on the third floor," Briggs said. "Ordinarily he'd be in the lockdown ward for prisoners, but they don't have the ability to segregate him there. Tell the guard at the door you're here for the contaminated linens. Make sure you're wearing double gloves and the mask. If the guard has any sense, he'll walk away from the room when you go after the linens."

"How do you know all this?" Lula asked Briggs.

"There's a protocol for patients getting radiation. It's nasty stuff. The drill with the laundry is that one of you stays just outside the room with the laundry cart and one of you goes in and empties the hamper and checks the bathroom. There are a bunch of security cameras past this point, so I'm going to stay here. You want to put your masks and gowns on now, and don't take them off until you're back here, out of camera range."

"We need names," Lula said to me. "I'm going to be Shaneeka. Who do you want to be?"

"Judy."

"Say what? That's a lame name for a secret-agent nurse."

"I'm not a nurse. I'm pushing a laundry basket."

"It don't matter. You still could take pride in your work. I think you should be Shandra."

"Okay, I'm Shandra."

We followed Briggs's instructions and took the service elevator to the third floor. Three men in rumpled gray suits and wearing earbuds were at the end of the corridor.

"Showtime," Lula said, setting her sights on the three men.

"We're going to keep a low profile," I said to her.

"Sure," she said. "I know that."

Lula stopped in front of the men and looked into the room. The door was closed, and on it was a sign with the international symbol for radiation.

"Shandra and me are here to get the contaminated linens in this room," she said. "We're sort of new at this, so you might want to stand back in case we accidentally spew some bad shit out at you."

All three men took several steps back.

I pulled on double gloves, took a large heavy-duty orange plastic bag with a radiation symbol on it from the cart, and went into the room.

Gardi was in bed, hooked up to a bunch of tubes that were dripping stuff into him. His eyes were closed, and his skin was the color of wet cement.

"Hey," I said to him. "How's it going?"

He half opened his eyes. "Great."

"Sorry about the polonium."

"Shit happens."

"I heard someone set you up."

"You heard wrong. I set myself up. It was a business deal. I needed money. Bad. Now I'm a dead man."

"There might be an antidote."

"You got one in your pocket?"

"Just saying. Who gave you the polonium?"

"Who wants to know?"

"Ranger."

"Figures. Look, I got nothing personal against him, even though he ruined my dinner with my friends."

"Then help me out here. Who gave you the polonium?"

"Some guy with a weird tattoo on his neck. I told the FBI, and they looked at me like I was nuts. I don't think they believed me."

"Does this guy have a name?"

"I didn't get one. He approached me. Said he knew I needed money. Said he had a lot of money and needed a job done."

"What did this guy look like?"

"Average height and build. He was wearing a hooded sweatshirt with the hood up. Caucasian, but I couldn't see his hair. He had on mirrored sunglasses, but I could see he had a scar above one of his eyes. He had some kind of accent. Sort of British. And he had that tattoo on his neck."

"What did the tattoo look like?"

"It was a skull with a flower."

"And he told you he wanted you to deliver the polonium?"

"Yeah. He said if I got it on me it was deadly so I should be careful. I guess he got that right."

"But you agreed to do it anyway."

"It was a *lot* of money. And it seemed safe. The canister had a timer on it. I pushed the button, and I had a half hour before it spewed out the shit. Except the stupid thing got busted in the scuffle with the Rangeman guy, and it all leaked out on me."

I went into the bathroom and gathered up his towels. "How did Skull and Flower pass the canister to you?"

"He got me a hotel room in New York. The Gatewell. The canister was in the room when I checked in."

"And the money?"

"Cash. Delivered to my . . . financial partners."

"Jeez, Emilio, this sucks."

"Is my hair falling out yet?"

"Not that I can tell."

"If I beat this thing, I'm debt free."

"Yeah, well, good luck."

I left the room and shoved the orange bag of linens into the cart.

"We all done here?" Lula asked.

"Yep. All done."

We put our heads down and walked the laundry cart to the service elevator. We got off at the ground floor, pushed the cart beyond the point where there were security cameras, and shucked our masks, gloves, gowns, and scrubs. We left the cart in the hall and exited the building. Connie and Briggs were waiting at the curb. A black SUV that I suspected was a Rangeman vehicle was idling across the street. Lula and I got into Connie's car, and she drove us back to the office. The black SUV pulled up behind Connie's car, and Hal got out.

"Ranger would like to see you," Hal said.

I got into the SUV, and Hal drove me to the safe house on Bender Street. I took the elevator to the third floor and found Ranger at his desk.

"You didn't have to make your one phone call," he said.

"No. I got in to see Gardi, and so far no one's come after me."

"How is he?"

"He looks terrible, but he was coherent. He's been talking to the FBI, but it sounds like they don't think the information is worth anything. Gardi doesn't have a name. He said it was a business deal. He needed money bad, and this guy came to him and offered him the job. Gardi saw the man once. The money was paid in cash to Gardi's business partners. The canister of poison was left in a New York hotel room for pickup. That's it."

"Did he give you a description?"

I told Ranger everything Gardi had told me, from the FBI interrogation to the guy with the scar and the tattoo.

"Let me guess," Ranger said. "It was a skull and a flower."

"Yes! Do you know him?"

"Only as Vlatko. Our paths crossed while I was on a search and rescue mission in North Korea, and he was a Russian SVR thug. SVR is the new KGB."

"Did you work together?"

"No. We were on opposite sides. He was Russian intelligence, and I was point man for a ground troops unit."

"And?"

"The operation was a success, but it wasn't clean. Troops were lost on both sides. I was captured and handed over to

Vlatko for torture. His specialty was disembowelment. He put a six-inch slice into my belly before I managed to get the knife from him."

"I thought that scar was from an appendectomy."

"If the knife had gone deeper, it would have been."

"And what did you do to *him*?"

"I stuck the knife in his eye."

"Wow, that's pretty horrible. North Korea was years ago. Have you heard from Vlatko since?"

"No. I thought he was out of my life."

"I guess he didn't like losing an eye."

"Go figure," Ranger said.

"The only other thing I got from Gardi was the name of the hotel in New York. It was the Gatewell."

Ranger tapped the name of the hotel into his computer.

"The Gatewell is on the West Side," he said. "It's a small boutique hotel. I'll do some research on it."

"Would that research involve hacking into their client database?"

"That would be illegal," Ranger said, "and difficult from this location, but we might be able to manage it."

Hal drove me back to the bonds office. I loaded Briggs into my car, and picked up a couple pizzas. Morelli was just returning from a walk with Bob when I rolled in. Bob rushed over, sniffed at the pizza boxes, and growled at Briggs.

I put the pizza boxes on the coffee table, and Morelli brought a roll of paper towels and a cold six-pack of Bud from the kitchen. He flipped the television on, and we dug in.

"Any luck finding Poletti today?" Briggs asked Morelli.

Morelli shook his head. "He's out there, but he's moving around."

"Big of you to let us stay here, considering the risk," Briggs said.

Morelli paused with a pizza slice in his hand. "Risk?"

"The probability that you'll get a firebomb shot through your window is really high," Briggs said.

Morelli looked surprised. Like he hadn't actually thought about it.

"If we don't advertise that you're here," I said to Briggs, "no one will know and no one will shoot a rocket through Morelli's window."

Briggs looked at the beer. "I don't suppose you've got a Heineken?" he asked Morelli.

"I've got Bud," Morelli said.

Briggs gave out a major sigh of disappointment and took a Bud. "Have you got a beer glass?" he asked.

"You didn't ask for a glass at *my* house," I said.

"My expectations are lower at *your* house," Briggs said.

Morelli got Briggs a glass. "Don't let the curtains on the windows and the toaster in the kitchen fool you. I'm even less civilized than she is."

It was a nice thought, but I wasn't sure it was true. I chugged my beer from the can and scarfed down two pieces of pizza.

"I need to go to my parents' house to get my laundry," I said to Morelli. "Grandma has my black suit airing so I can wear it to the funeral tomorrow."

Morelli looked over at Briggs. "What about *him*?"

"I was going to leave him here."

"You aren't just going to take off, are you?" Morelli asked. "You're coming back, right?"

"Yes. I'm coming back."

FOURTEEN

MY LAUNDRY WAS all neatly folded in the laundry basket. My black suit had been aired and pressed and was on a hanger. My red dress was at the cleaners. My mother and grandmother were the queens of clean and organized.

"Did you hear about Emilio Gardi?" Grandma asked. "Marjorie Barstock called and said he just died."

"Are you sure?"

"Marjorie's daughter works at the hospital, and she said there was a big to-do over it. The FBI was hoping he'd stay alive long enough for them to get more information out of him. Marjorie said her daughter thinks it was his heart that went kaput. That radiation stuff is bad. That's why you never stand in front of the microwave."

"Is there any dessert?" I asked Grandma.

"Your mother made vanilla pudding. I think there's one left in the fridge. And there's whipped cream to go with it."

I found the pudding, added a big glob of whipped cream, and ate standing in front of the sink.

"Where do you suppose they'll bury him?" Grandma asked. "Do they have to put him in one of them toxic-waste dumps out in Nevada?"

It seemed unlikely to me, but I didn't know for sure.

"Marjorie said the youngest Poletti boy was in the emergency room today too. Her daughter said he was high as a kite, and I guess he was smoking some weed, and he set his shirt on fire, and he got some burns on his hands trying to rip his shirt off. Here's the perfect example why weed is more dangerous than alcohol. Most of the time people don't set themselves on fire when they're drinking alcohol."

"I have to get back to Morelli," I said. "I left Briggs there."

Grandma helped me carry the laundry out to the car. "If you hear anything about the burial, let me know. And we need to be at the church tomorrow at eight in the morning. I don't need to get there early on account of I don't care where I sit for that."

I drove back to Morelli's house, parked at the curb, and lugged the laundry basket into the living room. Briggs, Morelli, and Bob were watching the ball game. No one was bleeding, so I took that as a good sign.

"You know what I could use?" Briggs said. "Ice cream."

Morelli cut him a sideways glance. "I don't have any ice cream."

"Somebody could go get some," Briggs said.

All three heads swiveled and looked at me.

"Okay, fine," I said. "Do you need anything besides ice cream?"

"Cookies," Briggs said.

I went to the convenience store a mile away on Hamilton. I got three tubs of ice cream, two bags of cookies, and Twizzlers. I now had zero money and a maxed-out credit card. I parked in front of Morelli's house and called Ranger.

"I need money," I said. "I need to catch Poletti. He wasn't at his mother's viewing, but he might try to attend the funeral tomorrow morning. Maybe he'll show up in disguise or he'll watch from a distance. I could use some help."

"How much help do you want?"

"Another set of eyes."

"Done."

I fished a Twizzler out of its packaging and bit off a piece. "Gardi died."

"I heard," Ranger said. "I have two men searching through data for Vlatko, but we're not turning anything up."

"How hard could it be to find a one-eyed guy with a skull and a flower tattooed on his neck?"

"There wasn't anyone with that description on Facebook or Match.com," Ranger said.

"What's next?"

"Field trip to New York."

I disconnected with Ranger, then called Lula and asked for her help as well. I needed someone to look after Briggs while I watched for Poletti.

· · ·

Morelli gave up on the ball game at ten o'clock.

"I have an early meeting tomorrow and my team's losing," he said.

Briggs was settled in on the couch. "I'm going to stay to see the end."

Morelli's house wasn't big, but it was comfortable for a single guy. Living room, dining room, kitchen, and half bath downstairs. Three bedrooms and bath upstairs. It would also have been comfortable for a married couple or a young family. It was *uncomfortable* with Briggs in it.

I was in Morelli's bed wearing panties and a T-shirt with the covers pulled up to my chin. Morelli was naked next to me.

"Is there a problem?" he asked.

"Briggs."

"He's downstairs watching television."

"I'm worried he'll just walk in on us to ask if we have organic taro chips or to tell us he needs to borrow a credit card to rent a porno film."

"He's watching the ball game."

"You don't know that for sure. He's little and sneaky. He could have crept up the stairs. Did you lock the bedroom door?"

"Yes."

"You're fibbing. It doesn't have a lock on it."

"Would you feel better if I pushed the dresser in front of the door?"

"Maybe. But he could still be listening."

Morelli was inching my panties down.

"Don't you care if he's listening?" I asked him.

"No." He kissed my bare shoulder and did some exploration under the T-shirt.

"I can't stop thinking about him," I said.

Although, I had to admit, Morelli had wonderful hands. And he was an amazing kisser. And I was liking what his hands were doing.

"Do you like this?" Morelli asked, and he ran a finger across my nipple.

"Mmmm," I said.

And then a vision of Briggs, listening to us on the other side of the door, popped into my head.

"I'm having a hard time focusing," I told Morelli.

"As you can tell, I'm not having that problem."

"I noticed. And there's a part of me that really would like to do this. And I mean *really* would like to do this. But I can't shake the feeling that Briggs is out there. I mean, what if the game suddenly ends?"

"There were two innings left."

"That's true," I said. "So maybe if we're super fast we can get it done before the game ends."

"There's no problem on my end," Morelli said.

There might be a problem on *my* end. "What if everyone gets struck out and the innings are over in record time? In fact, for all we know, they could be on the last inning *now*. It could be the *bottom* of the last inning!"

"Okay," Morelli said. "I was saving this for a special occasion, but maybe this is a good time to try it out."

He fumbled around in the nightstand drawer and brought out a neon blue and silver box. "I busted Ziggy Shestok last week. He was selling stuff out of the trunk of his Cadillac again, and I got this baby for two bucks. If you bought it on one of those shopping channels, you'd pay twenty dollars for it."

"Wait. You arrested Ziggy for selling hot appliances and then you bought one?"

"No. I arrested him for selling drugs. The appliances were just a sideline for him. He had toasters too, but I already have one of those." Morelli peeled the cellophane wrapper off the box, took the gizmo out, and held it up for inspection. "Batteries included," he said.

"Holy Toledo. What are all those nubby little things on it?"

"It says on the box that they're pleasure stimulators."

"Pleasure is good," I said.

"Damn straight."

Morelli turned it on. *BZZZZZZZZZZZ!*

"Whoa. It sounds . . . *powerful*."

"It's called the One-Second Wonder Tool."

He hit the go button again, the thing *bzzzzed* in his hand, and I felt the vibration run through his body and into the mattress.

I jumped to the other side of the bed. "That sounds like too much pleasure."

Morelli pulled me back to his side, threw a leg over me, and kissed me. "Be brave," he said. "It's got a money-back guarantee."

I squeezed my eyes shut and clenched my teeth. "Do it!"

BZZZZZZZZZZ! BZZZZZZZZZ!

"Yow!" I yelled.

Morelli rolled off me. "What? Are you okay?"

"Better than okay," I gasped. "That might have been the best second of my life."

BAM, BAM, BAM! "Hey," Briggs shouted from the other side of the door, "are you all right in there? I heard this weird buzzing. It sounded like a bunch of angry bees."

"Power surge," Morelli said. "It happens all the time. Go back to the game."

FIFTEEN

I **WAS IN** the kitchen enjoying my second cup of coffee when Briggs shuffled in.

"I couldn't sleep," he said. "I kept waiting for a firebomb to come through the window."

"A firebomb isn't going to come through the window. No one knows you're here."

"He'll find me. It's just a matter of time." He helped himself to coffee. "Where's Morelli?"

"Early meeting. He's already out of the house."

"What's with the black suit on you? You look like you're going to a funeral."

"I am. Jimmy Poletti's mother is getting buried today."

"I forgot. Do you think I should go?"

"Yes. We need to leave for the service in twenty minutes."

Briggs returned to the kitchen in fifteen minutes. He was

showered and dressed in clothes that were wrinkled but clean and smelling only slightly of smoke. He scarfed down his coffee and a bowl of cereal, complained about the quality of the orange juice, and we were out the door and on our way to get Grandma.

Grandma was wearing a royal blue pantsuit and black patent leather pumps, and she was carrying her large black patent leather purse. I strongly suspected she had her .45 long barrel in the purse.

I pulled the Buick into the funeral line at the church and had a funeral flag attached to my car. Lula slid in line behind me in her red Firebird. We all got out of our cars and gathered on the sidewalk. Lula was wearing five-inch heels and a stretchy black skirt and wrap top. Her hair had been toned down for the occasion from hot pink to magenta.

"So what's the plan?" Lula wanted to know. "We gonna hang the little guy out and hope someone takes a potshot at him?"

"That's plan B," I said. "We'll do that tomorrow if plan A doesn't work today."

"And plan A would be what?" Briggs asked.

"We go to the church service and the funeral and hope we see Jimmy Poletti lurking somewhere," I said. "We'll spread out and keep in touch by phone."

"I'm ready to take him down," Grandma said. "I've got the big boy with me."

"Keep the big boy in your purse, please," I said, "and call me if you see Jimmy. I'm going to hang outside. I want you and Lula to go inside with Briggs. Don't let anyone snatch him."

I crossed the street to get a better view of the church and

its surroundings. I'd fibbed a little about not hanging Briggs out for a potshot. Of course I was hanging him out. Everyone knew it, including Briggs, but I didn't think he wanted to hear me admit it.

My phone buzzed, and I looked down at the text message:
Babe.

Ranger was in place . . . somewhere.

Five minutes later, Grandma texted me. She, Lula, and Briggs were seated in the last row and could see the whole church, and so far they hadn't spotted Jimmy, but the Poletti boy was there with his hands bandaged.

Organ music drifted out to me. The big carved oak doors closed, and there was silence.

Another text from Ranger. *Two plainclothes cops inside, and one outside standing half a block from you.*

I looked down the block and waved at the guy on the corner. He grinned but didn't wave back. I looked around for Ranger, but couldn't find him. No surprise there.

I watched the passing cars and the side doors of the church. I didn't see any unusual activity. After a while the big double doors at the front of the church opened, and people began trickling out.

I got a text from Lula. *We're staying with the dead lady. So far no one's wanted short stuff, but he's gotten a bunch of dirty looks from a lot of people. He don't seem to be real popular.*

I waited across the street until Mrs. Poletti was eased into the hearse. The cop at the corner was still in place. Grandma and Lula were on the sidewalk by the hearse with Briggs squashed between them. No Ranger in sight. Grandma and Briggs went with Lula, I got behind the wheel of the Buick, and we all played follow the leader to the cemetery.

I parked on the road that led to the gravesite, got out of the car, and immediately got a text from Ranger.

Looking good.

I didn't know if he meant me in my little black suit, or if he meant that Jimmy Poletti was here. Either way, it was a good message. I followed the people who were walking to where a tent gave shelter to a few chairs. The cemetery was old and held generations of families. Grave markers varied from simple flat stones on the ground to elaborate granite statues of angels. The terrain was for the most part open grass fields, but there were also mature trees scattered over acres of graves.

The Poletti grave was on the side of a gently sloping hill. There were approximately fifty people at graveside. A few mourners were sitting on folding chairs, but most were standing. Lula, Grandma, and Briggs were at the outer edge of the crowd. I was a short distance away, with my back to the gravesite, watching the road.

I felt a change in my force field, caught a hint of Bulgari Green shower gel, and knew Ranger was near.

"You're looking in the wrong direction," he said, close behind me. "He's standing off to the side, by the maple tree."

I turned and picked out Jimmy Poletti, partly hidden by the tree, dressed in a dark suit, looking solemn.

"I feel bad that we're taking him down at his mother's funeral," I said.

"Babe, he shot a firebomb into your apartment."

"We don't know for sure that it was him."

"Do you want to let him walk?"

"No, but it would be nice if we could wait until the ceremony is over to grab him."

"I'm willing to wait, but I can't speak for the undercover guys."

"Do you think they see him?"

"Not yet, but it's only a matter of time, because he's creeping closer."

"How did he get here?"

"He has a car parked on the other side of the hill."

"And he's alone?"

"He was the only one in the car."

"How is it that you know all these things and I don't?" I asked.

"I know where to look."

I couldn't hear the priest from where I was standing, but I could see that he was going through the ritual. Briggs looked bored, shifting his weight from foot to foot. He couldn't see much in front of him. He was looking around, up at the sky, back at me, over to the maple tree. I saw him stiffen, and I knew he'd spotted Jimmy Poletti.

"Briggs!" I said to Ranger. "He sees Jimmy."

Ranger moved forward, but not in time to stop Briggs.

"It's *him*!" Briggs yelled, pointing to Poletti. "You son of a bitch!"

The priest froze midblessing, mouth open, eyes wide. Every

head swiveled to the maple tree. Poletti went deer in the head-lights.

"I got a gun," Lula said, shoving her hand into her purse. "Just everyone hold up until I get my gun."

The plainclothes guys were on the move, and fifty geriatric mourners scrambled to get away from the action, pushing and shoving, heading for their cars.

Poletti turned to go up the hill, saw a cop running down the hill toward him, and changed direction, running straight for the grave. A shot was fired and everyone hit the deck, except Lula, Grandma, and Briggs, who were holding their ground.

Lula had a two-handed grip on her Glock and was trying to get a sight on Poletti. Briggs was enraged, his face bright red, his eyes crazy.

"What the hell is wrong with you?" Briggs yelled at Poletti. "You blew up my apartment, you moron!"

"You fucked my wife!" Poletti yelled back, running full-tilt at Briggs. "I hate you."

"Everybody fucks your wife," Briggs shouted. "I don't see you blowing up *everybody's* apartment. It's because I'm short, isn't it?"

Lula fired off a shot that went wide, and Poletti charged Briggs. Grandma swung her purse just as Poletti swept past her. The big black patent leather bag caught Poletti on the side of the head, and Poletti staggered and crashed to the ground. Ranger cuffed him, and the three cops took over.

Lula and Grandma did a complicated high five.

"I did it," Grandma said. "I just ticked off one of the things on my bucket list. I just took down a bad guy. I got to put on some fresh lipstick. I'm going to be the talk of the wake."

"I could have taken him," Briggs said. "I would have ripped him to shreds."

"Yeah, you could have bitten him in the knee," Lula said.

"Don't underestimate a bite in the knee," Briggs said. "It could cripple someone."

SIXTEEN

RANGER AND I followed Poletti and the police down the hill to the cars and on to the police station. I waited while Poletti was booked in, I got my body receipt, and I returned to the parking lot, where Ranger was waiting. He was dressed in black slacks, a form-fitting black T-shirt, and a black blazer.

"You're not in Rangeman fatigues," I said. "Are you a businessman today, or is this just funeral attire?"

"I need to go to New York, and I thought the security guard look would be limiting. It would be helpful if you could come with me."

"I assume you're looking for Vlatko."

"Right now the hotel is my only lead."

I drove to the office and handed the body receipt to Connie.

"I'm going on a field trip with Ranger," I told her. "Poletti is off the streets. So Briggs can manage on his own now."

I don't get to New York as often as I'd like. Mostly because I have no time and no money. So even though this was business, I was excited about the trip. And let's be honest, I was excited about going to New York with Ranger. Plus I know this is shallow, but I was in his megabucks Porsche, feeling like I was in a James Bond movie.

Ranger took the Turnpike to the Lincoln Tunnel and parked in a lot on the Upper West Side of Manhattan not far from the Gatewell Hotel. It was midday, and the streets were crammed and the sidewalks weren't much better. The Gatewell was in the middle of the block, two blocks off Broadway. The doorman was dressed to look like Chairman Mao. The lobby was small but elegant. Lots of shiny black and white and silver with touches of red.

Ranger showed the manager his identification and his right-to-recover papers for Emilio Gardi.

"We have reason to believe he stayed in this hotel," Ranger said.

"The FBI have already asked about him," the manager said. "They were here yesterday."

"This is a different issue," Ranger said. "I represent his family and his bondsman."

"I don't have much information on him. He stayed here for one night last week. His room was prepaid in cash. There were no additional charges. No credit card on file."

"Do you have the name or phone number of the person who made the reservation?" Ranger asked.

"There's nothing on record, but one of the young men on

the front desk remembered the transaction. The man making the reservation did it in person two days in advance and pre-paid in full. He stood out because he had a slight British accent and an odd tattoo on his neck. A skull and a flower."

The hotel had a lounge off the lobby. We sat at a high-top table and ordered sandwiches from the bar menu.

"Is Vlatko British?" I asked Ranger.

"He's Russian, but he speaks fluent English that's more British than American."

"Do you speak Russian?"

"I understand some Russian, but I speak very little."

"There has to be a reason why he chose this hotel."

"There's a large Russian community here on the West Side," Ranger said. "I'm guessing he has ties to something nearby. A relative. A friend. A job. A woman."

We finished our lunch, and Ranger returned to the manager.

"Do you have many Russians staying here?" he asked.

"A fair amount," the manager said. "There's a satellite arm of the consulate one block south on Seventy-fifth Street. They host trade shows and small VIP parties, and they sometimes recommend us to visitors."

I followed Ranger out of the hotel and we walked one block to Seventy-fifth. We looked up and down the street but saw no Russian flags displayed. We walked east and studied the buildings we passed. We found the consulate on the second block. It was identified by a gold plaque fixed to the building. Writing was in Russian and English. The door was locked. There was a call box beside the gold plaque.

We crossed the street to get a better look. Five stories. Black wrought iron filigree on the lower-level windows. The windows on the upper floors were tinted and most likely impact glass. Security cameras scanned the street from the roof.

Ranger called Tank, gave him the consulate's address, and told him to research the week's events. Minutes later, Tank texted Ranger the consulate's schedule.

"There's a trade show going on this week for Russian vodka," Ranger said. "This consulate will be hosting a meet-and-greet party at five o'clock. That would be a good time for us to slip in."

We had some time to kill, so we went back to our high-top table at the Gatewell Hotel. We ordered drinks and received our complimentary bowl of bar nuts. We didn't touch any of this. We watched the room. There were four men at the bar. Two of them looked like cartoon versions of Russian vodka salesmen. Large red noses, too much flesh, laughing too loud, drinking vodka. And they were speaking Russian.

"You need to introduce yourself to those men," Ranger said. "It would help break the ice if you gave them more to look at. Something that would compensate for the fact that you don't speak Russian."

"What if they don't speak English?"

"They probably speak enough to get by."

I went to the ladies' room and looked at myself in the mirror. I was wearing a black business suit with a silky white shirt under it. My hair was pulled into a ponytail, and I was wearing heels. It was appropriately sexy for a funeral, but not so much for Russian vodka salesmen.

I opened enough buttons on the shirt that I was showing some cleavage. I wasn't sure if it was enough cleavage to compensate for my lack of Russian, so I stuffed some toilet paper into my bra. The cleavage got better, but I still wasn't anywhere near Lula cleavage. I walked around a little to make sure the toilet paper didn't rustle or shift in place, and then I shoved in some more. I was now bulging out of my bra, straining the fabric on my silky shirt, and there was no way I could button my jacket.

I jumped up and down to make sure I wouldn't unexpectedly have a wardrobe malfunction. I jiggled a little, and my nipples didn't pop out of my bra, so I figured I was good to go. I gunked up my eyes with a lot more mascara, added some eyeliner, and applied a fresh coat of blood red lipstick. I looked at myself in the full-length ladies' room mirror and worried that I still might not be compensating enough for my lack of language skills, so I pulled the scrunchie off my ponytail. *Whoosh*, my hair instantly expanded. I worked at it with water and hairspray until the natural curls were back. I now had a *lot* of hair, and a *lot* of it was frizz. This is why I usually wear a ponytail. Still, I thought it might be sexy, if you like the big frizzy-hair look. I mean, you see it in *Vogue* all the time, right?

I went back to the full-length mirror and took another look. *Yikes!* Good thing my mother wasn't here or I'd be grounded. I might have overdone the toilet-paper thing.

Ranger called my cellphone. "Babe," he said, "you've been in there a long time. Is everything okay?"

"Yep. It's peachy."

I hurried out of the ladies' room, took a deep breath, and set out across the room with what I hoped was a confident stride. Stephanie Plum, cunning sexpot, about to embark on a dangerous mission.

"What do you think?" I asked Ranger when I reached the high-top.

"Babe, you don't want to know what I'm thinking."

I actually had a pretty good idea what he was thinking, since his pupils were totally dilated. Like maybe we should forget about the two Russians at the bar and get a room. And now that I was slutted up and getting into the role, I was having similar thoughts. Problem was, undressing was going to be awkward.

"You do realize that I have half a roll of toilet paper stuffed into my bra?"

"I wouldn't share that with the men at the bar," Ranger said. He gave me a tiny earbud. "You can stay connected to me with this."

"Will you be able to hear what I'm saying?"

"Yes."

I stuck the earbud in my ear and sashayed over to the bar. I took the barstool next to one of the Russians and crossed my legs, letting my skirt ride up to a couple inches below my doo-dah, and asked the bartender for a champagne cocktail.

Conversation stopped, and both men looked my way. The man next to me smiled wide, displaying a gold-capped molar. He said something in Russian, and I did a palms-up display of

I no speak that language. I accompanied the palms-up with a giggle, and I jiggled around a little. It was like airhead bimbo–meets–ADHD Pomeranian.

"My name Leo Stolchi," he said. Heavy accent. "I sees you do not speak Russian."

"Honey, I have enough problems with English."

This got a big laugh, and his eyes tracked down to my boobs and from there went on to my crotch, which was demurely hidden by a small amount of black skirt fabric.

"You are very pretty," he said.

"Well, thank you," I said. "Aren't you sweet."

My drink arrived, and Leo told the bartender to put it on his bill.

"And *generous*," I said.

Leo looked unsure of "generous."

"What is 'generous'?" he asked.

"It's like . . . rich. You must be rich."

The smile was back. "Yes! Very, very rich."

"How did you make all your money?"

"Vodka," he said. "I makes the best."

I glanced over at Ranger and smiled. Jackpot.

"Do you know that man?" Leo asked.

"He's a friend of the family," I said.

"He look like a bad man."

"He has his moments."

No sound came over the earbud from Ranger, but I thought I sensed him smile.

"Are you staying at this hotel?" I asked Leo.

"Yes. It close to the consulate building where will take place the meetings. There is party soon."

"I love parties," I said.

"This a good one. They serving my vodka." He looked at his watch. "I should be going."

Damn! I was losing him. I put my hand on his leg. "That's too bad. We were just getting to know each other."

"It no will be long," he said. "Two hours."

My hand moved an inch closer to a place I really didn't want to go, and I leaned forward to give him a better look at the girls. "My friend has to leave, and I would be here all alone."

"I would stay but this important party."

Good grief, this guy was dense! "I could go with you," I said. "And then we can have our own private party when we come back to the hotel."

His eyes opened wide. "Yes! That is perfect plan."

"Last week I met a Russian named Vlatko," I said. "Do you know any men named Vlatko?"

"Vlatko is much common name in Russia."

"This man had an unusual tattoo on his neck. And he might only have one eye."

"I know a Vlatko what has his initials tattooed on forehead," Leo said. "This must be different Vlatko."

"Have you been inside the consulate building already?"

"Only for the short times yesterday. I went to register." He signed the tab over to his room and got off the barstool. "What about family friend?"

"Maybe he could come to the party with us. He loves vodka."

"I guesses that would be okay. He isn't going to have the party with us *after,* is he?"

"Not unless you want him to. He's gay, you know."

"He doesn't look gay."

"Of course he does. His skin is flawless and his haircut is perfect. And look at his slacks. Not a single wrinkle."

"How does he do that?" Leo asked. "I always get the wrinkles."

We stopped at Ranger's table and invited him to join us at the party. He dropped some money on the table and stood.

Leo stared at Ranger's slacks and gave me a sideways glance of acknowledgment. No wrinkles.

SEVENTEEN

THE MAN AT the consulate door checked Leo's invitation, and there was a brief conversation.

"No problems," Leo said to me. "You and your friend comes in. I very important vodka magnate."

The party was being held in a large room on the ground floor. The room was decorated in reds and golds. Oriental rugs. Antique-looking furniture in dark woods and brocaded fabrics. Very formal. Waiters in white shirts and black slacks were passing appetizers. A bar with two bartenders was set up at the far side of the room.

People were pouring in from the street. The men were in suits, and the women were in cocktail dresses. Average age for the men was fifty. More difficult to assess the women. It looked to me like a lot of the women were mid-level to high-end hookers. I figured I fit into the mid-level range.

Leo tugged me over to the bar. "You see bottle with red label? That is my vodka. You must drink some."

Ranger had already wandered off on his own to snoop through the five floors. I was left with the vodka king.

"It's a pretty bottle," I said.

"It made in China. They makes the best bottles. They add lead to make sparkle." He took two glasses of vodka from the bartender and passed one to me. He chugged his, and I sipped at mine. It burned all the way down, and I felt like my sinus cavities were on fire.

"Smooth," I said.

His eyes fixed on my bulging breasts. "Like mother's milk."

"Yep, that's what I was thinking." I looked around. "Do you know any of these people?"

His eyes were still focused on my chest. "I knows some of them. It is small world where is Russian vodka makers."

"If you'd like to talk to some of the people here, I'll be fine on my own. I'll just stay here and drink vodka."

"I should do this," he said. "Do not go away. I haves big plans. Leo that kind of guy. I much known to be big."

"Good to know."

He stepped away, and I checked in with Ranger. "Where are you?" I asked him.

"Third floor. Checking my email. Don't drink too much vodka."

"Just trying to increase my lead consumption. Over and out."

I had the bartender swap out my vodka for water, and I

155

JANET EVANOVICH

drifted around the room, eavesdropping. No one seemed especially interested in talking to me, but everyone stared at my chest. The women studied me with critical eyes. No doubt making surgical comparisons. The men smiled their approval. I didn't have the biggest breasts in the room, but I think I had the most enthusiastic. Almost everyone was speaking Russian, so I wasn't doing great in the information gathering department. I refrained from snacking on the appetizers that were being passed, just in case Vlatko had a grudge against vodka salesmen.

Leo looked at me from across the room, and I gave him a flirty finger wave. I felt a little bad about leading him on like this, but what the heck, he probably had a wife and five kids back in Russia, and he deserved to be lied to.

For lack of something better to do, I went in search of the ladies' room. I adjusted my toilet paper and put on fresh lipstick. I found some hair clips in my bag and used them to secure my hair so that it wasn't fluffing out all over my face.

"How's it going?" I asked Ranger.

"I'm on the top floor, and I'm limited by the security cameras everywhere."

As I ran water to wash my hands, my earbud fell out of my ear and went down the drain.

"Crap!"

I hauled my cellphone out of my bag and texted Ranger. *Bad news. Your earbud just went down the drain in the ladies' room.*

It was only a matter of time, he texted back.

I left the ladies' room, and as I stepped out into the long

156

hallway that led to the front of the building, a man came out of nowhere, slammed me into the wall, and held me there with one hand at my neck.

"I know who you are," he said. "Nice of Manoso to deliver you like this."

He had a slight British accent and a skull and flower tattoo showing just above his white shirt collar. It was Vlatko. He was younger than I'd expected. Not much older than Ranger. Slightly shorter and slimmer than Ranger. More boyish-looking. In fact, he could probably pass for a college student until you looked closely and saw the network of fine lines around his eyes. A psychopath you would be inclined to trust. Ash blond hair fell over his forehead. One of his eyes was covered with a black patch like a pirate's. The other was pale blue. A ragged scar showed above and below the patch.

I wanted to say something clever to show I wasn't afraid, but my heart was pounding so hard in my chest it was rattling my brain, and I was speechless.

"He's in the building," Vlatko said. "I saw him on the outside video feed. He's searching for me, isn't he?" He smiled. "In many ways this is much more fun than if everyone had been infected with the aerosol."

"Why are you doing this after all these years?"

"Convenience. I've kept an eye on Manoso, waiting for an opportunity to even the score and finish the job I started. And here it is. It was dropped into my lap. I had a job to do in Miami, where, as you know, Manoso has many relatives. And when my Miami job was completed I was scheduled to travel to

New York. It was perfect. I convinced my superior that I would need an extra canister for a test run, and then I sourced out someone from Miami who could place the polonium for me in the Rangeman building."

"This was a test?"

"It was a dry run of sorts to see if the polonium would work, and obviously the scheme was flawed. Truth is, we all had some doubts. Too many variables. And using an amateur to deliver a package like that is too unreliable."

"So you're done with Ranger?"

He gave a bark of laughter. "No. I'm only beginning. I'm going to kill him, but I'll torture him first. I'll let him watch you die, and then I'll finish the work I started on him in Korea. It will be even more satisfying than the radiation poisoning I originally planned. Although polonium is a very elegant assassination tool."

"That's sick."

"Not in my profession."

"Your profession is sick!"

"You need something to show Manoso," he said. "A small appetizer before he's treated to the main course."

He pulled a switchblade out of his pocket, flicked it open, and, still holding me against the wall with his left hand, slashed my right breast. The knife easily cut through the silky material of my shirt and my bra, and a huge wad of toilet paper fell out.

"Jeez," I said. "This is embarrassing."

"Unsatisfying and disappointing," Vlatko said, "but consistent with the intelligence report I got on you."

A woman left the party room and turned toward us. Two men also left the party room and walked toward the front entrance. Vlatko spun on his heel and, without another word, exited through a door across the hall.

I went back to the ladies' room and with shaking hands pulled the rest of the toilet paper out of my bra and buttoned my suit jacket. I texted Ranger that Vlatko was in the building and I was leaving. I would meet him in front.

I left the ladies' room and walked past the party room without even waving at Leo. He was going to have to figure it out on his own. I exited the building, and Ranger was moments behind me.

"He's probably watching us on the outside video feed," I said.

"I pulled the plug on the feed, but he could be watching from a window." He looked at the suit jacket buttoned over my vastly reduced chest. "You lost some weight."

"Long story. I'll tell you in the car."

Ranger gave me his keys. "Take the car and go home, and feel free to use it until I come for it. I'm going to stay and stake out the building. There's no rear exit. He has to come out this way."

"I can stay with you."

"Not necessary. I've already asked Tank to send men. They should be halfway here by now."

"Vlatko wants to finish the job he started in Korea," I said. "And I think there's something else going on. He said the episode at Rangeman was a dry run."

· · ·

I borrowed money from Ranger for parking and tolls and drove back to Trenton. Morelli called just as I was approaching my Turnpike exit.

"I'm driving," I said. "I'm not supposed to be talking on the phone."

"I grilled hotdogs for dinner, and I don't know if I should save the leftovers for you or feed them to Bob."

"Save one for me. I'm about an hour away."

Rush hour had come and gone, and traffic was light. I reached Morelli's house in just under an hour and parked Ranger's Porsche behind a bright blue RAV4.

Briggs was in the living room, holding on to his duffel bag, when I walked in.

"My cousin Eddie said I could stay with him now that no one wants to kill me," Briggs said.

"Is that your RAV4 at the curb?"

"Yeah. I was afraid to drive it when Poletti was looking for me."

"Do you have any job prospects?"

"No, but that's never an issue. I just play my short card and people are afraid I'll sue them if they don't hire me."

Briggs left, and I went into the kitchen in search of my hotdog. I removed my suit jacket, and I heard Morelli suck in some air. I looked down and saw that not only was my shirt slashed open, it was stained with dried blood.

"Psychopath encounter," I said to Morelli. "I think it's just a scratch."

"You don't know?"

"There was a lot going on." I checked myself out and verified that it wasn't serious. I added mustard, ketchup, pickles, and potato chips to my hotdog and took a bite. "I'm starving," I said with my mouth full of hotdog.

"About this psychopath," Morelli said.

"I went to New York with Ranger following a lead on the polonium thing. I had a run-in with this crazy guy named Vlatko who planned the poisoning, and he sort of slashed me."

"Where was Ranger when all this was happening?"

"He was snooping around in the Russian consulate."

Morelli was looking like his blood pressure was approaching stroke level. "Tell me you weren't in the consulate with him."

"It was a party. Technically I was there with a Russian vodka maker."

"How do you know a Russian vodka maker?"

"I picked him up in a bar."

"You've managed to do a lot in a short amount of time," Morelli said.

I washed the hotdog down with a beer. "We weren't able to catch Vlatko, but Ranger has him pinned down in the consulate."

"I don't suppose you brought the FBI in on this?"

"Not while I was there. It all happened too fast. I guess Ranger could have called them in after I left."

Personally, I thought chances of that were slim to none. Ranger would want to call the shots on this, and the FBI would freeze him out.

"So how did *your* day go?" I asked Morelli.

"*My* grandmother says *your* grandmother is stalking her."

"That could be true. Grandma made a bucket list, and getting your grandmother is on it."

"Did she say how she was going to get her?"

"I don't think she's decided."

"She wouldn't do anything crazy like shoot her or beat her silly with a baseball bat, would she? I don't want to have to arrest your grandmother."

"I'll talk to her."

EIGHTEEN

WHEN I WALKED in, Grandma was in the kitchen, chopping vegetables for soup.

"Help yourself to coffee," she said. "Would you like me to make you some eggs? Your mother is at mass."

"I already ate breakfast," I said, "but coffee would be great."

"I guess you're happy now that Jimmy Poletti's behind bars," Grandma said.

"Yep. Briggs is out of my life, and I can afford to get a car of my own. Thanks for helping with the takedown."

"I got a good start on my bucket list," Grandma said. "Not that I'm planning on getting planted anytime soon, but I figure why not get all that stuff out of the way, right?"

"There've been some rumors that you're stalking Joe's Grandma Bella."

"You bet I'm stalking her. I'm freaking her out. She tried to put the whammy on me a couple times, but I just whammied her back."

"You know how to do that?"

"I Googled it. I'm pretty sure I got it right."

Joe's Grandma Bella is the scourge of the Burg. She looks like an extra from a *Godfather* movie. Steel gray hair pulled back into a bun. No makeup. Ferocious black eyebrows. Eyes like a fish hawk. Five long black chin hairs. She's short and stooped and wears black shirtwaist dresses and flat black shoes. The longer she's lived in this country, the stronger her Sicilian accent has become. And she is feared for her ability to give people the eye. The eye is some weird Sicilian curse that makes your hair fall out, your face break out in warts, your teeth rot in your mouth, and your private parts shrivel. Intelligent people cross the street rather than pass too close to Bella. Grandma prefers to pass as close as possible and double-dare Bella to look at her cross-eyed. And Bella is happy to comply. The result is sometimes an ugly display of old lady bitch slapping. And God forbid they should simultaneously get to the cookie table at the funeral home with just one cookie remaining.

"I know getting the best of Bella is on your bucket list."

"You bet it is. I'm going to get her good. She's messed with me one time too many. Remember when she called me an old slut?" Grandma whacked a carrot in half. "Well, I'm not all that old. And she bumped me on purpose with her shopping cart at the grocery store. She said I wasn't moving fast enough. And then she tried to push in front of me in the checkout line."

My mom came into the kitchen at the end of Grandma's tirade.

"She's a silly old lady," my mother said. "You could be a good Christian and turn the other cheek."

"I'm a plenty good Christian," Grandma said, "but I got it on good authority that God wants me to get Bella for Him."

My mother made the sign of the cross and wistfully looked over at the cabinet where she keeps her booze. Being a good housewife and Christian woman, she knew it was too early in the day for medicinal help from Jack Daniel's.

"I have to get to work," I said to Grandma. "Don't do anything that'll get you arrested."

"Don't worry," Grandma said. "I'm going to be sneaky."

• • •

"Wow," Lula said when I got to the office. "Is that Ranger's car you're driving?"

"Yeah, it's a loaner."

"You must have done something real good to get that car as a loaner."

"Sadly, no."

"I have a new skip," Connie said. "It just came in. Gloria Grimley. She's in Hamilton Township."

"What did she do?" I asked.

"She held up the bakery on Nottingham Way. Armed robbery."

"How much did she take?"

"No money, but she cleaned out the cannoli display."

"And she got arrested for that?" Lula said. "That's just terrible. Obviously the woman needed a cannoli. I don't know what this world's coming to when you get arrested for needing a cannoli."

I took the file, paged through it, and stopped at her picture.

Lula looked over my shoulder. "What's that on her face in her mugshot?"

"I think it's chocolate," I said.

"At least she knows what she's doing when it comes to stealing cannoli," Lula said. "And that bakery on Nottingham was a good choice. They make excellent cannoli. And they stuff them with all kinds of shit, too. Not just the usual stuff."

I left Ranger's two-seater Porsche at the office and took Lula and the Buick. Gloria lived in Hamilton Township. I knew the area. Classic suburbia. Three-bedroom, two-bath ranch houses built in the sixties. Enough yard for a swing set. A driveway but no garage.

Her house was painted a cheerful yellow and white. A Honda Civic was parked in the driveway. Lula and I went to the door and rang the bell.

"This here's a house where happy people live," Lula said. "I can tell these things. I got a good feeling about this house. This woman probably just accidentally left her purse at home and needed to celebrate something with a pastry. I know the feeling. I've been there a couple times myself. 'Course I never robbed a store for a pastry, but only because I never forgot my purse."

I rang a second time, the door opened, and a fiend from hell looked out at us. She vaguely resembled the booking photo, but her hair was way beyond bed head, she had dark circles under her bloodshot eyes, she had a huge herpes sore at the corner of her mouth, and she was wearing a pink flannel nightgown with what looked like gravy stains splotching the front of it. Her nose was running, and she had a balled-up tissue in her hand.

"What?" she asked.

"Whoa," Lula said, backing up.

I held my ground. "Gloria Grimley?"

"Yes."

"Are you okay?" I asked her.

"Yes," she said. "I'm fine." And she burst into tears. "F-f-f-fine."

"Where's the happy people in this house?" Lula asked. "I was pretty sure this was a happy house."

"The son of a bitch left me," Gloria said, sniffing up some snot. "Just like that. One minute everything is roses, then he says he's met someone else, and he's sure she's his soulmate. Can you believe that?"

"What about this here cheerful house?" Lula asked.

"Rented," she said. "I'm stuck with a year's lease."

"Good news," Lula said. "You're up for armed robbery. By the time you get out of the pokey, your lease will be up."

This got another giant sob.

"I don't suppose you've got any of those cannoli left," Lula said.

"I ate them," Gloria said. "All of them. I was depressed."

"I saw the report, and that was a lot of cannoli," Lula said.

Gloria looked down at her nightgown. "Tell me about it. This is the only thing that fits."

"We need to take you downtown to get you rebooked and rebonded out," I said to Gloria. "It would be good if you could find something else to wear."

"Maybe you got some big-ass sweatpants or something," Lula said.

Gloria shuffled off to her bedroom and came back minutes later in jeans and a T-shirt. The jeans were only zipped halfway.

"That's got a advantage," Lula said, "being that you won't have to give them your belt."

"I forgot something," Gloria said.

She turned, went back into her bedroom, and *Bang!* Lula and I went dead still.

"Oh crap," Lula said.

Bang, bang, bang!

We ran to the bedroom and found Gloria pumping half a clip into a picture of her ex-husband.

She dropped the gun onto the floor, turned, and mooned the picture and farted.

Lula and I took a step back.

"Sorry," Gloria said. "I get gas when I eat too much sugar."

We loaded Gloria into the Buick, and I called Connie on

our way to the municipal building so she could rebond Gloria. An hour later we were all back at the office. Connie was at her computer. Lula was on the couch reading *Star* magazine. I was looking at used cars on Craigslist.

The door crashed open and Briggs staggered in, dragging his duffel bag. His hair was sticking out every which way, his eyes were bugged out, and he had black sooty smudges all over his face and clothes.

"Someone blew up my car," he said. "Lucky I wasn't in it. I have one of those remote starters so I can get the air-conditioning going if I want. I pushed the starter when I came out of my cousin's house and *kaboom*. It knocked me on my ass."

"Your ass is pretty close to the ground anyways," Lula said.

"It was a big fireball," Briggs said. "If I was any closer I'd be a cinder now."

"So how come you got your duffel bag with you?" Lula asked.

"It's my clothes. My cousin kicked me out of his house, being that someone still wants to kill me."

"Oh no," I said. "No, no, no, no."

"You gotta help me out," Briggs said. "It must not have been Poletti. I need a safe place to live."

"How about Florida?" I said. "You could rent a condo somewhere on a bus line so you don't need a car."

"I don't want to live in Florida. It's too hot. And they have big bugs and alligators."

"You want to see a big bug, you should go into the storeroom here," Lula said. "There's the roach that ate Tokyo back there."

"I don't get it," Briggs said. "I was sure it was Poletti. He tried to run me over. I saw him."

"Who else's wife did you sleep with?" Lula asked.

"Recently?"

Lula turned to me. "And we're supposed to be keeping him from getting a rocket up his butt why?"

I didn't have an answer to that one, so I stepped outside and called Ranger.

"Are you still in New York?" I asked him.

"I'm on my way home. Vlatko left the consulate this morning with two other men. They got into a car, and we lost them in traffic. I left Rich and Silvestor there to watch the building, but I doubt Vlatko will be back."

"Is there anything I can do for you?"

"Babe," Ranger said.

"Besides that."

I thought I heard him smile just before he disconnected.

I went back into the office, and Briggs was sitting in one of the cheap orange plastic chairs. His duffel bag was between his feet, and he looked depressed.

"Okay," I said, "let's think about this. Someone wants you dead. And it's someone who doesn't want to get his hands dirty. If you take Poletti out of the equation, you have two rocket-propelled firebombs and a car bomb. Very impersonal. Death from a distance."

"Or it could be someone who likes explosions," Lula said.

I looked at Briggs. "Do you know anyone who likes explosions?"

"All the poker players," Briggs said. "They were always going out to the Pine Barrens to blow stuff up. One time they blew up a refrigerator. Sometimes they took their kids. Like it was family fun day. Poletti's older kid never went, but the stoner loved it."

"There are three poker players left," I said. "Ron Siglowski, Buster Poletti, and Silvio Pepper. Out of those three, who wants to kill you the most?"

"I don't know," Briggs said. "I didn't boink any of their wives. Ron Siglowski and Buster Poletti don't even *have* wives. And Pepper's wife is comatose by noon."

"Sounds like your kind of date," Lula said.

"There are advantages," Briggs said.

"What about Scootch and Tommy Ritt?" Connie asked. "They were shot at close range. How does that fit?"

"It doesn't fit," I said. "Maybe we're looking at two different killers."

"So far, only one of them is a killer," Lula said. "And the other one has no luck at all."

"Maybe you could let me live here at the office for a couple days until I figure things out," Briggs said. "I could sleep on the couch, and if someone shoots a rocket through the window I'm close to the hospital."

"Not happening," Connie said.

"How about a motel room?" I said. "There are some inexpensive motels on the road to White Horse."

"I'd be a sitting duck in a motel."

"Maybe if you weren't such a sleazebucket you wouldn't be in this predicament," Lula said. "You ever think of *that*?"

"Talk about the pot calling the kettle black," Briggs said. "I never took money for sex acts."

"That's 'cause no one would pay you," Lula said.

Dillan Ruddick called on my cellphone.

"I have your apartment pretty cleaned up, and the claims adjuster is going to be here in ten minutes," he said. "I thought you might want to walk through with him."

"Sure," I told him. "I'm on my way."

"What about me?" Briggs asked. "Am I on my way too? What was that about?"

"I'm going to meet the claims adjuster at my apartment."

"I could be helpful," Briggs said. "I have a good head for finance. I could take notes for you."

NINETEEN

THE ADJUSTER WAS already in my apartment when I walked in with Briggs.

"This isn't so bad," Briggs said. "They've got your rug taken up already, and all the stuff's gone that was in the living room. It doesn't even smell bad."

Correction. The apartment didn't smell as bad as Briggs. Briggs smelled like burning rubber, and he looked like a train had run over him.

"Hey, I remember you," Dillan said to Briggs. "You're the little guy who was in the apartment when it got hit by the rocket."

"Yeah, lucky me," Briggs said.

The adjuster looked up from his clipboard. "Goodness," he said, "are you still wearing the same clothes?"

"No," Briggs said, glancing down at himself. "Different explosion. Some idiot blew up my car this morning."

173

"That's amazing," the adjuster said. "Two explosions in one week."

"Three," Briggs said. "Three explosions."

"Maybe you want to check out the rest of the apartment while I walk around with the adjuster," I said to Briggs.

"This is a fairly straightforward claim," the adjuster said. "Most of the significant damage was confined to one area. There's some smoke and water damage. And there's the hole in the wall. That's actually covered under another policy."

"Probably you don't get a lot of claims for damage done by handheld rockets."

"Not in this neighborhood. Mostly those claims are in the projects and in the area around Stark Street."

The adjuster left, and Dillan stayed behind.

"We're doing the same carpet and paint color as last time, right?" Dillan asked.

"Right."

"That makes it easy. I should have you all put back together in a week, depending on the carpet guy, the masons, carpenters, drywallers, and painters."

Dillan left, and Briggs went from the bedroom to the kitchen, looking in the refrigerator and the cupboards.

"There's even mustard in the refrigerator," he said. "And your dishes look okay. You could move back in."

"It's easier for me to live with Morelli," I said. "I probably need to get a new mattress, and I'd rather not live with the paint smell." Not to mention that Morelli has a toaster, his mom fills his refrigerator with lasagna and ricotta pie, and he is available for snuggling. Snuggling with Morelli is not to be underestimated.

"I don't mind paint smell," Briggs said. "I could live here until you want to come back."

This was much better than having Briggs live with Morelli and me. I was running the risk that eventually I'd have to eject Briggs at gunpoint, but I'd deal with that later.

"Sure," I said. "But you have to leave when the carpet goes in."

"Yeah, I know. Boy, this will be great. This is a terrific apartment."

"What's going on with *your* apartment?"

"They're saying six months to rewire and rebuild. So I was let out of my lease. There was also some mention of me being an undesirable tenant, being that people wanted to blow me up."

"Personally, if I was walking in your shoes, I'd take my chances with the giant bugs and gators in Florida."

"My life will be all straightened out as soon as you find out who's trying to kill me."

"That would be a job for a cop. I was looking for Poletti because he skipped out on his bond."

"But you're so good at this. I bet you could find the creep."

"Even if I wanted to help you, I have no idea where to start looking."

"How about talking to Buster? He's related to Jimmy Poletti. Maybe they were working together to off me. And Buster was involved in the Mexican business, so he might think I know something."

I narrowed my eyes at him. "Do you?"

"What?"

"Do you know something about Buster that would incriminate him?"

"No more than everyone else does. Everyone knew he was in Mexico. And now that it's come out about the girls, you could assume Buster was part of that. I guess I know more about the money."

"What about the money?"

"There was a lot of it."

"In Mexico?"

"Yeah," Briggs said. "But I don't know exactly where. Not exactly, only approximately."

"Good grief."

"So how about it? Maybe you could go talk to Buster."

"I can't just go talk to Buster. What would I say?"

"You could ask him if he's trying to kill me. And then you could tell him to cut it out or else."

I left Briggs in my apartment and drove back to the bail bonds office.

"Where's your little buddy?" Lula asked.

"I left him in my apartment. It's sort of habitable."

"Aren't you afraid someone's going to shoot another rocket through your wall if Briggs is living there?"

"Yes, but it was the best of all the alternatives."

"You better hope the police find this rocket shooter guy," Lula said.

I hiked my messenger bag higher on my shoulder. "I'm going to talk to Buster," I said.

"I'll go with you," Lula said. "Maybe I'll get a look at the killer Chihuahuas. And besides, I want to ride in Ranger's Porsche."

Ordinarily you wouldn't park a decent car on Stark Street, but Ranger's car was so expensive that it was protected against theft or vandalism. It would be thought that Ranger's Porsche belonged to either a high-level drug dealer or someone making a major drug investment. And the locals didn't want to mess with either of those kinds of people. The locals knew to protect the marketplace. Not to mention the Porsche had an alarm system that could be heard for miles. I found a parking place on Stark, and Lula and I marched over to Buster's building and rang the buzzer on his intercom.

"Talk to me," Buster yelled.

"It's Stephanie Plum," I said. "I came to show you my breasts."

"Come on up." And he buzzed the door open.

"That works good," Lula said. "That's better than the pizza delivery thing. I gotta remember this."

Buster was waiting for us at the top of the stairs.

"Two for the price of one," he said.

"Bad news," I told him. "I lied about the breasts."

"How about her?" he said. "I'd rather see hers anyway."

"Sure," Lula said.

She pulled one out of her tanktop, and I clapped my hands over my eyes.

"Holy crap," Buster said. "That's massive."

"And because I'm in a good mood," she said to Buster, stuffing herself back into her clothes, "I'm not even going to charge you for looking."

"About the real reason for this visit . . . ," I said.

"You got Jimmy behind bars," Buster said. "Now what?"

"I want to talk to you about Randy Briggs. Are you trying to kill him?"

"Gee, why would anyone want to kill Briggs? He's such a sweet guy."

"Actually, I don't care if you want to kill him," I said. "I just don't want another rocket shot into my apartment. And I don't want to find Briggs bleeding on my floor. So if you want to kill him, I'd appreciate it if you'd do it someplace far away from my apartment."

"I'll keep that in mind," Buster said. "You sure you don't want to show me your tits?"

"I'm sure."

"Do you want to see mine?"

"No!"

• • •

I stopped at a deli on lower Stark, and Lula made a sandwich run while I took a call from Briggs.

"I need to go food shopping," Briggs said.

"And?"

"I haven't got a car."

"Do you have feet?"

"Yeah, but there aren't any supermarkets nearby, and I can't carry a whole lot anyway. I swear this is the last favor I'll ever ask of you. Ever, ever, ever."

I dropped Lula at the office and picked Briggs up at the back door of my apartment building. He'd cleaned himself up as best he could, but his hair was singed, his face looked sunburned, and he still smelled slightly of smoking rubber.

"I just need some basic things," Briggs said. "And I want a bottle of wine."

"There's a liquor store next to Shop and Bag."

"This is a really nice car," he said. "I like riding in it. These seats are real leather, too. Do you get it on with Ranger in this car?"

"Ranger isn't my boyfriend. Ranger and I have a professional relationship."

"Yeah, but that doesn't mean you can't play hide the salami once in a while."

I punched XM Radio on, tuned in to an electronic dance station, and turned the volume up. Ten minutes later I swung into the Shop and Bag strip mall parking lot.

"You work on your grocery list, and I'll get the wine," I said. "What kind of wine do you want?"

"I want a cabernet. California is okay. And get me a Russian River pinot noir."

"Sure. What's your price point? Do you want something in a box or in a bottle?"

"How about you get the food and I'll get the wine," Briggs said.

I took his shopping list and looked it over. Seemed simple enough. Bread, milk, cereal, butter, coffee, some deli meat, cookies, and cheese. I added a bag of chips, a frozen pizza, a jar of peanut butter for me, and a chew toy for Bob. I was at the checkout when an explosion rattled the store windows. I left my shopping cart and ran outside. Black smoke billowed off a flaming inferno, and people were running toward something lying in the parking lot.

"Briggs," I said on a sigh. "And Ranger's Porsche."

A couple people got Briggs to his feet and walked him away from the fire toward the store. I met them halfway.

"What happened?" I asked Briggs.

"Boom," Briggs said. His eyes were glazed, and his hair was smoking. "Big boom."

"Are you okay?"

"I don't know," he said. "How do I look?"

"You look good," I told him.

That was a lie. He looked like an overcooked marshmallow. The one that got dropped into the fire and retrieved and was all sooty.

"Yeah," he said. "I feel okay. Did you get the cookies?"

"Yeah, I got cookies."

"I think the wine got blown up."

"That's okay," I said. "I'll get more wine. Maybe you should sit down over there by the store."

"It went *boom*," Briggs said. "There was a big boom."

I stayed with Briggs until the paramedics came and checked him out. He had some superficial burns and scrapes, but he was basically okay. I went back inside the store, paid for my groceries, and returned to Briggs with the bag of cookies.

Briggs selected a cookie. "I put the wine in the car and sat down in the passenger seat, and then I decided to see if you were finding everything okay in the store. So I got out of the car and next thing I hear *WHOOOSH!* and *KABBAM!* and I was flying through the air."

What was left of the car had been hosed down, and the fire truck was packing up. I'd given the police a preliminary report.

Ranger called on my cellphone.

"The tracking mechanism on my Porsche went dead," Ranger said. "Is there a problem?"

"There are some mechanical difficulties," I said. "It would be great if you could send someone to pick me up."

Fifteen minutes later, Briggs had eaten the entire bag of cookies, and Ranger arrived in a black SUV. He got out and stood looking at the smoldering lump of melted, mangled Porsche.

"I assume this is my car," he said.

"Yep," I replied.

"No one was hurt?"

"Nope. Briggs was a little rattled, but he's okay."

He wrapped an arm around me. "How about you? Were you rattled?"

"I'm always rattled."

"Do we know who did this?"

"No. I was in the grocery store, and Briggs was sitting in the car. He decided to come get me, got out of the car, heard a *WHOOSH*, and next thing he was flying through the air. He didn't see anything, but I think it sounds like the rocket guy."

"So this is the fourth attempt to kill him?"

"Yes. Three firebombs shot from some sort of rocket launcher, and one car bomb."

"Any suspects?"

"Several."

"We have two options," Ranger said. "We find the inept amateur who's doing this, or I put a bullet in Briggs's brain and we get on with our lives."

I was pretty sure Ranger wasn't serious about shooting Briggs, but then again, he had a point.

We looked back at Briggs. He was sitting on a bench with a blanket wrapped around him, and his feet didn't touch the ground.

"Your call," Ranger said.

"Boy, this is a tough decision."

A smile twitched at the corner of Ranger's mouth, and he kissed me just above my ear. "I suppose we should take him home. Where is he living?"

"In my apartment."

"Babe."

"I'm letting him stay there while it's under construction."

"And you?"

"I'm rooming with Morelli."

TWENTY

WE DROPPED BRIGGS and his groceries at my apartment building, and Ranger drove me to the bail bonds office, where the Buick was still parked.

"Have you heard from Vlatko?" I asked Ranger.

"No. With any luck, he's busy working on his primary assignment and I have time to find him before he goes on the attack after us. I had a contact comb through recently issued visas, and no one named Vlatko was on the list, so we can assume he's using a different name."

"We know he's working out of the Russian consulate in New York," I said. "Suppose I go back there and try to get a name."

"Do you have an angle?"

"I can go back with my lawyer and my slashed shirt and accuse Vlatko of viciously attacking me at the party."

"Who's your lawyer?"

"Briggs. When all else fails, he's good at playing the short card."

"I like it, but if something goes wrong, you're on foreign soil and a rescue will be more difficult."

"But not impossible?"

"Not impossible," Ranger said. "When do you want to do this?"

"Tomorrow morning."

I watched Ranger drive away, and I called Briggs.

"Do you have a suit?" I asked him.

"Did you say 'fruit'?"

"I said 'suit.'"

"Sorry, my ears are ringing from the explosion. I *had* a suit, but it went up in flames with everything else I owned."

"I need you to pretend to be a lawyer tomorrow morning, and you need to look the part."

"My friend Nick is my size. I might be able to borrow some clothes from him. What kind of lawyer am I?"

"Litigator."

"Oh man, I'm going to be a kick-ass litigator. Who are we suing? I can do this. I'll scare the crap out of the sonsabitches. I even thought about being a lawyer when I was in college."

"I'm not suing anyone. This is sort of a con."

"A what?"

"A con. A scam."

"Say again."

"A con," I yelled into the phone.

"A *con*. Even better!"

"Call me if you need a ride to pick up the clothes. Otherwise I'll come get you tomorrow at eight A.M."

Lula was on the couch, reading email on her smartphone, when I walked into the office.

"This here's from my cousin Joleen," she said. "She's gonna get married as soon as her boyfriend gets a parole. He's got a hearing coming up in a couple weeks, and they're thinking about a December wedding if everything goes right."

"Gee, that's great," I said. "What's he in for?"

"Armed robbery with intent to kill, but it wasn't his fault. He was on a lot of drugs."

"And he's off them now?"

"Yeah. Drugs are expensive in prison, and he don't have a good source of income there."

"I need to have another conversation with Buster," I said. "Do you want to ride along?"

"Sure," Lula said. "As long as we get back by five o'clock. I got a big date tonight, and it might take me some time to get beautiful."

I drove past Rangeman on the way across town. The crime scene tape had been taken down, but several vans from a variety of government agencies were still in place.

"This whole thing gives me the creeps," Lula said. "I don't like no radioactive shit leaking out in my neighborhood. Excuse my language, but there's no other way to say it. It's scary as snot."

I cut back to State Street, turned up Stark, and parked across the street from Buster. It was late in the day, and people were lining up for pizza.

We crossed the street, I pushed the intercom buzzer, and Buster answered.

"It's me again," I said.

"Is the chick with the big tits with you?"

"Yeah."

"Come on up."

"That's sweet," Lula said. "He remembered me."

Buster was standing at the top of the stairs, wearing a red chef's apron and holding a spoon.

"What's up?" he said. "I'm in the middle of making dinner."

"What are you making?" Lula asked him.

"Red sauce. I'm having spaghetti. I got some nice parmesan and some fresh basil."

"We need to talk," I said. "Someone just shot a rocket into a very expensive Porsche because Briggs was in it. Was that you?"

"No shit," Buster said. "Did Briggs get blown up?"

"No, he was thrown clear."

"Bummer," Buster said.

"So?" I asked him.

"Not me. I don't do rockets."

"Who would do rockets?"

Buster shrugged. "Could be anyone."

"Let's take this from another direction. Who would want Briggs dead?"

"Just about everyone I know. He snooped where he shouldn't be snooping. He messed around with other people's wives. He was damn annoying. And he can't drive. He's a menace on the road. He kept smashing into my Mercedes with his stupid blue RAV4. I hated that car."

"Omigod," I said. "You're the car bomber."

"Right now I'm the spaghetti maker," Buster said. "Do you ladies want to stay for supper?"

"I got a date," Lula said, "but I'll take a rain check. That spaghetti sauce smells good."

I drove Lula back to the office and continued on to Morelli's house. Morelli wasn't home, so I took Bob for a walk, straightened up the kitchen, fed Bob, and made myself a grilled cheese sandwich.

Morelli rolled in at seven o'clock. He grabbed me and kissed me, and scratched Bob behind his ear. He got a beer out of the fridge, chugged it, and belched.

"Long day," I said.

"No kidding. Do we have food?"

I assembled two more grilled cheese sandwiches and set them into the fry pan. I wasn't any kind of a cook, but I could make grilled cheese.

"Ron Siglowski turned up today," Morelli said. "He floated down the Delaware and washed up onto the shore by the Route 1 bridge embankment. A homeless guy found him at four o'clock. He was decomposed, but it was obvious he'd taken a bullet in the head."

"That leaves just two poker players."

Morelli looked around. "Where's Briggs?"

"He's staying in my apartment while it's under construction. I thought it was better than having him here."

"If I had to live with him another day, you could add me to the list of people trying to kill him."

I slid a grilled cheese onto a plate and added pickles and some chips. "Do you have a lead on the shooter?"

"Nothing worth anything. Buster and Pepper are suspects only because they're the last two men standing, but it could just as easily be someone on the outside. All these guys associated with bad people. They were all involved in human trafficking and who knows what else. They might not have been as deeply invested as Jimmy Poletti, but they all knew what was going on."

"It sounds like Buster was boots on the ground in Mexico. And Silvio Pepper had his trucks going in and out of Mexico."

"The feds are involved in that part of it. Not sure how much progress they're making."

"Speaking of feds, I drove past Rangeman today. They've removed the crime scene tape, but there were still a bunch of vans on the street."

"My understanding is that the poison was pretty well contained in the one small room where Gardi was being held. If the polonium had been released directly into the ventilation system as planned, it might have done more damage, although even that's doubtful. What I'm hearing is that because of the system Ranger uses, the poison would have had to be introduced at a more central point to actually circulate. I imagine they'll let everyone back into the building tonight or tomorrow."

"Ranger has a lot of sensitive technology in that building. There are probably agents at his console checking up on their girlfriends."

Morelli finished his second sandwich and pushed back from the little kitchen table. "Not likely. Ranger's had his guys in hazmat suits on all seven floors 24/7. And word is that he was able to lock down his system from offsite. I know he has a very elite clientele, and they're willing to pay a premium for his services, but even at that, you have to wonder if there's more going on in that building than local security."

"Like what?"

Morelli shrugged. "I don't know. All I know is that his building is more secure than it needs to be, and the technology he uses is expensive, complicated, and not readily available. I used to think he was a dangerous whackjob. Now I'm not sure *what* he is."

No need to tell Morelli I was still helping Ranger track Vlatko, right? Why cause him additional stress?

• • •

Grandma called at eight o'clock.

"I'm at the Rickert viewing," she said, "and I could use a ride home. I don't suppose you could come get me? There's a lot of people here, and it's going to be a big traffic mess, so you

189

could pick me up on the side street by the driveway going to the garage area."

"Okay," I said. "I'll be right there."

Fifteen minutes later I turned onto the side street and saw Grandma crash through a hedge that bordered the funeral home driveway and wave me down. I stopped the Buick, and she grabbed the door handle, wrenched the door open, and jumped inside.

"Go, go, go," she said.

I took off and gave her a sideways glance. "What's this all about?"

"I didn't feel like talking to anybody. And the cookies weren't so good either. By the time I got to the cookies there were only Fig Newtons left, and they get under my dentures."

When I drove up to my parents' house, my mother was standing on the sidewalk with her arms crossed over her chest.

"Uh-oh," Grandma said. "I've never seen your mother standing there like that."

"She looks mad."

"Yeah, I wonder what brought that on."

"Did you try to pry the lid open on a casket again?"

"No way," she said. "The lid was already up."

"Did you stick the dead guy with a pin to make sure he was dead?"

"I didn't do that either. And I only did that once, when Mabel Sheindler looked so lifelike. And I didn't knock over any vases or set anything on fire."

I parked and got out of the car with Grandma.

"What's up?" I asked my mother.

"I just got fourteen phone calls about someone hitting Joseph's Grandma Bella in the face with a chocolate cream pie when she was walking out of the funeral home. They said she was going out the side door for some reason, and someone came out of nowhere and hit her with the pie."

"Did they know who did it?" Grandma asked.

"Bella said it was you."

"That's a fib," Grandma said. "I bet she never even saw who did it. I bet someone lured her out through the side door and then sneaked up behind her and reached around and smushed her with the pie. Those chocolate pies are a big gooey mess. She would have had pie in her eyes when that person was running away. She just *thinks* it was me, because I have her spooked. She don't know for sure."

"Were there witnesses?" I asked my mother.

"I don't know," my mother said. "Nobody mentioned witnesses."

"Well, there you have it," Grandma said. "It's her word against mine."

My mother narrowed her eyes at Grandma. "I *know* you did it."

"No need to get your panties in a bunch," Grandma said. "It was just a pie. And anyway maybe it was an accident. Maybe the pie slipped out of someone's hand and landed in Bella's face."

"Is that the story you're going with?" my mother asked.

"Yeah, I think I'll stick with that one," Grandma said.

• • •

Morelli and Bob were watching television when I walked in.

"My mother called," Morelli said. "Someone got Bella with a chocolate cream pie. A full-on face job."

I squeezed in between Morelli and Bob. "Seems like a waste of a perfectly good pie."

"I wouldn't want to be in the shoes of whoever did it," Morelli said.

"Do you mean because of the curse thing?"

"I mean because of the Sicilian revenge thing."

He hooked a finger under the hem of my T-shirt, lifted it up, and peeked under.

"This is going to be fun tonight," he said. "Just you and me."

"Are we going to use the One-Second Wonder Tool?"

"No. We're going to do it the old-fashioned way. We're going to use *my* wonder tool."

Oh boy.

TWENTY-ONE

I WAITED UNTIL Morelli was out of the house before I showered and dressed in my black all-purpose suit and high-neck stretchy pink shirt. I pulled my hair back into a ponytail and went with the fresh-face look. A swipe of mascara and some lip gloss. That's as natural as I get. I stuffed my sliced-up bra and my white shirt with the gash in it into my messenger bag. I told Bob he should be a good boy and that Morelli would be home at lunchtime to let him out. And I chugged off in the Buick to get Briggs.

Briggs was waiting for me by the back door of my apartment building. He was dressed in a tan suit that almost fit him, a light blue dress shirt, a yellow and blue striped tie, and the running shoes he always wore.

"Sorry about the shoes," he said, climbing onto the passenger seat. "They're all I've got right now. But what do you think about the suit? It's not bad, right?"

"It's great. I appreciate your help."

"What?"

"I appreciate your help."

"No, I don't need any help," Briggs said. "Where are we going? Are we going to the courthouse? Do you have an office set up for the scam?"

"We're going to the bail bonds office to meet Ranger," I yelled at him. "And then we're going to New York to the Russian consulate on the Upper West Side."

"Are you shitting me? We're going to scam the Ruskies? I'm there. I'm ready."

"That's not exactly it. I need information on someone I believe is associated with the consulate. I only have a description of him, and I need his name, so we're going to say I was at a party two nights ago and this guy attacked me. If I can get someone to pull his dossier, I might be able to create a diversion and steal it."

Briggs nodded, but I wasn't sure he'd understood a word I'd said.

"What about Ranger?" Briggs asked. "What's his role?"

"He's driving us in and waiting outside for us. He's security."

"He's a secretary?"

"Security. SECURITY."

"Cool," Briggs said. "Security. We're going to kick some Ruskie ass."

A black Rangeman SUV was already parked in front of the

bail bonds office. I pulled in behind it, and Briggs and I got out and got into the SUV.

I buckled myself in next to Ranger and we drove in silence to the Turnpike, through the tunnel, up Tenth Avenue to the Upper West Side. Ranger parked in the lot we'd used before and called the man he had in place watching the consulate.

"Business as usual," he said to me. "No sign of our friend. I'm going to hang back, but I'll keep you in sight. Pretend I'm not here." He gave me a new earbud. "If you get into trouble, feed Briggs to the dogs and run."

"What?" Briggs said. "What about Briggs?"

"He has some hearing loss from the blast," I told Ranger.

"Babe," Ranger said.

I figured that pretty much covered it, so I stuck the earbud into my ear and yelled at Briggs to walk with me.

We got to the consulate, I pushed the intercom buzzer, and I told the voice at the other end that I needed to speak to someone in charge. The door was buzzed open, and Briggs and I were in.

A man in a suit came forward and asked if he could help me.

"I was at a party here two nights ago," I said, "and one of the men attacked me. I got frightened and left, but I'm back today with my lawyer."

The man gave Briggs a curt nod. "I'll see if I can find someone of authority."

Five minutes later we were taken to a second-floor office. It was a small room dominated by a large oak desk, and a large Russian man sat behind the desk.

"My name is Sergei Yablonovich," he said. "Please have a seat."

The two seats in front of the desk were brown leather, overstuffed, and big enough for Paul Bunyan. I perched on the edge of mine, and Briggs stood looking at his. I imagined he was wondering how he was going to get in it and, more to the point, how he was going to avoid looking ridiculous. After a long moment he sacrificed dignity, climbed up onto the chair, and sat back with his legs sticking straight out in front of him.

"Comfy chair," he said.

"My associate tells me you had an unfortunate experience at our consulate two nights ago," Sergei said to me.

"I came with one of the men who was here for the trade show. It was a nice party, but I went to the ladies' room down the hall, and when I came out a man I had never seen before jumped out at me and held me at knifepoint. He put his hand on my breast and said that if I didn't cooperate he'd kill me. I tried to get away, and he slashed at me with his knife."

I took my bra and shirt out of my bag and made sure Sergei could see that my hands were trembling. Truth is, it wasn't hard, because I was close to hyperventilating sitting in this guy's office, trying to pull this off.

"I brought my clothes to show you," I said. "I was lucky I wasn't badly hurt. Some people came out of the party room just as he went after me with the knife, and he ran away. I was so scared that I left the building without even saying goodbye to my date."

Sergei shook his head at the sliced shirt. "This is terrible. Have you gone to the police?"

"Yes, and they said I should come to you about it. I didn't want to come alone, so I brought my friend Randy Briggs. He's also a lawyer, and he's advising me on the matter. I think someone should find this man. And someone should at least pay for me to get a new blouse."

At the mention of his name, Briggs craned his neck up so he could look over the edge of the desk.

"Was this man with the trade delegates or the consulate?" Sergei asked.

"I don't think he was with the trade delegates, because I didn't see him at the party. He spoke English with a slight British accent. He had an odd tattoo on his neck and a patch over one eye. I would definitely know him if I saw a photo."

Sergei hit a speed dial button on his desk phone, and a woman answered on speakerphone.

"I'm looking for a man with a patch over one eye who might be associated with the Russian vodka trade show or with this consulate," Sergei said to the woman.

"Viktor Volkov wears a patch over his eye," she said. "He's a representative of the Russian Ministry of Industry and Trade. He was sent here from our Miami office for the vodka trade show taking place in Atlantic City."

"I'd like to see his dossier."

He disconnected from his call and turned back to me.

"Ordinarily I myself would have welcomed our vodka makers at that party," Sergei said, "but we have a very important

general arriving, and I had to personally see to his accommo-
dations. He'll be speaking at the international trade show in
Atlantic City. He travels with several aides and much security,
and we had to take over an entire floor of the hotel."

A very competent looking woman with short brown hair
and a pleasant, makeup-free face knocked once on the open
door and walked into the office with the dossier. She handed it
to Sergei and left without a word.

Sergei read through the file, found the photo, and showed it
to me. "Is this the man?"

"Yes!"

I clapped a hand over my mouth and gave my best shot at
looking horrified and terrified, and to my credit I think I might
have even gotten a little teary.

"I can assure you we'll look into this," Sergei said.

"Yeah, but what about her blouse?" Briggs said. "Who's
going to pay for the blouse?"

"I'm not actually authorized to reimburse her," Sergei said,
"but when we conclude our investigation I might be able to
recommend some compensation."

Briggs cupped his ear. "What?" He looked at me. "What did
he say? Did he say something about condensation?"

"He has a temporary hearing loss," I said to Sergei.

"Yeah," Briggs said. "Someone blew up my car, and I was
standing too close."

"It was a political act," I said to Sergei. "I'm sure you
understand about these things."

"So what about the blouse?" Briggs said. "There was no condensation on it. Just handprints. And my good friend and client here has a big scar on her tit from where this Viktor guy went after her."

Briggs was having a hard time seeing Sergei, so he got up and stood on the chair seat.

"We demand action," Briggs said, jumping up and down. "Action, action, action!"

He lost his balance on the third jump, fell off the chair, and crashed to the floor.

"*Ow!*" he yelled. "My leg. I broke my leg. I need a doctor. Call the paramedics."

He was rolling around on the floor, holding his leg and moaning.

"I feel sick," he said. "I'm gonna throw up. I need air. Someone get me some air. This office is closing in on me."

He crawled to the door, dragging his broken leg behind him, making gagging sounds. Sergei was on his phone again, calling his assistant, telling her to call for an EMT. Briggs made it into the hall. Sergei hovered over him, not sure what to do. And as soon as I was left alone in the office, I took photos of the three-page dossier on Viktor Volkov with my smartphone.

I went into the hall and looked down at Briggs. "Are you sure your leg is broken?"

"I thought it was broken," Briggs said. "But now it's feeling better."

"He has panic attacks," I explained to Sergei.

"You might think about getting a new lawyer," Sergei said.

I grabbed Briggs by the arm and hauled him to his feet. "Upsy-daisy," I said.

Briggs gingerly tried his leg. "It's a miracle!"

"Oh gosh, look at the time," I said. "I have to be at work. Thank you so much for looking into this for me. I'll check back next week."

"I didn't get your name," Sergei said.

"Joyce Barnhardt."

Briggs was already in the elevator, holding the door for me. I jumped in, and Briggs hit the button for the first floor.

We passed the brunette on our way out. She was at the door, presumably waiting for the EMTs.

"False alarm," I said to her. "So sorry."

A black Rangeman SUV rolled down the street and stopped in front of us. Briggs and I got into the backseat. Ranger was in the front seat, and one of his men was driving. A second Rangeman SUV was behind us.

I removed my earbud and gave it back to Ranger. "It looks like you're ending surveillance on the consulate."

"I am. I don't see Vlatko returning."

"We did good, right?" Briggs said to me. "Did you see the brilliant way I diverted the Ruskie's attention away from his desk so you could steal the dossier? That was an Academy Award–winning performance. I should be a movie actor. I'd make all those other Hobbits look like crap."

Ranger turned in his seat and looked at me. "Did you get the dossier?"

"I photographed it." I pulled the document photos up on my phone and sent them to Ranger, and he downloaded them into his phone.

"Viktor Volkov," he said, reading off his phone. "He's here as a representative of the Russian Ministry of Industry and Trade. A government liaison to the Russian spirits trade mission."

"Vodka," I said.

"Yes, among other liquors, but primarily vodka. This gives a Moscow address as his permanent residence, and several contact addresses while he's in this country. The contact addresses are all hotels. One in Miami, the Gatewell Hotel, and a hotel in Atlantic City."

"There's a big international trade show coming to Atlantic City," I said. "The Russian vodka makers will be part of it. The consulate official I spoke to said he was there making arrangements for some important general who would be speaking."

"From the little I know about Vlatko, I'm guessing almost everything in this dossier is cover and not true. He probably has a local handler who knows more, but the consulate staff would know only what they see here and take it at face value. Russian bureaucrats learn not to ask questions."

"But we know he's going to Atlantic City," I said. "He might not have stayed in the hotels he gave, but he *was* in Miami and New York. And it looks like his cover was created to bring him into contact with the vodka makers. So maybe his primary target is one of the vodka makers."

"That's too simple," Ranger said. "Someone went to a lot of trouble to get Vlatko here. He's a Russian government assassin and a specialist. He's been sent here to eliminate someone who's difficult to reach, or he's been sent here to create chaos."

"He's off to a good start in Trenton," I said.

"Fortunately, there was only one death. It looks like McCready is going to be okay. And I should be back in my building sometime tomorrow."

TWENTY-TWO

RANGER DROPPED BRIGGS off at my apartment.

"Thanks," I said to Briggs. "You were great."

"What? I need a mate?"

"No! You were great!" I yelled. *"Thank you!"*

"Yeah, anytime," Briggs said. "I could use some wine when you get back this way. Mine went when the car blew up."

"Okay," I said. "I'll make sure you get wine."

"I could have someone pick him up and drop him off in North Carolina," Ranger said.

I declined the offer, and parted company with Ranger at the bail bonds office.

"Hey, look who's back," Lula said. "Is everything secure in Rangerland?"

"Pretty much. I think he'll be able to go back into his building tomorrow."

"I have a new skip for you," Connie said. "Forest Kottel. He's a low-level bond, and there's no rush on it. Gives his address as a cardboard box on Geneva Street, off Stark. Wanted for shoplifting in a grocery store on Stark."

"That's just sad," Lula said. "A man finds a nice box to live in, you'd think he could put it someplace better than that corner."

"Vinnie bonded out a homeless person?" I asked Connie. "How did this guy secure his bond?"

"A relative in Cleveland wired the money."

I took the file and shoved it into my bag. "I'm going to mooch lunch from my mom," I said. "I'll probably stop back later this afternoon."

"I got a better idea," Lula said. "How about if I go with you, and then after you mooch lunch we can look for Forest? His box is a block away from the pizza place in Buster's building. If we get there in the middle of the afternoon, I bet there's no line, and we can waltz right in and get pizza."

"Sounds like a plan."

My mother was ironing when Lula and I walked into the kitchen.

"Hey, Mrs. P.," Lula said. "How's it going?"

"She's ironing," Grandma said. "That's how it's going. She's been ironing for four hours."

"I guess you're needing some mental health time, eh?" Lula said to my mom. "I know how that is. And ironing is real calming. Although you might want to think about how you're scorching that shirt you're working on."

"She's been ironing the same shirt for forty-five minutes," Grandma said. "She's run out of clothes."

"Maybe you want to switch her over to alcohol before she starts to smoke," Lula said.

"It's Bella," Grandma said. "Even though she has no good proof that I was the one who pied her, she's going all over telling everyone I did it."

"Well, were you the one?" Lula asked Grandma.

"I don't want to admit to anything, but I might have done it."

"So what's the problem?"

"Everyone's scared she'll put the eye on them, so we got disinvited to Amy Shute's wedding shower, and I got a phone call that the Bingo game was all full tonight, and when your mother went to mass this morning, no one would sit on that side of the church with her."

"Before you know it, everyone will forget about it," I said.

"As long as you're already getting the heat, I think you should hit her again," Lula said. "I think you should TP her house."

My mother looked up, wild-eyed, and took off after Lula with the iron. "That's the devil talking!" she shouted.

The plug popped out of the wall, and Lula put the kitchen table between herself and my mom.

"Take it easy, Mrs. P.," Lula said. "You're gonna get your blood pressure up and you'll burst a blood vessel. That happened to my Aunt Celia, only she was working at the time being a 'ho."

"No kidding?" Grandma said. "I guess it can be hard work being a 'ho."

"You're all lunatics," my mother said.

"I don't mean to be disrespecting or nothing, but you're the one who got the iron," Lula said. "How about we get you a pill or something?"

"I didn't realize I still had it in my hand," my mother said, looking at the iron.

"Happens to me all the time," Lula said, "but usually it's a gun or a donut."

"Do you want me to go get the blood pressure machine?" Grandma asked my mom. "I got one upstairs for when I watch *Naked and Afraid*."

"Not necessary," my mother said. "I just had a moment." She put the iron back on the ironing board. "Ironing doesn't do it for me anymore. Maybe I'll take up knitting again."

"I don't know if you want to be handling knitting needles while you're having another one of them moments," Lula said. "How about baking cupcakes? That's a real good activity."

"And my daughter's a real good cupcake maker," Grandma said. "Did you girls come over for something special?"

"Nope," I said. "We were in the neighborhood and thought we'd say hello."

"Yeah, just stopped by to say hello," Lula said.

Grandma walked us to the door. "Are you going after bad guys now?"

"Yep," Lula said. "We're going to make the city a safer place."

I wasn't sure rousting a homeless guy out of his cardboard box was all that noble, but it was my job, and I was going to do it . . . probably.

We got into the Buick, and I turned to Lula. "I didn't think this was a good day to mooch lunch."

"Hell," Lula said. "I'm not even hungry no more. And that hardly ever happens."

We roared off with the V8 guzzling gas at a furious rate. I drove through town on autopilot and turned up Stark. Buster lived in a manageable part of Stark, not the best and not the worst. Forest Kottel lived two blocks up in an area that was not the worst but getting there fast. It was open range for gangs, crazies, and drugged-out zombies. Geneva Street was the demarcation line for Lula and me. We didn't stop the car beyond Geneva if we could possibly avoid it. No FTA was worth it.

We passed the pizza place, drove two more blocks, and didn't see a cardboard box on the corner of Stark and Geneva. I left-turned onto Geneva, and half a block in we ran into a city of cardboard boxes, plastic tents, and patched-together one-man shanties that had been erected in the alley cutting the block.

"Used to be you had to get on a plane to see a slum of this quality," Lula said. "This is better than the tent city they got going under the bridge abutment."

I parked the Buick at the corner and shoved pepper spray into one pocket and my stun gun into another. I hung handcuffs from my waistband and slung my messenger bag across my chest. For the most part I've found that homeless people aren't violent, but many of them are crazy and unpredictable, especially when they live this far up Stark.

"Do you have your gun with you?" I asked Lula.

"Hell, yeah."

"Do you have it someplace you can reach it in a hurry?"

Lula searched through her huge purse, found the gun, and shoved it into the waistband of her black spandex skirt.

Forest Kottel's photo was stapled to the second page of his file. Weathered face. Lots of tangled hair. Squinty eyes. His description had him at 5' 10" and 170 pounds. Caucasian. Connie had listed the color of his eyes as red.

We approached the first box and were at a loss what to do next. No doorbell. No name on the box. Lots more boxes in the alley. No way to know if there was something alive in the box.

"Knock, knock," I said.

No answer.

"I'm not touching it," Lula said. "That box got the skeebies. I can tell just by looking at it."

I toed the box with my sneaker.

"Go away," said someone from inside the box.

"I'm looking for Forest Kottel."

"Well, you haven't found him."

"Thanks," I said. "Sorry to disturb you. Have a nice day."

"He lives in a box," Lula said. "How nice could his day get?"

We tiptoed past several bedraggled tents and stopped at another box.

"Hello," I said. "Anybody home?"

I walked around the box and looked inside through a door cut into the cardboard. Empty.

"Hey, look at that beauty of a box that's alongside the dumpster," Lula said. "It must be from one of them doublewide refrigerators. Now, *that's* a box a man could be proud of."

She took a step toward the box, and a little brown creature with big ears crept from behind the dumpster. It was followed by a second and then a third creature, all with teeth bared, softly growling.

"Chihuahuas!" Lula said. "It's the rabid Chihuahuas from hell! *Run for your life!*"

Lula took off in her five-inch heels, waving her arms and shrieking, and I ran after her. She reached the Buick, wrenched the door open, and jumped inside.

"Did you see them?" she asked when I got behind the wheel. "Did you see their glowing eyes?"

"No. I didn't see any glowing eyes."

"They were from hell."

"I don't think so," I said. "I think they were from someone's cardboard box."

"Yeah, but they looked ferocious."

"They were only three pounds each."

"Like big rats."

"They didn't look like rats. I thought they were kind of cute with their big ears."

"I did like their ears," Lula said. "But what about the creeping and growling?"

Okay, I had to admit I was freaked about the creeping and growling.

"Now that I'm thinking about it, I bet those dogs just need some bacon," Lula said. "Everybody feels happy when they got bacon."

"So you think if we gave them bacon, they'd be friendly?"

"Remember when we had to get past that alligator in whatshisname's apartment? We just kept feeding him chicken wings. Our problem was we didn't bring enough wings."

. . .

I drove back down Stark, turned onto State Street, and pulled into a fast-food drive-thru. They didn't list bacon on their à la carte menu, so I did the next best thing and got a bagful of bacon cheeseburgers.

"Those cheeseburgers smell pretty good," Lula said. "I might have to test drive one or two of them. And personally, I think those Chihuahuas would have liked some fries."

"You can have *one burger*. The rest are for the dogs."

Kottel wasn't a high-end bond, but when added to the Poletti capture money, my recovery fee would keep me going for a while. Problem was, I was having a hard time focusing on Forest Kottel when Ranger was tracking a psychopathic assassin who had me at the top of his hit list. I wanted to get Kottel as quickly as possible so I'd be free to help Ranger or maybe to go underground if necessary.

I returned to the alley off Geneva, parked the car, and set off with my bacon cheeseburgers. We approached the big box next to the dumpster, and two attack Chihuahuas circled the box and growled at us. I tossed a burger at them, and eight more dogs instantly appeared. All ten dogs pounced on the burger, devoured it, and then sat back on their tiny haunches looking at me expectantly.

"You got their attention," Lula said. "You just better hope they don't figure out there's more burgers in the bag or they'll be on you like white on rice."

A shaved bald head popped out of a flap on the top of the box, followed by a lanky body dressed in a grungy black bathrobe. It was Forest Kottel.

"Who goes there?" he asked. "Who approaches my private lair and disturbs my minions?"

"This guy's a whackadoodle," Lula said. "We should have brought the butterfly net."

"Stephanie Plum," I said. "I represent your bail bondsman. You missed a court date, and you need to reschedule."

"You remind me of someone," Lula said.

Forest stood ramrod straight. "You may remember me from when I stole the moon. Or from when I saved the world from El Macho."

"That sounds real familiar," Lula said. "Like I read it somewhere or saw it on the news."

"It's an animated movie," I said. "He's Gru from *Despicable Me*."

"Lies!" Forest said, wild-eyed. "All lies. El Macho turned my minions into Chihuahuas using a top-secret formula known as Chihuahua Maker Number 42. They might look like Chihuahuas, but underneath they're one hundred percent minion."

"That explains it," Lula said. "You want a burger? We brought some burgers for you and your minions."

Forest disappeared inside the box, a door scraped open on the other side, and he crawled out. He unfolded a red and white checkered plastic tablecloth, laid it on the ground, and sat cross-legged on it. The dogs trotted over and sat beside him.

"Will you ladies be joining us for dinner?"

"Actually," I said, "I thought you could feed your minions and then eat your burger while I drive you to the police station to reschedule."

"I can't leave Daisy," Forest said. "Daisy gets anxious when I leave. And Ronald and Scooter will go off and chew the corners off other people's boxes. And then there's Mitzy and Brownie and Puddles and Boomer . . ."

"Boy," Lula said. "You got a lot of minions."

"I started with two."

"You might want to think about minion birth control," Lula said.

"How do you feed all your minions?" I asked Forest. "How do you feed yourself?"

"There's a church truck that comes around and gives out sandwiches. If I get in line twice, there's enough for all of us. The minions don't eat a lot."

"Suppose I found good homes for the minions," I said. "Would that work for you?"

"It would be okay with me, but the minions have minds of their own, and they're very attached to me."

"That's on account of minions are loyal," Lula said, "but that don't mean deep down inside they wouldn't rather go with the guy with the bag of bacon cheeseburgers."

I handed the bag of burgers to Forest. "I'll be back," I said. "I need to look into some options for the minions. They're house-broken, right?"

"Perfectly. They have never once piddled in my box."

Lula and I returned to the Buick and drove back to the office.

"How are you going to find homes for those minions?" Lula asked. "Do you know anyone who wants a minion?"

"I need to give it some thought."

"You need to start asking around," Lula said. "There's Morelli's dog, Bob, who could use a minion. And there's your granny. I could see her with a minion."

"How about you?"

"It seems like a big responsibility," Lula said. "I don't know if I could take that on. I'd have to feed him and walk him and pick up minion poop. Of course, minion poop would be real small. I might have to get reading glasses just to see it. And reading glasses would ruin my image of perfection."

Connie had closed the office for the day, so Lula got into her Firebird and drove home, and I took a call from Morelli.

"I need ice cream," he said. "Lots of it."

"What flavor?"

"Every flavor."

"Jeez, you must have had a really bad day."

"Some idiot found a judge and bonded out Jimmy Poletti, and some other idiot shot him dead. Do you have any idea the kind of paperwork this creates?"

"Do you know who bonded him out?"

"I imagine it was Vinnie, but I haven't gotten that far in the investigation. This thing's created a media storm. I had to attend the press conference. I had to brief the mayor. I had to stop for antacids and Excedrin. Poletti was shot an hour after he got out of jail. An hour!"

"Do you know who did it?"

"If I knew who did it, I wouldn't need the antacids, Excedrin, and ice cream."

"Are you done working? Are you home?"

"I'm home, but I'm not done working. I came home to walk Bob and get something to eat, and then I'm going back to the station."

"And you need ice cream."

"It's a temporary substitute for liquor," he said.

"I'm on my way."

I stopped at the deli next to the bakery and got tubs of chocolate, butter pecan, coffee, and chocolate chip, plus a large bag of dog food for the minions.

Morelli was in the kitchen eating a ham and cheese sandwich when I walked in. He looked in the ice cream bag, then grabbed me and kissed me and fondled a breast.

"Is this big display of affection and passion a result of the ice cream, or are you happy to see me?" I asked him.

"I'm happy to see you, but the ice cream enhances the moment."

He finished his sandwich and dug into the chocolate.

"Where was Poletti when he got shot?" I asked.

"In Buster's apartment."

"Get out!"

"I swear to God. He was in Buster's apartment. Buster phoned it in."

"Where was Buster when all this went down?"

"He was at the eye doctor getting his eyes checked. Rock solid alibi. They dilated his eyes, so he had a friend take him and bring him home. They walked into Buster's apartment and found Poletti sprawled out on the living room rug. A bullet in the head and two in the chest. The rug will never be the same."

"Buster needs to change his lock."

"Yeah. And then he needs to get a condo in Panama where the shooter can't find him, since there are only two poker players left."

"Have you talked to Silvio Pepper?"

"He's on my list."

Morelli fed me a spoonful of chocolate ice cream, kissed me again, stepped away, and checked his phone for messages.

"I have to go," he said. "Hopefully this won't take too long. Save me some butter pecan."

"You got it."

• • •

215

Grandma Mazur called at seven-thirty.

"I'm at the funeral home," she said. "I came with Marie Zajak, but she had to leave early on account of she had an irritable bowel attack. I was hoping you could give me a ride home."

"When do you want to get picked up?"

"The viewing is over in a half hour. I thought it would be good if you waited for me on the side street like last time. I don't see Bella here, but I thought it wouldn't hurt to sneak out the side door just in case. I heard a rumor that she was waiting at the front door with a pie."

I parked on the street a couple minutes early, cut the engine, and looked around, on high alert for Vlatko. The sun was setting, and the side yard of the funeral home was in deep shade. People were walking to cars that were parked in the small lot to the front of the building and at the curb on Hamilton Avenue.

I heard a heart-stopping shriek that levitated me off the car seat. The shriek was followed by a lot of yelling and cussing, and then Grandma Mazur stomped into view. She was soaked from head to toe, and water dripped from the tip of her nose. She wrenched the passenger side door open, got in, and slammed the door shut.

"Take me home," she said.

"What happened?"

"Devil woman turned a hose on me."

I cranked the engine over and put the car in gear. "Are you sure it was her?"

"I don't want to talk about it."

"I guess the rumor about the pie was wrong."

"She tricked me. I tell you, she's evil."

I watched to make sure Grandma got into my parents' house without anything else going wrong, and then I went back to Morelli's.

A half hour later Morelli came home.

"What's new?" I asked him.

"An early ballistics report indicates the same weapon was used on Scootch, Ritt, and Poletti."

"So all you have to do is find the gun."

"Yeah, that's all I have to do."

I followed him into the kitchen. "Do you think these could be contract killings?"

"You're thinking Buster hired someone to kill Scootch and Poletti when he was away from his apartment."

"He could have called Scootch and Poletti and told them to come to his apartment, and when Scootch and Poletti got there the shooter was waiting for them."

"Motive?"

"Get rid of everyone who could implicate him in the slave trade."

"So you think Pepper is next?"

"Unless they're working together."

Morelli pulled the butter pecan ice cream out of the freezer and got a spoon out of the silverware drawer. "What about Briggs?"

"From what I can see, everyone hates him. Poletti tried to run him over, and Buster tried to kill him with a car bomb."

217

"What about the rockets?"

"Wild card."

"That's as good as anything I've got," Morelli said.

I got my own spoon and went to work on the chocolate chip ice cream. "I had an interesting night. I picked Grandma up at the funeral home after *your* grandmother turned a hose on her."

"Are you kidding me?"

"It's going to take days for the Buick to dry out. She was *soaked*."

"At least they aren't shooting at each other like the Hatfields and McCoys."

"Not yet."

TWENTY-THREE

IT WAS SUNDAY, and Morelli and Bob had breakfast and took off to help Morelli's brother, Anthony, put a swing set together for his kids. I waved them off, had a second cup of coffee, and called Lula.

"I'm going to visit Forest," I said. "Want to ride along?"

"Sure," she said. "Nothing much doing here."

I took my big bag of dog food out to the car and drove to Lula's apartment. I hadn't heard from Ranger, so I had no idea what was happening with Vlatko. The possibilities sent a wave of nausea through my stomach, and I watched my rearview mirror, making sure I wasn't being tailed by a guy with one eye and a sharp knife.

I picked Lula up and drove to Stark Street, slowing when we got to Buster's building. The CSI van was parked curbside, and a single strip of yellow crime scene tape fluttered at the apartment's front door.

"Did you hear about Jimmy Poletti?" I asked Lula.

"Hard not to hear. It was on every news station. They even interviewed his wife, who didn't seem that broken up. Maybe she's the one shooting all these guys. Maybe she has a bad hair day and she pops someone. And she could specialize in poker players. She might have been traumatized by a poker player when she was a kid."

Considering how congested Trudy Poletti's schedule had to be with the Pilates classes and the boinking every man she could get her hands on, it was hard to believe she had time to murder poker players.

I turned at the corner of Geneva and parked. I left Lula with the Buick, grabbed the dog food, and walked it to Forest's box. It was a nice sunny morning, and Forest was sitting outside, leaning against his dumpster. The Chihuahua pack was snoozing at his feet. All heads came up when I approached.

"I brought food for the minions," I said to Forest.

"Do you hear that, my teensy minions? The nice lady brought us food."

Some of the minions started to vibrate.

"Why are they shaking?" I asked Forest.

"Minions do that. They're very excitable."

I put the bag on the ground and kept my distance. I didn't want the minions to feel threatened by a big advancing human.

"Now that the little critters have lots of food," I said to Forest, "I thought you might be willing to let me bring you in."

"I can't leave my minions unprotected. Starman will barbecue them."

Crap. I had two alternatives. The first was to stun-gun Forest and drag him to the car. I went with the second.

"I'll take care of the minions," I said. "I'll get you booked in at the police station, and I'll babysit the minions until you can secure a bond."

Forest turned to the minions. "What do you think? Would you like to go with the nice lady for just a little while so Forest can get arrested?"

"Lula is waiting at the cross street," I said. "Do you have something we can put the minions in?"

"The minions run free."

Great. Free-running minions.

I walked Forest to the Firebird with the minions goose-stepping around us.

"What the heck's this?" Lula asked.

"We're taking Forest to the police station, and then I'm taking the minions home with me. I'll stash them in my apartment until someone springs Forest. They haven't put the carpet down yet, and Briggs is there to babysit."

Forest loaded the Chihuahuas into the Buick. "Be good minions. No dookey or peepee in the nice lady's box."

I cuffed Forest, buckled him into the backseat with the Chihuahuas, and drove to the police station. I left Lula with the dogs and walked Forest into the building. I collected my body receipt and returned to Lula.

"Remember I got a big date with Stanley Kulicky tonight,"

Lula said to me. "We're going to see that movie about the end of the world coming and then just in time the world's saved by one of them Transformers."

"What time will it be over?"

"We're going to the eight o'clock movie, so it'll be over around ten. I'll call you when we're walking out."

I dropped Lula off at her apartment, and as soon as I got behind the wheel of the Buick, the dogs started yapping. As I drove through town, they yapped louder. They scrambled over the seat and jumped at the dashboard. They were on my lap, on the back of my seat, gnawing on my ponytail. They snarled at one another, snapped at passing cars, and looked at me bug-eyed.

I whipped into the drive-thru at Cluck-in-a-Bucket, got a bagful of bacon cheeseburgers, and stuffed the bag into the glove compartment. I gritted my teeth, hunched over the steering wheel, and headed for my apartment.

I lured the dogs out of the car and into the building with the bag of burgers. We took the stairs, hurried the short distance down the hall, and I shoved my key in the lock with one hand and held the burger bag over my head with the other. For small dogs they could jump impressively high when they smelled burgers.

I held the door open with my foot, threw a burger into the kitchen, and the dogs rushed in and pounced on the burger.

Briggs ran in from the bedroom. "What the heck's going on?"

"Roommates," I said. "I need to leave them with you."

"They look vicious."

I handed him the bag of burgers. "Just give them a burger once in a while and you'll be fine."

"They're dogs, right?"

"Yeah."

"I don't want dogs in my apartment."

"It's not *your* apartment," I told him. "It's *my* apartment."

"It's sort of mine."

"Wrong, wrong, wrong. There's no part of this apartment that's yours."

"Yeah, but I got rights. I'm living here."

"You have *no* rights. And if you want to *keep* living here, you'll take *very good care of the dogs.* And anyway, it's only for a short time."

Easy to understand why everyone wanted to kill him.

I drove to Walmart and went straight to the pet department. I got ten lightweight leashes, ten Chihuahua-size harnesses, a box of plastic poop bags, ten little chew toys, and a giant bag of dog food.

I hauled everything back to my apartment and let myself in. All ten dogs rushed at me, yapping and snarling. I opened the bag of dog food, threw some nuggets at them, and they snapped them up.

"Jeez," Briggs said, "I thought you'd never show up. These dogs are creeping me out. They keep shivering and looking at me with big bugged-out eyes."

"It's a Chihuahua thing," I told him. "They're excitable."

"Yeah, me too. I'm excited you're here to take them away."

"Turns out they're not going away today. I can't get their owner bailed out until Monday." Maybe never.

"Are you shitting me? What am I supposed to do with them?"

I dumped the dog stuff on my kitchen counter. "First thing we have to do is take them for a walk, so help me hook them up."

So much for the free-running minion experience.

By the time we got the dogs out of the elevator they were hopelessly tangled. I had three leashes in each hand, and Briggs had two in each hand.

"These are the dumbest dogs ever," Briggs said. "It's like they never walked on a leash before."

"You might want to walk them two at a time after this," I said.

"It'll take me all day. And I'll be a sitting duck out here."

"I'll give you a break on the rent."

"I'm not paying any rent."

"Exactly."

We walked them around the block, and they all peed and two out of ten pooped.

"How often do I have to do this?" Briggs asked.

"Four times a day. They don't have to always go for long walks. They just need a chance to piddle."

We dragged the dogs up the stairs, and I set out bowls of water for them and gave them a quilt to use as a bed.

"I need a television," Briggs said. "There's nothing to do here."

"You could look for a job."

"I don't have a car. How am I going to get around?"

"Taxi. Skateboard. Drone pickup. Figure it out!"

TWENTY-FOUR

I DROVE AWAY feeling agitated. I hated that Forest was locked up in jail. I didn't like leaving the dogs with Briggs. I was terrified that something horrible was going to happen to Ranger. And I had a sick feeling in my stomach that I was going to get disemboweled by Vlatko.

All morning I'd been fighting the urge to call Ranger. I wanted reassurance that he was okay, but I didn't want to overstep the boundaries of our relationship. Ranger wasn't a chatty person, and we didn't make casual phone calls. Truth is, if I made a phone call every time I was worried Ranger's life was in danger, I'd spend half my life on the phone. Still, this felt different. This was bigger and crazier and scarier.

Morelli's green SUV wasn't in front of his house when I pulled to the curb. He was still helping Anthony. I let myself in and realized there was no Bob. Bob was usually the first to greet me. I went to the kitchen in search of lunch, knowing there were good things waiting for me in Morelli's refrigerator.

Morelli had started out as the bad kid in the neighborhood. He was every teenage girl's dream and every mother's nightmare. He'd done some time in the Navy, joined the Trenton police, set a record for barroom brawls and one-night stands, and miraculously emerged from the devastation as a disease-free, mostly mature and responsible adult. Go figure.

I'd had a less tumultuous transition from childhood to adulthood, but somewhere in my twenties I feel like I got stalled in the process and now I'm drifting, marking time without any great passion to move forward. It could be that I'm just liking where I'm at and want to stay there a while longer. Still, it would be helpful if I could get motivated enough to buy a toaster.

I pulled a half-eaten tray of lasagna out of the fridge, carved a chunk off for myself, and ate it cold. I called Morelli and got a progress report on the swing set. It sounded to me like there was more beer drinking going on than bolting and wrenching. I went upstairs, brushed my teeth, and dabbed at the lasagna stain on my T-shirt. I gave up on the shirt, changed into a new one, and went downstairs. For lack of anything better to do I thought I'd go back to my apartment and help Briggs with the dogs. I went to the kitchen to get my messenger bag and froze in the middle of the room, unable to move, unable to breathe, my thoughts momentarily scrambled.

My messenger bag was on the counter, and next to it in a

smear of blood was what looked like a human heart. The little sticky note next to it said, *I'll have yours next.*

I looked around. No broken or open windows. The back door was locked. With shaky hands I got the key from the red coffee mug in Morelli's over-the-counter cupboard, unlocked the drawer next to the sink, and removed Morelli's spare Glock 9.

I stood with my back to the kitchen wall and called Ranger.

"I'm alone in Morelli's house and someone just left a bloody heart on the kitchen counter," I said. "I have a gun, and I'm in the kitchen, and I'm not going to move until you get here."

"I'm fifteen minutes away, but I'll have one of my men in your backyard sooner than that."

I hung up and called my parents' house.

"Just checking in," I said when Grandma Mazur answered. "How's everything going there?"

"We just finished lunch, and now your father's sleeping in front of the television."

I called my sister. I called Briggs. I called Connie and Lula. No one was missing a heart. I looked outside and saw that two Rangeman guys were at attention in Morelli's yard.

I debated calling Morelli. It was his house, and he should be told about this. Problem was, it would create a firestorm of unwanted activity. If I blurted out the whole story, it would get tied to the polonium and the feds would take over. There'd be CSI trucks and crime scene tape and hours of interrogation. If I didn't blurt out the whole story, I'd be withholding information in a federal investigation. And my biggest reservation was that the feds wouldn't be as efficient as Ranger when it came to solving the problem. In fact, they might only complicate things. I had confidence that Ranger would find Vlatko and eliminate him. The feds, not so much.

My cellphone rang, and Ranger told me he was at the front door and coming in. I heard the door open and close, and moments later Ranger walked into the kitchen. He glanced at me and then at the heart on the counter.

"Have you cleared the house?" he asked me.

"No."

"Stay here while I do a walk-through."

Minutes later he returned to the kitchen.

"All the doors and windows were locked," I told him. "I went upstairs to brush my teeth and change my shirt, and when I came down the heart was on the counter."

"Are you sure you locked the front door when you came in?"

"Absolutely."

"It was unlocked when I arrived. Morelli could use a better locking system, although I suspect if Vlatko wants to get through a door he can find a way."

Ranger went to the counter and looked down at the heart. He tapped a number into his phone and gave the person on the other end Morelli's address and told him to use the back door.

"I'm not an expert," Ranger said, "but this looks like a human heart."

"You've seen a lot of hearts?"

"How many is a lot?"

"One," I said.

"Yeah, I've seen a lot of hearts. Have you called Morelli?"

"No. Not yet."

"If it's a human heart, we have to call him," Ranger said. "If it's something other than human, I'd rather not make the call. It'll further complicate the Vlatko search."

"Are you making any progress?"

"I've been researching Viktor Volkov. Volkov is a common Russian surname. There are several Viktor Volkovs in New York and New Jersey. One of them lives in Atlantic City."

"That's a convenient coincidence."

"The Atlantic City resident has been in the U.S. for several years, working as an independent contractor for a heating and air-conditioning company. Fifty-two years old. Single. Renting a house in a low-income neighborhood. Two eyes. Obviously not Vlatko. He doesn't answer his phone."

"Are you going to Atlantic City to talk to him?"

"Yes. I would have gone today, but we moved back into the building and I needed to be there."

A narrow-faced, pockmarked guy in Rangeman black fatigues knocked on the back door. Ranger let him in and nodded toward the heart.

"Tell me about this," Ranger said.

"It's a heart," the guy said.

"What kind?"

"Human. You can tell by the shape. It's adult-size. It appears to have been frozen and recently defrosted. The liquid on the counter is from the defrosting process. Cells breaking down."

"Anything else?" Ranger asked.

"It appears to have been healthy, but that's all I could tell you without slicing into it."

"Thanks," Ranger said.

The Rangeman guy joined the two who were still standing at parade rest in the backyard.

"Who the heck was that?" I asked Ranger.

"Rodriguez. He's a specialist."

"I bet."

"Make the phone call," Ranger said.

"Maybe you should leave."

He shook his head. "I'm staying."

I blew out a sigh and called Morelli.

"Hey," I said. "How's it going?"

"We hit a snag on the sliding board, but I think we have it figured out."

"I'm at your house, and I have a sort of situation here."

"What sort of situation?"

"Sort of a home invasion situation. I'm fine and Ranger is here, but we thought you'd want to check out the . . . problem."

"Oh man, did someone shoot a rocket into my living room?"

"Nope. No rocket. Your living room is just like you left it. It's the kitchen that was sort of invaded."

"Okay, I'll round Bob up and come home."

"This probably isn't going to go well," I said to Ranger.

· · ·

231

Bob bounded into the kitchen, slammed into me, and sniffed at Ranger. Morelli followed. He nodded to Ranger and focused on me. His gaze traveled down my arm to my hand, and I realized I was still holding his Glock.

"On the counter," I said.

Morelli shifted his attention. "It's a heart," he said.

"We think it's human," I told him. "Someone broke in while I was upstairs and left it here with a note."

Morelli walked to the counter and read the note. *"I'll have yours next."*

He looked at me, and I could see the checked anger in the set of his mouth. "Do you know what this means?"

"Probably," I said. "We think it relates to the polonium."

"I'm listening."

"When I was with Special Forces," Ranger told Morelli, "I had an encounter with an SVR agent named Vlatko. He's an assassin and an interrogator, and he's in this country on some sort of mission. He used Rangeman for a practice run. I've tracked him to the Russian consulate in New York, and have some leads, but he's still in the wind."

"What has this got to do with me?" Morelli asked. "Why do I have a heart on my kitchen counter?"

"It has nothing to do with you," Ranger said. "It was left for Stephanie. He's targeting her because she's worked for me. Eventually he'll come after me. In the meantime, he's playing with the people around me."

"Do the feds know about the Vlatko connection?"

"Not from me," Ranger said. "But they followed all the

same initial leads that I followed. Since they don't share their information with me, I have no idea where they're at in the investigation."

"If it's a human heart, it has a body somewhere," Morelli said. "At the very least, it needs to be tested and registered as a crime."

We all looked over at the kitchen counter. No heart. Just a watery smear of blood and a trail of drops on the floor leading into the dining room. We followed the drops through the dining room and into the living room, where Bob was gnawing on the last remnant of the heart.

"*Bad Bob*," Morelli said, shaking his finger at Bob. "That's not Bob food."

Bob obviously had a different opinion, because he snatched the mangled piece of meat and ran upstairs.

Morelli ran after him, there was a lot of yelling and growling, and Morelli came down empty-handed.

"He ate it," Morelli said.

I was horrified to the point of gagging. Ranger stared down at his shoe, making a monumental effort not to laugh. And Morelli stood hands on hips, staring at the bloody splotch on his rug. The splotch sort of blended in with the rug pattern and various other food and beverage stains.

We were all carrying guns, and no one wanted to say the wrong thing and start World War III, so no one said anything.

"This never happened," Morelli finally said.

"I didn't see anything," Ranger said.

I agreed. "Me either."

Morelli turned to Ranger. "If anything happens to her, I'm holding you responsible."

"Understood," Ranger said.

"Excuse me?" I said. "I'm an adult. I make my own decisions. And *I'm* responsible for my well-being. Is that clear?"

"No," both men said in unison.

"I have to get back to Anthony before he wrenches his own thumb off," Morelli said. "He's no Mr. Fix-It."

Bob slunk down the stairs and stared up at Morelli with soulful eyes. He was sorry he'd eaten the evidence.

"That was bad," Morelli said to Bob. "You know you're not supposed to eat off the counter."

A shoestring of drool hung from the side of Bob's mouth, his eyes got glassy, he planted his four feet, and *GAK* . . . he barfed up the heart.

"Maybe you can still test it for DNA or something," I said to Morelli.

Ranger grinned. "You're going to need a snow shovel to get that up."

• • •

Morelli and I were snuggled together on the couch, watching television, when Lula called.

"We just got out of the movie," she said. "He's getting one last tub of popcorn for the ride home, and then we're going to start to waddle out to his car."

"He has a car?"

"It's his dad's. I wouldn't put him in my Firebird on account of he'd ruin my suspension system. Anyway, I thought I'll get him to take me home, and I'll get him out of the car with the promise of sex. And if that don't work, I'll tell him I got pot roast and gravy upstairs. Soon as I get him out of the car, you can jump out from the bushes in my front yard and snap the cuffs on him."

"Sounds like a plan," I said, and disconnected.

"What's a plan?" Morelli asked.

"Stanley Kulicky is FTA, and Lula just had a date with him. She's going to hold him over at her house until I can get there."

"Have you seen him lately? He must weigh three hundred pounds."

"Yep, he's a big boy."

"Bring the extra large flexi-cuffs."

"Check."

Lula lives in a low-to-no-income neighborhood that has a lot less crime than Stark Street. There's some gang and drug activity and a bunch of fourteen-year-old pregnant girls, but Lula is happy with the rent, and the commute to the office is manageable. She lives on the second floor of a small lavender house with elaborate trim that was just recently painted pink. For the most part the house is graffiti free.

I parked the Buick one house down and waited with the engine running, the windows up, and Morelli's Glock on my lap. The neighborhood didn't worry me, but Vlatko had my intestines in knots. I'd picked up two Rangeman tails when I left Morelli's house. One was now parked directly behind me, and another drove past me, made a U-turn, and parked across the street.

A big SUV rolled past me and parked in front of Lula's house. I grabbed the cuffs from my bag, cut the engine, and got out of the car. I shoved the Glock under the waistband of my jeans at the small of my back and crouched behind the car in front of me. Stanley got out of the SUV and opened the door for Lula. Lula got out and fumbled with her purse.

"Oh my," Lula said. "I hope I have my house keys."

I rushed Stanley, cuffed him, and asked Lula about the movie.

"The movie was excellent," Lula said. "RoboGod saved the world, but not before a lot of awesome shit went down."

"This sucks," Stanley said to Lula. "You took advantage of me. I want my money back for the movie ticket."

"I didn't have nothing to do with this," Lula said. "She figured this out on her own. I swear to RoboGod. And anyways, I bought the first two buckets of popcorn, and I let you fondle my knee."

"I'm not going to jail," Stanley said. "They make you take your clothes off and they look up your poopoo hole."

"Dude," Lula said. "You were sitting naked on your garage roof. Every time you turned around or bent over, everybody looked up your poopoo hole. That ship sailed."

"I don't care," Stanley said, sitting down on the sidewalk. "I'm not going."

"We need a forklift," Lula said.

I had something better than a forklift. I had Rangeman

guys. I motioned to the SUVs that I needed help, and two big guys emerged from each shiny black Rangeman vehicle.

"I need to deliver Mr. Kulicky to the police station," I said.

Two of the men lifted Stanley and carried him to the SUV that was parked behind my Buick. He was buckled in, doors were closed, and we were ready to roll.

Lula and I got into the Buick and led the parade.

"I wasn't going to come with," Lula said, "but those Rangeman guys are hot. Not as hot as Ranger, but they're totally acceptable."

"What about Stanley?"

"Stanley is cuddly. There's a difference between cuddly and hot. Hot trumps cuddly."

I wasn't sure that hot trumped cuddly. I liked cuddly a lot. Lucky for me, Morelli was both. I didn't know about Ranger. I hadn't had much cuddle time with Ranger.

We handed Stanley over to the docket lieutenant, I got my body receipt, and Stanley made another movie date with Lula.

We drove back to Lula's house, Lula got into Mr. Kulicky's SUV, and the parade took the SUV home. It was almost eleven o'clock, but lights were still on in the Kulicky house. I rang the bell and explained to Mr. Kulicky that Stanley was okay, and we'd bond him out first thing Monday morning. I handed him the keys to his car, took Lula home, and returned to Morelli with my Rangeman escort following close behind.

"How'd it go?" Morelli asked when I flopped onto the couch beside him.

"Smooth as silk."

"You realize you have a tail, right?"

"It's all your fault."

"He would have done it anyway."

This was true.

"I hope you didn't exhaust yourself on that capture," Morelli said. "Because I have plans for the rest of the night and possibly tomorrow morning."

"I hope the plans for tomorrow morning involve a trip to the bakery."

"Kinky," Morelli said, "but I might be able to work it in."

TWENTY-FIVE

MORELLI, BOB, AND I sat at the little kitchen table, drinking coffee and eating donuts fresh from the bakery. The two Rangeman guys in the backyard were also drinking coffee and eating donuts. And the two Rangeman guys in the SUV in front of Morelli's house were drinking coffee and eating donuts.

"They better hope Ranger doesn't catch them eating donuts on the job," I said to Morelli. "The closest you come to dessert at Rangeman is an apple."

"At the risk of seeming unappreciative, four armed guards patrolling my property feels excessive."

"Welcome to my world. I've got Rangeman tracking devices mysteriously dropped into my pockets and stuck to my cars." I pushed back from the table, rinsed my coffee mug, and put it in the dishwasher.

"It's my Uncle Lou's birthday today," Morelli said. "The

239

whole family will be at my cousin Maddie's house for dinner tonight. You're invited."

"No way. Your Grandma Bella will be there. She scares the heck out of me. And I'm sure she's still got a vendetta against Grandma over the pie thing. She'll secretly put the eye on me, and I'll get my period nonstop for a month. Besides, I have my own chores. I need to do some food shopping for Briggs, and I'm going to help him walk the dogs."

"What dogs?"

"The ten Chihuahuas that were living in a box with Forest Kottel."

I grabbed my messenger bag, waved at the two men in the backyard, gave Morelli a fast kiss, and headed out.

I stopped at the supermarket, and two Rangeman guys watched over the Buick and two followed me around the store. I got a week's worth of staples for Briggs plus some ice cream and chips and a paperback mystery.

One of the Rangeman guys carried my groceries to my apartment while another followed close behind, his hand on his holstered gun, ever ready.

I knocked once, opened the door, and Briggs came forward, surrounded by prancing dogs.

"Groceries," I said.

"What's with the armed guards? You win the lottery?"

"Ranger thinks I need security."

Briggs stood on a small step stool and emptied the bags.

"A book?" he asked.

"Yeah, remember before television and computers we used to do this thing called *reading*?"

The dogs were milling around in the kitchen, watching Briggs.

"How's it going with the minions?" I asked him.

"Most of them have the leash figured out. Gracie is hopeless. She always wants to run. I have to find a dog park for her. Bernie should be a circus dog. He can walk on his back legs forever. The bony one with the white tip on her tail is a real picky eater, but if I put a little cheese in with her food she gobbles it. Give me a couple days and I'll have her fattened up."

"You like them!"

"Except for Blinky. He bit me in the ankle. I think he has trust issues."

"I was going to help you walk them."

"That would be great! Maybe you can run a little with Gracie. I can't keep up with her."

We got Gracie and three of the others hooked up and took them outside. Me, Briggs, four teeny-tiny dogs, and two heavily armed men. A new black Porsche 911 Turbo was parked next to the two Rangeman SUVs, and Ranger was standing beside it talking to his men.

"What's up?" I asked Ranger.

"It's a nice day. I thought I'd go to Atlantic City."

"You weren't going to sneak off without me, were you?"

"That was the plan."

"Can I talk to you in private?"

I handed the dogs off to a Rangeman guy, and Ranger and I walked a short distance away.

"A sick psychopathic freak broke into Morelli's house and left his gruesome message on the kitchen counter," I said to Ranger. "I don't like it. I don't like that he wants to kill me. I don't like that he wants to kill you. And I don't like that Morelli is now involved. I want this creep found and eliminated. I'm in. I know what he looks like and what he sounds like and what he smells like."

"What does he smell like?" Ranger asked.

"Burning sulfur."

"I understand your emotion, but you'd serve no purpose today. You'd be a liability."

"Gee, that's so flattering. Let me get this straight. You only have me tag along when I serve some useful purpose, like being a dumb bimbo in a bar."

"Yes."

"You are such a *jerk*."

"Babe."

I was pretty sure this time "Babe" meant I was giving him a cramp in his sphincter.

He grabbed me by the arm and yanked me to his car. "She's coming with me," he said to his men. "Jose and Rodriguez, follow me. Stay a quarter mile back. Keep channel 1 open. Roger and Mario, help Briggs walk the dogs and then return to Rangeman."

"I need my messenger bag," I said to Ranger.

"Why?"

"Identification, lipstick, cellphone, and Morelli's gun, which has bullets in it."

"Get it."

• • •

It takes about an hour and a half to get from Trenton to Atlantic City. For the most part it's open highway, so if you're riding in Ranger's Porsche and he has his radar detector and laser scrambler up and running, you can make it in just over an hour.

We were flying low today, with Ranger in his zone, driving in silence. The Porsche had paddle shifters, but Ranger rarely used them. Not even Ranger could shift as efficiently as the Porsche computer.

I assumed that we were going to check on Viktor Volkov. I also assumed that Ranger had a full report on the trade show and that at some time in the near future he'd share that information with me. For the moment I wasn't messing with his Zen by asking questions.

He turned off Route 30 onto Dr. Martin Luther King Boulevard and then left onto Fairview, into a neighborhood that was upper class if you were using ghetto standards.

Viktor Volkov lived in a small cinderblock bungalow stuck between two other small cinderblock bungalows. Across the street was a two-floor cinderblock motel that rented rooms by the hour. Viktor's house was painted a bright turquoise, his windows had iron security bars cemented into place, and a rusted-out junker car of indeterminate paint color was abandoned half on the road and half on what would have been, in a better part of town, a lawn. In this part of town it was hard-scrabble yellow dirt.

Ranger parked at the end of the block, and we sat watching the Volkov house and its surroundings for a half hour. One car pulled into the motel. That was it for traffic. No activity around any of the houses. No cats. No dogs. No kids. No gunshots.

"According to my information," Ranger said, "Volkov has a van that he uses for his business. I don't see it here, so he probably isn't home."

We left the Porsche and walked to Volkov's house. The front door and back door were both locked. No answer to our knocking. No answer when we called his cellphone. Ranger used a pick on the front door lock and had it open in thirty seconds.

The house was dark inside. Living room, eat-in kitchen, two bedrooms, bathroom. Shabby furniture that you would expect in this level rental. Black heavy-duty plastic body bag in the second bedroom. Looked like there was a body in the bag.

"I have a box of disposable gloves in the car," Ranger said. "Stay here. I'll be right back."

"No way. You stay here. I'll get the gloves."

I returned with the gloves and stood back while Ranger unzipped the bag. I saw that the body was covered with lime, but even with a thick layer of lime it didn't smell great. I inched my way out of the bedroom and across the living room to the front door. I mean, someone has to guard the door, right?

Ranger came out after a couple minutes, snapped his gloves off, and bagged them.

"Male. Partially decomposed, but I could see enough to guess that it's Volkov," he said. "The corpse is clearly missing a heart, so that's one mystery solved."

He pulled on new gloves and went room by room, opening drawers and looking in closets. He bagged the gloves with the first pair when he was done, and we left the house, closing the door behind us.

"No way to lock up," he said. "There weren't any keys in the house. No house keys and no car keys."

"Vlatko wanted the van."

"And the identity. If you don't have a stooge to bring airborne poison into a building, you might come in as an HVAC tech. I'm sure Vlatko learned from Rangeman. He'll be smarter if he attempts to use the polonium again."

"Are you going to call this in to the police?"

"I'll have someone make an anonymous call from a phone card. I don't want to be involved."

We walked the short distance to the Porsche, Ranger made a U-turn back to Dr. Martin Luther King Boulevard, and we headed for the beach.

"The trade show is at the Roland Atlantic Hotel," Ranger said. "It gets a lot of the smaller conventions. There are seven hundred attending this one. Approximately half are from overseas. There's a large bloc from Eastern Europe. I combed through the registration list and came up with several possible targets for Vlatko. He could also be here to take out someone who looks benign but is secretly an enemy of the state."

"The eye patch puts him at a disadvantage," I said. "There

aren't a lot of men walking around who look like they're seventeen and only have one eye. I doubt the woman in the consulate would have remembered him if he hadn't had the eye patch. Maybe you should be working with the police to find him."

"If the police arrest him he's inaccessible to me," Ranger said, "and I don't trust the system to permanently lock him away. It will be hard to tie him to the Rangeman incident, since the only witness is dead. If they catch him with the polonium he could be charged as a terrorist, especially if I testify against him. For obvious reasons, I'd prefer not to do that. I'd rather not have my black ops history made public. If they suspect him of murdering Volkov but can't prove it, he'll have his visa revoked and he'll come back under a new identity to kill me and everyone associated with me."

"So we're on our own."

"More or less. I have an FBI contact I trust. He'll be working with me. And I have Rangeman."

TWENTY-SIX

THE ROLAND ATLANTIC was toward the end of the vast Atlantic City boardwalk. It was an older hotel that had been expanded, given a fresh coat of badly applied stucco, and painted to resemble a birthday cake. The interior décor was also birthday cake with a splash of Easter basket.

Ranger parked in the ten-tier garage that was attached to the hotel by a pedestrian bridge on the third floor and a covered walkway going directly into the ground-floor casino. He called Jose and Rodriguez and told them to find him in the garage. Minutes later, they parked beside him. Jose and Rodriguez stayed in the garage, and Ranger and I took the elevator and entered the hotel directly into the casino. It was almost noon on a Monday, and the gaming area was packed. Most of the people were senior citizens. More women than men. The younger crowd would come out at night.

The noise from the slots was deafening, the flashing lights were seizure-inducing, and the amount of fat ass hanging over the chairs attached to the slot machines was horrifying. Because smoking was now prohibited, the overriding smell was that of whiskey slopped onto the Pepto-Bismol pink, Gulden's mustard gold, and poison green carpet.

"Unzipping that body bag didn't bother me," Ranger said, "but I'm going to have nightmares over this casino."

"What are we looking for?"

"Nothing special. I wanted to see the space."

We moved from the slots to the tables, mentally cataloging exits, making note of the bars and dining areas. We took the escalator to the second-floor lobby. Check-in desk. Concierge station. More slots. Another bar. A restaurant advertising an all-day breakfast buffet and Bingo. The ballroom, conference meeting rooms, and a pedestrian bridge to the conference center were on the mezzanine level. The ballroom was empty of people but filled with round tables and chairs. It was set for a wedding party. White tablecloths with huge pink bows and pink and white artificial flower centerpieces, a two-foot riser with a long decorated table for the bridal party, a smaller round table next to the riser. The smaller table supported a massive wedding cake that was being cooled by a standing fan.

"This is so romantic," I said to Ranger. "Does it give you ideas?"

He wrapped an arm around me, dragged me close against him, and kissed me on the forehead. "Yes, it gives me ideas, but not about marriage. Mostly about setting fire to this atrocity."

"It's not that bad. It's sort of growing on me."

What was really growing on me was hunger. I hadn't had any lunch, and I was ready to kill for a chunk of the wedding cake.

"I want to see the meeting rooms and the conference center," Ranger said. "And then we need to look at the mechanicals."

"I'm thinking what we need is the all-day breakfast buffet."

Ranger glanced at his watch. "You have thirty minutes."

I went for the good stuff first. Waffles, bacon, sausage, home fries, scrambled eggs, slices of ham, and a sticky bun. Ranger went with fresh fruit and a whole-wheat bagel with smoked salmon.

I cleaned my plate and pushed back from the table.

"You still have ten minutes," Ranger said.

"I'm stuffed. I can't eat any more."

"Then let's move. I have a lot of ground to cover."

I tagged after Ranger, up the escalator to the mezzanine. He looked in every meeting room and crossed the bridge to the convention center.

"Why do we need to see all this?" I asked him.

"The trade show opens tomorrow at eight o'clock and ends Thursday at five o'clock. We think Vlatko is going to attempt to kill someone at the trade show. My best chance to catch Vlatko will be when he's in this building occupied with his assignment. I have blueprints of the building, but I need to see some of the public area for myself."

"This is a big building. How are you going to find him if he's in an air duct somewhere?"

"Assassins only crawl around in air ducts in the movies. He'd be making a lot of noise and he wouldn't fit. And after he dropped the polonium, there'd be the risk of self-contamination if he couldn't get out fast enough. He's going to use his disguise to get into a room or to gain access to the air handler that services the room. That's assuming he's going with the airborne polonium again."

"I get the value of polonium at Rangeman. He wanted to infect everyone who worked for you. Why the polonium here? Why doesn't he just shoot his target?"

"There are advantages to something like polonium. It kills slowly, so there's not likely to be an immediate investigation. In fact, the death might not even be ruled a homicide. And if polonium is suspected as the agent of death, it sends a terrifying message to whoever else is involved."

We pushed through the double doors leading to the convention center and walked out into what looked like a food court with slot machines. The food vendors were shuttered. The slot machines were open for business. We took the escalator down to the cavernous first level and saw that hotel employees were setting up partitions and folding tables in numbered stall areas. Cases of booze were being wheeled around on hand trucks and deposited in stalls.

"Hard to believe this room would be involved," I said to Ranger. "It's so big. Vlatko would have to have a ton of polonium to do the whole space, and I don't see how he'd be able to target just one stall."

"I've been told that Gardi carried enough polonium to infect all of Rangeman and everyone in it, if it had been properly disseminated. The total volume of this room plus the second-level food court is more than the total volume of Rangeman, but Vlatko could probably dump enough contaminant into the system to make a lot of people sick."

"Do you think that's his goal? To make people sick?"

"No. I think he needs to eliminate someone."

We left the convention center, and I recognized one of Ranger's men loafing against the side of the building. He was dressed in tan shorts and a powder blue three-button knit shirt, and he looked like a rhinoceros dressed up for a golf date.

"Clever disguise," I said to Ranger.

"It gets better. I have a man on every exit, and I think Ramon is wearing a hotdog suit, handing out coupons to Good Dogs."

We walked the boardwalk to the casino entrance, cruised past more slots, and Ranger steered me to the bank of elevators going to guest rooms.

"I'm told I have a room on the seventh floor," he said.

"How do you know all this stuff?"

He pointed to the earbud in his ear. "I can hear, but I'm not sending right now. Tank is at Rangeman coordinating efforts with my FBI contact. Hal is in the room, coordinating here at the hotel."

"Is your FBI contact onsite?"

"No, but he has men here. They're working their way through the hotel, floor by floor, checking all the air handlers."

"This is a big operation."

"Bigger than I would like it to be, but public safety is involved."

"Out of morbid curiosity, what happens if the FBI does the takedown on Vlatko?"

"They talk to him, and then they accidentally turn him over to me for safekeeping."

"And he'll escape from you, never to be seen again."

"This isn't going to help my karma," Ranger said.

We took the elevator to the seventh floor, walked to the room at the end of the hall, and Ranger rapped twice on the door. Hal opened the door, and we stepped into a one-bedroom suite decorated in the same birthday cake style as the rest of the hotel. Pink and green wallpaper. White and gold furniture. Pictures of big pink flowers on the walls. Pink sateen bedspread that would discourage an erection from the most manly of men.

A dining room table seating six was positioned in front of the wet bar. On the table were stacks of files, a MacBook Air, a small printer, and rolls of blueprints.

A slim Hispanic guy in jeans and a T-shirt was at the Air.

"Ryan hacked into the hotel's system," he said, handing a paper to Ranger. "I have the room numbers you wanted."

Ranger took the paper, selected a file from the stack, and went to the couch. "Has Viktor Volkov registered yet?"

"No, but he has a room reserved."

"With the help of the FBI we've designated seven men as

being possible targets," Ranger said to me. "All but General Semov have checked in."

"Is he the guy getting the white glove treatment from the consulate?"

"Yes. He has the entire tenth floor. High security."

"Why is he so special?"

"He went to soccer camp with the Russian president. He's powerful. He's rich. He's ruthless. Some say he's too ambitious."

"Who would want him dead?"

"The list is long, and it includes his best friend, the president. It's whispered that the president is worried about job security."

"So is Semov at the top of our list?"

"He's at the top for motivation but near the bottom for being realistic. He's constantly surrounded by his military aides. It's like Fort Knox on the tenth floor."

"What about the ventilation system?"

"Every floor has a mechanical room with air handlers, and the polonium would have to get placed in the air handler for that floor. It's not difficult to do. You can accomplish it with a screwdriver. Ordinarily it wouldn't be a problem, but as of a couple days ago, the tenth floor has been sealed. An HVAC tech would have to be thoroughly vetted and then have a guard with him. I don't think Vlatko's cover would stand up to that kind of scrutiny."

"Why is Semov here?"

"He's been invited to give the keynote speech at lunch tomorrow. He owns a distillery in Moscow."

"So who's number one if it's not Semov?"

"I don't have a number one."

"They have cameras all over the place in these casinos. Do you have someone watching the monitors for a guy with one eye?"

"The feeds are being watched at Rangeman."

"And nothing?"

"Nothing."

"Maybe we should go downstairs and circulate," I said to Ranger. "We could mingle. Keep our eyes open." Have a gelato.

Ranger stood and stretched, his black T-shirt rode up, and I caught a glimpse of two inches of brown skin and hard abs and almost had an orgasm.

"Babe," he said. "Are you okay?"

"Yep. Why?"

"You sort of moaned."

"Gas."

"Understandable."

We took the elevator to the lobby and looked in at the bar. Filled with men speaking Russian.

"Jackpot," Ranger said. "Go do your bimbo thing."

I sidled up to a couple men but didn't get much response. I tried my luck at the other end. Nothing happening. I went back to Ranger.

"No one wants to talk to me," I said.

"Maybe it's because you're wearing a T-shirt advertising beer and these men all make vodka."

I looked down at my shirt. "This was supposed to be my day off. I wasn't dressing for success."

Ranger slung an arm around my shoulder. "Let's see what they've got in the hotel shopping arcade."

Three stores. One selling magazines and candy. One selling beachwear. One selling bimbo clothes. Perfect.

"We just need to swap out the T-shirt," Ranger said. "The jeans are good."

"They fit better before lunch."

Ranger pulled a white T-shirt off the rack. "Try this."

It was a stretchy little job with a low scoop neck, cap sleeves, and HOT STUFF spelled out in rhinestones across the boob area.

I tried it on and it fit okay. I had a little cleavage that was all my own. I wasn't sure I lived up to the message.

I peeked out of the dressing room at Ranger. "What do you think?"

"I'd give you the keys to my car."

"You do that all the time anyway."

"Ever hopeful," Ranger said.

I marched over to the bar and got into a conversation with one of the men.

"Nice shirt," he said. "Is it truly?"

"Yeah," I said. "I'm smokin'. Are you one of the vodka people?"

"Yes. I'm a very big vodka man."

"I have a friend with the trade show. He has a patch over one eye." I covered my eye with my hand. "Like this," I said. "Do you know him?"

"I don't know this patch."

I moved down the bar to another Russian.

"Howdy," I said. "Do you speak English?"

"Yes. Very good English," he said. "I mostly speak to hot girls."

Fifteen minutes later I said adios to the last Russian at the bar and returned to Ranger.

"That was fast," Ranger said.

"When you advertise hot on your chest like this, the conversation progresses pretty quickly. No one's seen Vlatko."

TWENTY-SEVEN

THE LOBBY WAS relatively empty. No one checking in or out. Two older women talking to the concierge. He gave them a map and they walked away. A service elevator to the side of the concierge desk opened, and six men in regulation military uniforms stepped out, followed by a man in a more elaborate uniform.

"General Semov," Ranger said.

Semov looked fit. Ranger had already briefed me on him, so I knew that he was fifty-three years old and had been married for twenty-three years. His inner circle knew he was unfaithful in a way usually seen in rock stars and NBA players. FBI intelligence knew that his more talkative girlfriends suffered unfortunate and fatal accidents. People who were close to him suspected regular Botox injections and an occasional peel. His face was said to be as smooth as vanilla custard.

Personally, from this distance I thought he looked a little scary.

The seven men crossed the lobby to the guest elevators, where an elevator was being held with the door open. The men got into the elevator, the door closed, and presumably the elevator whooshed Semov up to the tenth floor.

"So much for the Semov experience," I said to Ranger. "Was the FBI able to get onto the floor to check his air handler?"

"Yes."

We traded the lobby level for the casino level and wandered around. I didn't expect to see Vlatko here, but we checked anyway.

Morelli called at five o'clock.

"It's hell here," he said. "It's started to rain and we're all locked in the house with the kids running around screaming about Transformer zombies. And Bella is on a rant about your grandmother. I can't tell if Bella's overmedicated or undermedicated. Where are you? What's with all the bells and gongs going off in the background?"

"I'm in a casino in Atlantic City with Ranger."

"This must be Torture Joe Day."

"It's business. We're looking for Vlatko."

"And that's supposed to make me feel better?" There were some fumbling sounds from the phone and I could hear Morelli yelling, "Anthony junior, don't feed him any more candy."

"Is Anthony junior feeding candy to Bob?" I asked Morelli.

"No. He's feeding it to Uncle Manny. You remember Manny, right?"

"A hundred years old, no teeth, drools, smells like canned peas."

"Yeah, that's him."

"We found a guy who's missing a heart."

"Only one?"

"So far."

"Let me talk to Ranger," Morelli said.

"No. You're going to yell at him."

"I'm not going to yell at him. I'm going to threaten him with police brutality and dismemberment Italian style."

"That's sort of yelling."

More phone fumbling noise. *"Bob, drop it!"* Morelli shouted.

"Now what?"

"He's got my Aunt Momo's dentures. She takes them out when she eats. I have to go. He ran upstairs with them."

I disconnected and put my phone back into my pocket.

"Everything okay in Trenton?" Ranger asked.

"Yep. Same old, same old."

Ranger put his finger to his ear. "Tank has a visual of Vlatko. Mezzanine level, convention center."

We were standing near the front door. Ranger turned and ran out of the casino, down the boardwalk, and into the convention center. He crossed the floor to the escalator and took the steps two at a time while I scrambled to keep up. He stopped at the top of the escalator, and I came up behind him, gasping for air.

"Tank lost him," Ranger said, moving toward one of the concession stands. "He exited through the door by the frozen yogurt bar."

Ranger unholstered his gun, and we opened the door and looked into a service area with two elevators and a stairwell. No cameras. This was a major security flaw, but not unusual. The hotel had cameras only in areas available to guests. We took the stairs to the ground floor and then down one more level. We opened a door onto a maze of hallways, mechanical rooms, and storerooms connecting to the main part of the hotel.

"He can move around undetected down here," Ranger said to Tank. "Call Mac and tell him you had a visual and he needs to have a man go through the belowground service area."

"Is Mac the FBI guy?" I asked.

"He's not my primary contact. He's boots on the ground." Ranger holstered his gun, and we stepped out of the service area and into the casino. "I want to go back to the room so I can look at the hotel blueprints."

. . .

Hal was in the suite, but the computer guy was gone. Ranger unrolled the blueprints, found the lower-level print, and set a couple bottles of water on it to keep it from rolling back up again.

"Do you think you have him trapped?" I asked Ranger.

"I'm not counting on it. He's insane, but he's not stupid. I'm sure there are ways to slip out of that underground maze." He marked the blueprint with a red marker. "These are the exterior exit points. Two are to the rear of the building. A loading dock and a single door. I have a man on both of those. Plus the hotel has extra security there because Semov and his entourage are using the back door. Employees for the most part enter through a side door and go to various locker rooms. Eventually the locker rooms lead to the underground service corridors."

"And you have a man on the employee entrance?"

"Yes."

"What about the elevators and stairwells?"

"They go to all floors, and on each floor they empty out into the service pantry. Extra linens and toiletries are kept there. Room service passes through there. And next door to the service pantry is the mechanical room with the air handlers, among other things."

"Can you go directly from the service pantry into the mechanical room?"

"No. They're side by side, but you have to go out one door and in another. And when that happens you're caught on camera."

"So now we sit and wait?"

"Yes."

"Do you want to go for a gelato?"

Ranger looked at me like I had corn growing out of my ears.

"I'm just saying, they have a gazillion flavors of gelato at this little kiosk next to the all-day breakfast place," I said. "And I thought it might be refreshing."

Ranger smiled. "There are times when I seriously consider marrying you, but then I get yet another black mark on my path to enlightenment and forgiveness and I scratch marriage off my bucket list."

"Really? You think about marrying me?"

"Marrying you might be extreme, but once in a while I think about sharing my closet."

"You have a really great closet."

It was a big walk-in with beautiful cherry cabinets and wall-to-wall carpet. Ella kept Ranger's clothes perfectly pressed and orderly. She folded his underwear and matched his socks. She lined his dress shirts up with the hangers all going in the same direction. Of course it was all made easier by the fact that Ranger only wore black.

"So about the gelato?" I said.

"Sure."

"I don't mean to be listening in or anything," Hal said. "But if you're bringing gelato back, I like Banana Sunrise."

This two-hundred-and-fifty-pound guy who looked like the Hulk, if the Hulk wasn't green, liked Banana Sunrise gelato.

We stepped into the hall, and Tank told Ranger he had another visual. Vlatko was on the ninth floor, moving from the service pantry to the mechanical room. And he didn't have the patch. He was wearing dark glasses.

Ranger went through the seventh-floor service pantry and ran up two flights of stairs. I ran behind him and hit the service pantry just as he was out the door. By the time I reached the hall he had his gun drawn and the mechanical room door unlocked.

Cautioning me to stand back, he pushed the mechanical room door open and stepped inside. I moved to the open door and waited there while Ranger searched the room.

"He's not here," he said. "You can come in."

I stepped in, and the door locked behind me. "Did Tank see him leave this room?"

"No. There must be a way out that doesn't show on the blueprint."

"The window," I said.

The window was frosted and closed but not locked. Ranger opened the window and looked out. A wrought iron ladder ran up the side of the building, from the second floor to the roof. An emergency fire escape. Even if the building was burning I'm not sure I could bring myself to use it.

Ranger closed and locked the window, went to the air handler, and used his penknife to remove the side panel.

"If Vlatko wants to use the aerosol polonium, this is probably how he'll do it," Ranger said. "Or at least this is how he'd hoped to do it. He could put the canister in here, on the coils, set the timer, and the air handler fan would blow the polonium into the guest rooms."

"Do you think he's changed his plan? He has to know we're here looking for him."

"If he was sent here to get a job done, and he was sent with a very specific weapon, like the aerosol polonium, he might not have a lot of flexibility. And unless he has sophisticated listening equipment, which I doubt, he has no way of knowing how many people are looking for him."

"Wouldn't he assume you'd be working with the FBI after he set the polonium off at Rangeman? That's considered nuclear terrorism."

"I'm pretty sure I know his mindset, and he'd assume I was hunting him on my own. Vlatko works alone, and he sees me as his Western counterpart."

Ranger screwed the panel back in place. "I'm sure there's access to the roof from inside. There are water-cooling towers there for the air conditioners, and those units need maintenance. So there has to be a stairwell going to the roof from the tenth floor, and it would be part of the behind-the-scenes service network."

"So Vlatko could be avoiding cameras by using the outside ladder to get to the roof and hook up with the service stairwell there."

"Looks like it. He's also more difficult to spot without the eye patch."

We left the ninth floor, rode the elevator to the lobby, and Morelli called.

"You're not coming home, are you?" he asked.

"It's doubtful. We know he's here. He gets picked up on the hotel security feed once in a while, but we can't get to him fast enough."

"I'd be happy to help, but I suspect you've got a small army there."

"I'm not sure what we have here. I'm not totally in the loop. And I think you don't want to be either. It sounds like you survived the party."

"Barely. And Bob chipped a tooth off Momo's uppers. It's going to cost me a fortune. So what are you doing right now?"

"Ranger and I are in the lobby. We came down for gelato."

Silence on Morelli's end.

"But before this we examined the air handler on the ninth floor," I said.

"You aren't sleeping with him, are you?"

"Of course not."

"Good to know," Morelli said.

"You trust me."

"I do. But I don't trust him."

"You're pretty smart for a Trenton cop."

"I finished the Jumble today."

"Impressive."

I said good night, and looked over the list of gelato flavors.

"There are so many," I said to Ranger. "I can't choose."

"Do you want me to choose for you?"

"No!"

He looked at his watch. "You have thirty seconds."

"I want Tiramisu. No, wait, Strawberry. Maybe Caramel Swirl."

"Ten seconds."

"Mango, Coffee, Chocolate Marshmallow . . ."

"She'll have Tiramisu," he said to the girl at the counter. "And a large Banana Sunrise." He turned to me. "Always go with your first instinct."

"You're not having any?"

"My first instinct is to pass."

TWENTY-EIGHT

I ATE MY gelato and commandeered the bedroom while Ranger and Hal worked at the dining table. I watched television, ordered room service, and shut the door against the stream of men coming and going, reporting in to Ranger.

I called Connie and told her I was on a job with Ranger and might not be in the office tomorrow. I called Lula and asked her to look in on Briggs and the dogs. I got a call from Grandma Mazur asking for a ride home from Bingo.

"Sorry," I said. "I'm in Atlantic City on a job with Ranger."

"I wouldn't mind being in Atlantic City," Grandma said. "I like those all-you-can-eat lunch buffets. And I could spend some time playing the slots. I haven't done that in an age."

"I'm not doing any of those things. I'm working."

"Did you have a swirly frozen yogurt?"

"No, but I had a gelato."

"Then it wasn't a total waste," Grandma said.

From the level of activity in the other room I could guess that there weren't any more Vlatko sightings. I changed back into my comfy T-shirt advertising beer, crawled into bed, and switched the light off. I woke up at sunrise with Ranger next to me. Naked. No surprise there. Ranger always slept naked.

"I suppose I should be happy I don't have half of Rangeman and an FBI SWAT team in bed with me," I said.

"They have a room next door, and Hal's on the couch. If you're *really* happy, I could get rid of Hal."

"I'm not that happy. I'm wondering why I felt compelled to do this. It's not like I have something to contribute."

"The day isn't over. And none of us have been especially effective with the exception of Tank, who spotted Vlatko twice."

Ranger rolled out of bed and went into the bathroom, and I was sorry the room was dark and I couldn't see him better. I heard the shower running, and I went back to sleep. I opened my eyes an hour later and dragged myself into the shower. When I came out of the bathroom there was a bag from the bimbo store on the bed. A new shirt and some lingerie. The shirt was red, with rhinestones that spelled out ATLANTIC CITY. The lingerie was black and lacy.

"Thanks," I said when I came out of the bedroom. "It's great to have clean clothes. I'm surprised the store is open this early."

"Only for you," Ranger said. "Rafael did the shopping."

Rafael was obviously the slim guy at the computer. He looked up and smiled wide. "I know what the ladies like," he said.

Hal was at a second computer. He grinned and shook his head.

Ranger was dressed in Rangeman black fatigues. Ready for action. He was leaning against the breakfront with a coffee cup in his hand. He was armed.

"You look like you expect something to happen today," I said to him.

"Intel has picked up chatter that there'll be an event involving Semov. Mac has two extra men on him. One with Semov, and one checking Semov's environment. Semov is scheduled to remain in his suite until eleven forty-five, at which time he and his entourage will make their way to the ballroom, where he'll give the keynote address. He's vulnerable when he's moving. He could get swept along in the crowd, and Vlatko would only need to come in contact with him for a few seconds to deliver the polonium. Personally, I don't care if Semov lives or dies, but I don't want to miss the opportunity to take Vlatko down.

"I need to put you on the mezzanine level this morning. It's going to be a mob scene when everyone leaves the convention center and moves into the ballroom for lunch. Find a place where your back is to the wall and you can watch the people entering the ballroom. Vlatko has probably changed his appearance. Colored his hair, ditched the patch, added a beard, whatever, so you need to look for other things, like suspicious behavior and the tattoo. You have an advantage because you've actually seen him."

"How soon do you want me out there?"

"I'd like you in place by ten o'clock."

A buffet had been set out on the dining table. Croissants, bagels, smoked salmon, cream cheese, little jars of jam, pots of coffee, a large platter of fresh fruit. A container of orange juice. No waffles drenched in syrup. No donuts. No eggs Benedict.

I poured myself a cup of coffee and selected a croissant.

"Have there been any more Vlatko sightings?" I asked.

"No," Ranger said. "I have someone watching the ladder running up the side of the building, but Vlatko hasn't used it."

"Maybe he's already infected his target and he's on his way back to Russia."

"That's possible," Ranger said. "That's why the polonium is so useful. You can eliminate someone and no one necessarily knows for days, maybe weeks or months."

I took a call from Connie. "I can't find anyone to bond out Forest," she said. "He's homeless, and he stole food to feed his dog pack, so I don't think he's looking at a lot of time. I expect he'll get a week in the workhouse at the most. Problem is, he won't come to trial for weeks. Are you good with his dogs until then?"

"I've got Briggs babysitting. He seems to be doing okay. I asked Lula to look in on him."

"I haven't seen Lula. Maybe she went to your apartment before coming here. How's it going? Where are you, anyway?"

"Atlantic City."

"The hardship assignment."

"Yeah, I'm here with Ranger, drinking coffee and eating croissants."

"I hate you. Did you sleep with him?"

"That's a complicated question."

"You did!"

"No."

"Okay, I don't want to know any more, but I expect details when you get back."

I hung up and called Lula.

"Where are you?" I asked. "Did you check in with Briggs?"

"Yeah, I'm in your parking lot. He's turned into one of those dog nuts. And I tell you I can't blame him. Those critters are cute as anything. And they aren't even demons. I mean, they don't have rotating heads or glowing eyes or nothing. One of them tried to nip at me, but Briggs says that dog has trust issues, so I didn't take it personal. The rest were all dancing around and looking happy. And I'm even getting used to the way they vibrate. I mean, I like things that vibrate anyway, you see what I'm saying?"

Oh yeah.

"I'm stuck here in Atlantic City," I said. "I'm hoping to get home later today or tomorrow, but maybe in the meantime you could make sure Briggs has enough food. He's stuck there without a car."

"He said he had a job interview today. I don't know how he's getting there. Taxi, maybe. He didn't ask for help."

I hung up and called my mom.

"Just checking in," I said. "I'm out of town on a job with Ranger. Is everything going okay there?"

"Your father is out with the cab. And your grandmother is on one of those senior trips for the day, so it's nice and quiet here."

"Where's Grandma going?"

"Atlantic City. She said she felt lucky."

Crap! Double crap!!

"When did Grandma leave?"

"About a half hour ago. Your father took her to the senior center. They have a good deal. She gets the bus trip, a roll of tokens for the slots, and a ticket for the all-you-can-eat buffet."

"Do you know what casino she's going to?"

"No. The seniors get a bunch of deals. They don't always go to the same casino."

I hung up and called Grandma. No answer.

Okay, what are the chances it would be this casino? Slim. It was a crummy casino. And it was filled with booze salesmen. There were lots of other casinos in Atlantic City. So I shouldn't worry, right?

• • •

Ranger gave me an earbud a little before ten o'clock. "I have this set so you can communicate with me and with Tank. He'll be watching the video feeds."

I took the elevator to the mezzanine and found a place in the hall where I could see the doors to the ballroom and also the mechanical room door at the far end of the hall. The doors to the ballroom were closed, and the hallway was empty. I recognized a Rangeman guy standing by the bridge that led to the conference center.

I was in the hall for about fifteen minutes when Grandma called.

"Where are you?" she asked.

"I'm still in Atlantic City. Where are you?"

"I'm in some traffic on the road to Atlantic City. I'm with Lula."

"Mom said you were going on a seniors bus."

"It broke down before we even loaded onto it, so I called Lula to see if she felt lucky today, and here we are on the road. We're trying to decide on a casino. I like the new one with the jungle theme, but Lula says she's partial to Caesars. What casino are you at? We could come visit you."

"No visits! I have to work. And I'm not at a great casino anyway. Go to Caesars, and I'll call you later."

After an hour I was blind with boredom. I paced the hall. I counted the overhead lights. I tried a door to the ballroom. Locked. Guess they were worried some boozehound vodka dealer would steal the silverware or sit in an unassigned seat.

"This is boring," I said.

"Boring is good," Ranger said into my earbud.

People began drifting in from the convention center at 11:30. A few here. A few there. They gathered in clumps. They conducted business on their smartphones. They looked at their watches and looked at the closed ballroom doors. Hungry.

I watched a man come up the escalator. He didn't nod

or wave, but he exchanged a silent communication with the Rangeman guy. He was wearing a blue button-down shirt, tan slacks, scuffed brown shoes. FBI, I thought. He looked pleasant. I could see a slight gun bulge under his sport coat, and an earbud attached by a curly wire to a battery pack. Not high-tech like mine. FBI. He'd be jealous of my earbud.

"Hello," I said. "Anybody home?"

"Babe?" Ranger said.

"Where are you?"

"I'm waiting at the service elevator for Semov."

"On my floor?"

"Yes. And then I'll stay with Semov."

"Okay. Over and out."

The man in the blue shirt ambled past me. He went to the end of the hall and used a key to open the door to the mechanical room.

"A guy in a blue shirt just went into the mechanical room," I said.

"I've got him," Tank said. "He's FBI going in to check on the air handler."

"Just saying."

"Hang tight," Tank told me.

People poured out of the convention center and filled the corridor. The noise level rose. Men pushed against the ballroom doors and tested the doorknobs. Everyone looked happy. Lots of laughing. I figured there was vodka tasting going on this morning in the convention center. Probably they had a vodka fountain at the breakfast buffet.

"Moving out," Ranger said into my earbud.

The door to the service pantry opened and Semov's six aides strode out, followed by Semov, followed by Ranger, followed by two men with the old-school earbuds who I figured were FBI. They cut a path through the crowd, a door opened at the far end of the ballroom, and they disappeared inside.

Moments later the remaining doors to the ballroom opened and everyone stampeded in. I looked down the hall at the mechanical room.

"Did the FBI guy come out of the mechanical room?" I asked Tank.

"I didn't see him come out. He might have been told to stay there until the banquet is over. I can't talk to him. He's not on my frequency."

I walked down the hall and knocked on the door. "Hello," I said. "Are you okay in there?"

The door opened, an arm reached out and grabbed me, and I was yanked inside.

"Oh shit!" Tank said into my earbud.

TWENTY-NINE

I CAUGHT A glimpse of someone in a ball cap, and I was hit in the face and knocked off my feet. It was Vlatko. He looked down at me. His hair was dark brown under the ball cap, and he had sunglasses stuck over the brim. His injured eye was horrible, stitched together in a ragged, bunched-up scar that sliced through his eyebrow and ran into his cheek. He was wearing a lightweight gray hoodie and jeans. I could see the odd tattoo on his neck.

I tasted blood, and I didn't know if it was from my nose or my mouth. I was on my hands and knees, still fuzzy from being hit.

"What?" I said.

The earbud was on the floor. Vlatko picked it up and smiled. "Are you listening?" he said into the earbud. "I have your girlfriend, and she's going to be my ticket out. If anyone comes near me, I'll gut her. You know I can. She's already bleeding. It wouldn't take much to finish her off."

Vlatko dropped the earbud onto the floor and crushed it under his heel. He grabbed me and dragged me to my feet. I looked past him and saw the FBI guy on the floor in a pool of blood. His neck had been slashed so that his head was almost completely severed from his neck.

"That could easily be you," Vlatko said.

"You killed him."

"He came in at the wrong time. I was placing the polonium."

I looked over at the air handler. "You're going to poison everyone in the ballroom?"

"Clever, don't you think? An act of terrorism. A political statement rather than a planned assassination of a single political figure. I admit it hasn't gone as smooth as I'd hoped, but the job is done. And I have you. You'll get me out of here, and then I'll skin you alive and leave you for, what's his name now, Ranger?"

The dead agent, the blood, the skinning alive, were mind-numbingly terrifying. I was telling myself to focus, to be alert, not to be overwhelmed by the fear and the horror. When the opportunity came, I had to be ready to run. Yeah, right. My legs were shaky, and my heart was beating so hard my vision was blurred. Running wasn't currently an option.

"It won't work," I said. "They know we're in here. Someone will burst in any second and stop you."

"It's too late. The polonium's in the system. In fifteen minutes it will reach the ballroom."

"All those people . . ."

"Dead," Vlatko said.

Acting more from instinct than coherent thought I staggered back, flung my arm out, and pulled the fire alarm that hung on the wall. Vlatko yanked me away, but the alarm was already wailing, red ceiling lights flashing in the mechanical room. He put his knife to my neck and shoved me into the storage cabinet in the corner, and I realized how he'd managed to get into the room undetected. There was a hole punched into the wall between the mechanical room and the service pantry.

I went through the hole, into the storeroom, and attempted to scramble away, but he was too fast. He half dragged me, half shoved me into the stairwell. There were footsteps on the stairs below us. Men running.

"Up," he said, the knife to my throat again.

I stumbled on the first step and felt the knife bite into my neck. I managed to get to the fourth-floor landing, I looked over at him, and I saw no panic. No nervous sweat, no fear, no confusion. He was stone cold calm, calculating what to do next. He moved us into the fourth-floor supply room, went to the window and opened it.

"Out," he said.

"Out where?"

"Onto the ledge."

"Are you crazy? Do I look like Spider-Man? I'm not getting on that ledge. It's like a foot wide."

"You can die here, or you can go out the window."

"Where am I going once I get out there?"

"You're going to inch your way over to the covered pedestrian bridge to the parking garage."

"And then?"

"You're going to drop onto the bridge."

"No way!"

"It's not that far. Go!"

I crept out the window and carefully stood with my back pressed tight against the building. I'm not great with heights, and I was paralyzed with fear.

Vlatko was out of the window, standing next to me, his hand wrapped around my wrist. "Start moving," he said in his strange British accent.

"My f-f-feet won't move."

"I'm going to count to three, and then I'm throwing you off this ledge. You're in my way."

I moved one foot, then the other.

"Faster," he said.

The covered bridge to the parking garage wasn't far away. A few more steps. Don't look down, I told myself. Concentrate on the bridge. It wasn't a far drop, and it had a nice wide, flat roof. I could do it.

"Keep moving until you're in the middle of the bridge," Vlatko said. "I'll tell you when to jump. We're going to jump together."

"Aren't you afraid of a sniper?" I asked him. "The FBI probably has you in their sights."

"You're my insurance policy. If they shoot me now, you'll go down with me."

"Surely you don't think you can get away."

"It's not over until it's over. I've been in worse spots. And if I'm captured I'll be extradited to Russia, where I'll get bonus pay. I came here on a diplomatic visa, and I have friends in very high places."

I reached the middle of the bridge and allowed myself to finally look down. The cement roof was about four feet below me. If for some reason I skidded off the roof, I'd fall three stories to the street. Not a good thought.

"Jump," he said, stepping off the ledge, taking me with him.

I landed hard, my legs buckled, he pulled me up and yanked me forward.

The parking garage was a ten-story reinforced concrete structure that wasn't totally enclosed. At each level the thick outer wall was five feet high, leaving five feet of open space between the top of the wall and the beamed structure of the next concrete deck. In theory this should have allowed the wonderful sea breeze to waft through the garage. In practice, the hotel blocked the sea breeze, and what wafted through the garage was the smell of fried food spewing out of the kitchen ventilation system on the second floor.

The pedestrian bridge very nicely opened onto the third-floor parking deck, but if you happened to be on the *roof* of the bridge, there was no easy access. The bridge's roof connected to the five-foot very solid wall of parking deck number 4. Even with a knife to my throat and adrenaline surging through me, I had no ability to get over the five-foot wall. Maybe with a running start, but that wasn't going to happen.

"Here's what's going to happen," Vlatko said. "I'm going to give you a boost up, and before you even hit the ground on the other side, I'm going to be over the wall. So don't think about running away. If you even attempt to run, I'll catch you and kill you."

He gave me a boost that belly-flopped me onto the top of the wall and tumbled me off onto the floor on the other side. I landed on my back, and looked over at Ranger pressed flat against the wall. Vlatko swung himself over, and Ranger snatched him out of midair. There was the flash of Vlatko's knife blade, and in the next instant Ranger flung Vlatko off the fourth floor of the parking garage.

I was still on my back, and Ranger knelt beside me.

"Is anything broken?" he asked.

"Holy crap," I said. And a tear leaked out of my eye.

Ranger brushed the tear away and lifted me to my feet. We went to the wall and looked down at Vlatko, sprawled on the road below us.

"Do you think he's okay?" I asked.

"Babe," Ranger said. "He's one inch thick."

"Your arm is bleeding."

"He tagged me when I grabbed him."

"How did you know we'd be coming over the wall?"

"I was listening to you the whole time. I didn't trust you to hang on to the earbud, so I had a mini-microphone sewn into your shirt. It's just under the rolled hem on the neckline."

I glanced at it. "I thought it was just another rhinestone."

Men were running at us from all directions. Uniformed Rangeman guys, two guys in suits and ties that I knew were FBI, a hotel security guard.

The Rangeman guys secured the perimeter a short distance from us. The two FBI agents went to the wall and looked down at Vlatko and then looked over at Ranger.

"What happened?" one of the FBI guys asked.

"He jumped," Ranger said.

The agent nodded. "I figured. I could tell by the way he sailed out into space."

"He released the poison," I said. "He told me it would reach the ballroom in fifteen minutes."

"The fire alarm emptied the entire hotel," the FBI guy said. "The ballroom emptied in less than ten. Right now we're waiting for the hazmat team to suit up and go into the mechanical room to retrieve the canister. We'll know more when they get the canister out and take air quality readings in the ballroom."

I looked down at my bloody shirt and jeans. "My face hurts all over," I said to Ranger. "Where's all the blood coming from?"

"You're getting a bruise on your cheek. You have a small cut on your lower lip. You were bleeding from your nose, but that seems to have stopped. You have a puncture wound on your neck."

"I'm a mess!"

Ranger wrapped his arms around me and held me close. "You're beautiful. You evacuated the hotel and you delivered Vlatko."

We stared down at the street. It was clogged with police and firemen and vodka salesmen. No one was being allowed back into the hotel.

"What's next to us?" Ranger asked the hotel security guard.

"It's the new hotel that's all jungle theme. The Monkey Pod."

Ranger told Tank to get a suite and an extra room at the Monkey Pod. And he asked him to get us new clothes and to bring a first-aid kit from one of the Rangeman cars. We took the elevator to the ground level and exited the garage from the rear, away from the crowd. Ranger's men came with us, and the FBI went to check out Vlatko.

The Monkey Pod manager met us in the hotel lobby and escorted us upstairs. There were monkeys everywhere. Monkey wallpaper, monkey designs on hall carpets, and monkey sconces. It was worse than the birthday cake hotel. It was dark, and the monkeys didn't look happy.

Ranger took the key cards and assured the manager that everything was wonderful. He gave one card to the two men who accompanied us, and they went next door.

The suite had the same monkey theme as the hall. Monkey lights, monkey candy dishes, monkey wallpaper. At least it was large and everything was new and clean. And it felt far away from the horrors that had just happened in the poor birthday cake hotel.

My cellphone buzzed in my pocket. Grandma.

"Hey," I said.

"Hey, yourself," Grandma said. "I hope you're not missing all the action at that hotel that looks like a birthday cake. First off, the fire alarm sent everybody out. And then some guy went *splat* on the road. Nobody knows if it was a suicide or what. Lula and I were at the Monkey Pod when it all happened, and I got out in time to see the guy before the police roped it all off. He was flat as a fried egg, and his head was burst open like a ripe melon. It was terrible . . . in a fascinating kind of way."

"Poor man."

"Yeah. One of the people there said the smushed dead guy just broke up with his girlfriend and they had a big fight in the casino. Where are you, anyway? Did you get a chance to see all the commotion?"

"I'm at the Monkey Pod. Just checked in."

"We're out on the boardwalk. Boy, I'd kill to see one of those rooms. Do they have the monkey theme like the casino?"

"Yep. There are monkeys everywhere."

"I don't suppose we could come up just to take a peek?" Grandma asked.

"Sure. Just to take a peek, but this is actually Ranger's room and he's working, so you can't stay long."

"We'll be in and out."

I gave her the room number and hung up.

"Grandma and Lula want to see the room," I said to Ranger.

Ranger's shirt was soaked with blood. "I'm going to rinse off in the shower," he said. "I can't tell how deep this slash is on my arm. You're welcome to join me."

"Tempting, but I'll wait here for Grandma and Lula. They said they'd be right up."

I went to the powder room, switched the light on, looked

in the mirror, and had to steady myself with my hands on the vanity. I looked like something from a horror movie. I washed my face, neck, and chest as best I could. I scrubbed my arms to above the elbow. I couldn't do anything about the blood on my shirt and jeans, but at least the shirt was red from the start.

The suite had a doorbell that sounded like a monkey screaming. I opened the door to Lula and Grandma.

"Look at this," Lula said, pushing past me. "This is the shit. This is the bomb. It's got a dining room table. I bet the Queen of England lives like this. Like when she goes on vacation, I bet she stays in places like this."

"There's a separate bedroom," Grandma said, rushing into the bedroom. "And it's got its own television. And it's got monkey lamps and a monkey bedspread with a bunch of monkey pillows."

"Yeah, but that's nothing," Lula said. "It got a kitchen area with bottles of wine and packages of crackers. And there's a basket with Snickers in it, and all kinds of shit."

I understood their excitement. This was a high roller suite, and we weren't high roller people. Unfortunately, I'd just gotten punched in the face and thought I was going to swan dive off a ledge, so I was having a hard time getting excited about the Snickers and the monkey pillows. The adrenaline rush had burned off, and I was exhausted.

"They even got two bathrooms here," Grandma said. "There's a powder room, and then there's this bathroom here off the bedroom."

"Do you want this Snickers?" Lula asked me. "Because if you don't want it, I might want it for the ride home. And what about Granny? Does she want anything here?"

I looked around. I didn't see Grandma. She was in the bedroom, and she'd mentioned the bathroom, and *Oh my God!*

"*Babe!*" Ranger shouted from the bathroom. "Come get your grandmother."

Ranger was standing in the glass-enclosed shower with the door open, looking out at Grandma. He was dripping wet and seemed not especially concerned that he was naked.

"It's like she's paralyzed," he said.

"Amazing," Grandma said, eyes wide, staring in unblinking stupefaction.

I yanked Grandma out and closed the bathroom door.

"It was mesmerizing," Grandma said. "It was like staring into the eye of a cobra. I don't care if I do anything else on the bucket list. This was awesome. It was like a biblical experience."

Lula stared at my shirt and my face. "What the heck happened to you?"

"There was a little skirmish," I said. "It's all okay."

"You got a nasty bruise shaping up on your face. You didn't get that from anybody I know, did you?"

"Nope. We took down a bad guy. Where are you going now? More slots?"

"We didn't get to Caesars yet," Grandma said. "That's our next stop. And we're going home after the dinner buffet. Call if you need a ride."

I walked them to the door and locked up after them. Ranger was out of the shower when I went into the bedroom. His hair was damp, and he was wearing a hotel robe.

"Sorry about Grandma," I said. "She got away from me."

"She just stood there staring. It was eerie. I was afraid she'd had a stroke."

A stroke of good fortune, I thought. Not everyone was lucky enough to see Ranger naked.

"I heard a text come in while you were in the shower," I said.

Ranger looked at his phone. "It's from Mac. This was a more sophisticated delivery system than the one they were going to use on Rangeman. The timer actually showed the start time, and they calculate that the ballroom emptied well before the gas reached it. Plus Mac immediately shut the ventilation system down, so much of the polonium was trapped in the duct."

Rafael came to the door with a couple bags of clothes. "I did the best I could," he said, "but everything downstairs has monkeys on it."

"Thanks," I said. "I'm sure they're great."

THIRTY

RANGER NEEDED TO stay in Atlantic City to debrief with the FBI, but I was free to leave with Grandma and Lula. I might have been more inclined to stay with Ranger but for the fact that I was wearing head-to-toe monkeys. The day had been traumatic enough, and the day before hadn't been all that good either, and now I had monkey underpants on. The saying "Out of sight, out of mind" didn't apply to monkey underpants. I wanted to go home and try to feel normal and convince myself that the threat was gone.

Rafael and Hal walked me from the room to the hotel drive court and made sure I was securely belted into Lula's Firebird. Hard to tell if Ranger was still afraid for my safety, or if he was afraid I'd change my mind and come back to the room with Lula and Grandma.

Lula pulled away from the hotel and headed for the freeway.

"I must have ate a million shrimps at that buffet. And the cocktail sauce had just the right amount of horseradish."

"Yep," Grandma said. "This was a real good day. We should do this more often. I wouldn't mind having another day just like this one."

I was in the backseat with an ice pack on my bruised cheek, and I didn't ever want to repeat my day.

. . .

It was close to nine o'clock when I walked into Morelli's house. He was on the couch watching television with Bob, and they both looked happy to see me. Then Morelli took a closer look, and his expression changed from happy to heartburn. Good thing he hadn't seen me before the shower and clean clothes.

I dumped my messenger bag and clothes bag on the floor and squeezed in next to Morelli. "It looks worse than it is," I said. "The important thing is that it ended well. Vlatko is gone and will never come back. And I'm here with you and Bob."

"You have a monkey on your shirt," Morelli said.

"I have a monkey on my everything. What happened today? Did I miss anything good?"

"Miriam Pepper had a few too many Manhattans for breakfast, and her bathrobe caught fire while she was attempting to scramble some eggs. She managed to get herself out of the bathrobe, but in the process she set her kitchen on fire and half her house burned down."

"Is she okay?"

"Yeah, but here's the good part. When the fire marshal went into the basement, he found bricks of high-grade Mexican marijuana stacked up like cordwood, plus some rocket launchers and stuff to make firebombs. They started to question Pepper, and he lawyered up. When they questioned Miriam, she said the marijuana was for personal use and medicinal purposes."

"What about the rocket launchers?"

"She said they were used for family fun outings."

"Did she say anything about Briggs?"

"Yeah. She said Silvio hated Briggs. Briggs was driving Silvio nuts with his nitpicking all the transportation expenses. And Silvio told Miriam that Briggs hums when he works. Briggs would come in to do the books, and he'd hum."

"Pepper was trying to blow Briggs up for humming?"

"That's one theory."

"So let me get this straight. No one wanted to kill Briggs because he knew about Poletti's money stash and about the cooked books. Everyone wanted to kill Briggs because he's annoying."

"That's what we're hearing."

"It's a real accomplishment to be *that* annoying."

"I don't buy it," Morelli said. "There has to be more."

"What about Scootch, Siglowski, Ritt, and Poletti? Do you have a lead on the shooter? I was going with Silvio Pepper."

"The gun wasn't found in Pepper's house or office."

"Too bad. That would have tied things up nice and neat."

. . .

Morelli was long gone by the time I rolled out of bed. I had a bruise on my face and a Band-Aid on my neck. The cut on my lip was slightly swollen but not terrible. I made myself a peanut butter sandwich and washed it down with two cups of coffee. I slung the messenger bag over my shoulder, told Bob to be good, and went to the front door. There were two black SUVs at the curb and two Rangeman guys. One SUV was an Escalade, the other was a small Mercedes. I was handed the key to the Mercedes.

"Ranger wanted you to have this," one of the men said.

I texted *Thank you* to Ranger and got behind the wheel. I had money to get another car, but this made my life instantly better. I was spending a fortune on gas for the Buick, and sourcing out a good used SUV would take time.

First stop was my apartment, to check on Briggs. I ran into Dillan, the super, in the hall.

"We're painting on Friday, and your carpet is supposed to get installed the following Monday," he said.

"That's great," I told him. "Thanks."

I let myself into the apartment, and the dogs rushed over to me.

"Hey, look who's here!" Briggs said. "It's Aunt Stephanie."

He was dressed in the tan suit, and it looked like he'd gotten a haircut.

"What's with the suit?" I asked him.

"I have a job interview, so Nick let me keep it a while longer. What happened with the Russian guy?"

"The problem is solved."

"I bet."

"Dillan said the rugs are going in next Monday, so that means I'll be able to move back in."

"No problem. I got my new credit cards, and I got some insurance money, and my old apartment building gave me a good chunk of money as encouragement to live someplace else. So I'll go apartment hunting after the job interview. My cousin Bruce is going to drive me around."

"I'm only counting eight dogs," I said to Briggs.

"Mrs. Brodsky on the first floor took one. And Mr. Grezbek down the hall took one."

Someone hammered on my door, and I looked out the peephole at Oswald Poletti.

I opened the door, and Oswald slouched in. "Hey," he said. "What are you doing here?"

"This is my apartment," I told him.

"No shit? I thought this belonged to the little turd. What are you two, a couple or something?"

"He's an acquaintance. I let him stay here because someone firebombed his apartment."

"Yeah, that was me," Oswald said. "I was trying to run him out of town so he wouldn't ruin everything for Miriam. But then he moved here, so I shot off another rocket, only I didn't count for wind and my aim was off. Sorry about the hole in the wall."

Briggs and I were momentarily speechless.

"What about the two cars?" Briggs asked.

"I don't know about two cars. I just shot a rocket into one

291

car. A Porsche. It was awesome. Freaking awesome. I got a freaking boner over it."

"Miriam?" I finally said. "Are you talking about Miriam Pepper?"

"Yeah, she's a real nice lady. She makes a bad Manhattan, man. I mean, they're so bad you could drink until you pass out. And she's got good Mexican dope too."

"How do you know Miriam?"

"Her old man kept all the ammo for the shooting range in the Pine Barrens. Man, those were the days. I'd cart all the shit down there for him, and then we'd all get stoned and blow the shit up. Refrigerators, televisions, you name it and we blew it up."

"Do you see the difference between blowing up a refrigerator and sending a rocket into an apartment?"

"What do you mean?"

"You could have killed someone."

"It was just a refrigerator. There wasn't no one in it."

"I mean the apartment!"

"Yeah, but I thought it was *him* in the apartment. And anyway that didn't work so I came over here to tell him to leave Miriam alone."

"I don't even know Miriam," Briggs said. "Are you high?"

"Well, yeah," Oswald said, smiling. "Of course I'm high. Miriam said you were going to ruin everything. She said nobody trusted you, and you were going to talk to the police, and that would be the end of the Manhattans and weed. So I said, 'Don't worry, Miriam, I'll take care of him.'" Oswald looked around. "I'm starving, man. You have any chips, or something?"

"I ate all the chips," Briggs said.

"Then I guess I have to kill you," Oswald said. "So what do you have? Weed? Demerol? M&M's?"

"How about a puppy?" Briggs said. "You could give it to Miriam."

"Where?"

"Here," Briggs said, pointing to the Chihuahuas sitting at his feet. "Pick one. They're up for adoption."

"They look like rats with big ears."

"Watch what you say about my dogs," Briggs said. "They're very sensitive."

"Sorry, man. I wasn't thinking."

"Miriam probably doesn't want a dog right now," I said. "She sort of burned her house down."

"Yeah, she's like living in the garage," Oswald said. "It's got air-conditioning and everything, but the cops took all the weed and rockets. It's like such a bummer."

"Jeez, this has been a terrific conversation," Briggs said, "but I have stuff to do. And don't worry about Miriam. I won't bother Miriam."

"Do you need a ride?" I asked Oswald.

"No. I got a car. I'm sort of supposed to be at work, but the kitchen's loose, being that nobody else'll work the fry station."

I pointed Oswald in the direction of the elevator and closed and locked the door behind him.

"Boy," Briggs said, "I didn't see that one coming."

"There's no limit to your unpopularity."

I called Morelli and told him to pick Oswald up in connection with the firebombings.

"I have to run," Briggs said. "Bruce is probably already out there, and I don't want to be late for my interview. This would be a great job. Can you lock up for me?"

"Sure. Good luck."

I watched Briggs run down the hall and get into the elevator, and then I turned to the dogs.

"Okay," I said, "try not to vibrate too much until Briggs gets back. You don't want to go into a seizure or anything."

I stepped into the hall, closed and locked the door, took five steps, and the dogs started yipping. Considering they were such small dogs, the yipping was pretty loud.

I unlocked the door and stepped inside. "You can't make noise like that," I said to them. "The neighbors won't like it."

They all settled down and calmly stared up at me with their bug eyes.

"All right, then," I said.

I moved into the hall and closed the door, and instant yipping! I jumped back into the apartment, got the dog biscuits from the cupboard, and threw a bunch of them at the Chihuahuas.

I ran out of the apartment, got almost to the elevator, and the yipping turned into yelping.

Damn!

Five minutes later, the dogs were leashed and in the back of the Mercedes SUV. I drove to the office and brought the dogs in with me.

"What's with the minions?" Lula asked.

"I'm babysitting."

"Looks like you brought the little critters in a shiny new Mercedes," Lula said. "We should take it to lunch."

I looked at my watch. "It's early for lunch."

"Then we should take it to breakfast or brunch or whatever the hell. I woke up thinking about pizza. I don't know what it is about the pizza at the pizza place in Buster's building. I got a real craving for it."

THIRTY-ONE

I TOOK LULA across town and parked opposite Buster's building.

"It isn't even eleven o'clock and already there's a line here," Lula said. "Ordinarily I don't do lines, but this is different. I bet I could eat a whole pie. What kind are you going to get?"

"I'm going to skip the pizza. I just had a peanut butter sandwich. I'll wait here with the critters."

Lula got into line, and I relaxed in Ranger's Mercedes. Vlatko was out of the picture. Ranger was safe. I was wearing my own underwear. Life was good.

A Camaro with tinted windows parked on the other side of the street, two doors down from Buster. The driver got out, walked to Buster's door, unlocked the door with a key, and let himself in. The man was stocky. Black hair, dark skin. T-shirt and jeans. Hoodie over the T-shirt. Odd, since it was almost eighty degrees. My first thought was that he was hiding a gun.

My second thought was that I needed a new life because lately I thought *everybody* was packing a gun, and I was usually right.

Lula hustled out of the pizza place with a big pizza box.

"Fresh out of the oven," Lula said. "I had to pay extra for it because they said they were in a position where they had to pay extra for the herbs. Not that I care, because you know how important herbs are in pizza."

She opened the lid and I looked at the pizza. It was spectacular.

"Maybe just one piece," I said.

"Help yourself."

I took a bite and sighed. "Yum."

"You can say that again. This here's my favorite pizza place of all time. It's got something special about it. It must be those herbs."

I looked at the pizza. Basil leaves, oregano, something else.

"You see these green things?" I asked Lula. "What are they?"

"Herbs."

"Yes, but what kind?"

"I'm not actually up on my herbs," Lula said.

I suspected it was weed. Anything this good had to be illegal. I picked them off my piece.

The dogs were restless in the back of the SUV.

"I'm going to walk the pack," I said.

"You need help?"

"I'll be fine. Briggs has been working with them, and they're much better on the leash. Stay here and enjoy the pizza."

I walked one block toward State Street and turned the

corner. I knew there was an empty lot with some scraggly grass halfway down the block. I got to the lot and commanded the dogs to tinkle. They didn't look immediately motivated, so I walked them around a little on the grass and got most of them emptied out. I came back to the Mercedes and found a note on Lula's seat.

Got tired of sitting here so I took the last two pieces of pizza to Buster. Maybe I can get him to adopt a dog. Bring the dogs up when you get back.

Crap.

I looked up at Buster's windows and called Lula. No answer. I didn't trust Buster, and I had no idea what was going on with the hoodie guy. He didn't look any different from the rest of the men on the street, but truth is, those guys were sort of scary-looking.

I crossed the street and pushed the intercom buzzer. No answer. I pushed it again.

"Yes," someone said. Not Buster.

"Is Buster there?"

"No. Come back later."

The intercom went dead.

I leaned on the button.

"*What?*"

"Is Lula there?" I asked.

"Who?"

"Lula."

There was some static and muffled talking. And the door buzzed open. I stepped inside, took Morelli's gun out of my messenger bag, and crept up the stairs, feeling like an idiot. I had eight Chihuahuas and a gun in my hand. Could it get any more ridiculous?

I stopped at the head of the stairs and listened. Dead silence. I stepped into the apartment and my heart flipped. Buster was sitting on a chair from the dining table with his arms handcuffed behind his back. Lula was out cold on the floor, twitching. The hoodie guy had a gun trained on me.

"What's going on?" I said, trying hard to control my voice so I didn't sound like Minnie Mouse.

"Put the gun down," the hoodie guy said.

"Nope."

"I'll shoot you."

"Maybe I'll shoot you first," I said. "Who are you anyway?"

"Miguel."

"What happened to Lula?"

"Stun gun," Miguel said. "I think she knocked herself out when she went down. She got no muscle coordination. What's with the dogs?"

"We thought Buster might want to adopt one."

"Buster's not going to be in shape to take care of a dog. You don't pay up to your creditors, you die. That's our message. We give him girls and drugs, and we expect payment. That's fair, right?"

The Chihuahuas were in a pack, pressed against my ankles, shaking bad enough for their eyes to pop out of their heads and roll across the floor.

"Yeah," I said, "that's fair, but he can't pay you if he's dead."

"Our accountant writes it off as a bad debt and we move on," Miguel said. "You can only spend so much time on these losers. Time is money."

"Okay," I said. "So how about if I drag Lula out of here and let you get on with your business transaction."

"No can do that. It wouldn't be good for my health to leave witnesses like this. I'm going to have to kill all of you. Good thing I got a lot of bullets."

He clearly thought this last statement was hilarious, and he totally cracked himself up.

"Wha," Lula said, the twitches turning to thrashing. "Whaaaa's happening?"

"I might have to shoot her *first*," Miguel said.

Lula's eyes slid half open. "Jesus?"

"No. I'm Miguel," he said.

Lula pushed herself up to a sitting position. "I'm all tingly."

"Stun gun," I said.

"Oh yeah, now I remember. That asshole stun-gunned me."

She got to her feet, tugged her ultrashort spandex skirt down over her ass, adjusted the girls, and glared at Miguel.

"What the hell's the matter with you?" Lula said. "Didn't your mama teach you anything? You got no manners. And where's the rest of my pizza?"

The Chihuahuas had stopped vibrating and were at rigid attention, focused on Miguel, their tiny lips pulled back in a snarl.

"Move to the wall," Miguel said to Lula. "Hands on your head."

"What if I don't want to?"

"I'll shoot cutie pie here."

"Why you gonna shoot her and not me?" Lula asked.

"She's got a gun."

I was still holding the gun on him, and I was feeling freaked. Not only was I totally incompetent with a gun, but I had the gun in one hand and a fistful of leashes attached to Chihuahuas in the other. I dropped the leashes to have better control if I had to shoot, and the Chihuahuas flattened themselves to the floor and stalked Miguel.

"That's friggin' creepy," he said.

"You better believe it," Lula said. "Those aren't any ordinary feral Chihuahuas. Those are minions. Those are trained killer Chihuahuas."

"Maybe I need to shoot them," he said.

Lula went into angry rhinoceros stance. *"Kill!"* she said to the Chihuahuas.

The dogs lunged at Miguel and sank their tiny Chihuahua teeth into his pant legs and held on.

"What the fuck?" Miguel said, trying to shake the dogs off, swinging his gun at them.

I caught movement from my peripheral vision, and Morelli stepped into the room.

"Police," Morelli said. "Drop your weapon."

Miguel turned on Morelli and fired. Morelli and I fired back, and Miguel dropped to the floor.

"Are you okay?" I asked Morelli.

"I swear I felt that bullet skim my ear, but yeah, I'm okay."

Miguel was on the ground, bleeding from a single chest wound. The Chihuahuas were crowded in a corner, vibrating again. A second cop appeared and went to Miguel, cuffing him, checking on the gunshot wound, calling for backup and an EMT.

"Where the heck did you come from?" I asked Morelli.

"I've had Buster's apartment under video surveillance. Mike saw you go in with the dogs and called me. It was dumb luck that I was already on Stark."

"We both fired, but I only see one gunshot wound."

"You took out Buster's toaster. You need to spend more time on the practice range."

"This is just a shame, what with him doing all this bleeding," Lula said. "This looks like a brand-new rug."

. . .

I had the little kitchen table set when Morelli strolled into his house at 5:30. He wrapped his arms around me and kissed me, and lifted the lid on the casserole warming on the stove.

"Beef stew," he said. "Did you make this?"

"Nope. Your mom brought it over."

He got a beer from the fridge and chugged some.

"I'm dying to hear more about Buster."

"Yeah, sorry I couldn't get free to call you. Turns out all the poker players were in business together. Pepper would send his trucks down, and girls and pot would come back along with the salsa. Scootch, Siglowski, Poletti, Ritt, and Buster all had their hands in it. When Poletti got arrested and things went sour, there was a lot of money owed the Mexicans. They sent an enforcer, Miguel, up to collect, and he systematically shot the players when they didn't pay."

"Why didn't they just pay him?"

"The money wasn't there. It wasn't liquid. Briggs had talked Poletti and Pepper into long-term investments and land deals. The Mexicans wanted cash."

"Briggs said Poletti had a ton of money stashed somewhere."

"Not stashed. Invested in a chicken processing plant in Nogales. The plant was a total rust bucket infested with salmonella."

"How's Miguel?"

"He'll live."

"What's going to happen to Buster and Pepper?"

"I don't know. That's for the feds to sort out."

Morelli got a dish and spooned out some stew.

"This is nice. I like coming home to you and stew."

"Maybe we should enlarge our family. What would you think about adopting an attack Chihuahua?"

"By the time I questioned Briggs late this afternoon, there

were only two dogs that hadn't been adopted. And he wanted to keep those two. And he said to tell you he got the job. He's the new weatherman on the evening news. Some cable station. I didn't get all the details. Might have been the local Fox affiliate."

"Briggs is going to be on television? He's only three feet tall. How is he going to reach Chicago on the blue screen when he does the weather?"

"I don't know, but I'm sure it's going to be worth watching."

Morelli finished his dinner and pushed back from the table.

"Briggs said it was his dream job to be on television, and it was number twelve on his bucket list."

"What's with this bucket list thing? Suddenly everyone has a bucket list."

"Don't you have a bucket list?" Morelli asked.

"No. Do you?"

"Yeah."

"Can I see it?"

"It's not written down."

I raised an eyebrow.

"Most of it involves you," Morelli said.

"Oh boy."

Morelli got a pad and a pen from the counter and returned to the table. "I'll write it out for you, but if you read it, you have to do it."

"No way! What kind of bucket list is this?"

"It's my bedroom bucket list."

I wasn't surprised that Morelli would have a bedroom bucket list, but I *was* surprised that there was anything left to put on it.

He slid the pad over to me so I could read the list.

I looked down and grimaced. "I'm definitely not doing this first thing."

"How about if you're asleep?"

"No!"

"Drunk?"

"Under no circumstances."

"I figured," Morelli said, "but it was worth a shot."

"And you're going to have to explain that second thing. I've never heard of the Romanian Slippery Unicorn."

Morelli grinned. "Clear the table and take your clothes off. I'll get the egg timer and a spoon, and I'll demonstrate."

"You're making this up."

"Does it matter?"

"What's the spoon for?"

"The Marshmallow Fluff."

I kicked my shoes off and stripped my shirt over my head. Morelli and Marshmallow Fluff. My kind of dessert.

From
#1 *New York Times* **bestselling author**

Janet Evanovich

and bestselling author LEE GOLDBERG

**Turn the page to start reading
a short story featuring
Kate O'Hare and Nicolas Fox:**

PROS AND CONS

PROS AND CONS

FBI SPECIAL AGENT Kate O'Hare sat in her cramped cubicle at the Federal Building in West Los Angeles and stared at her computer screen. She had an empty Domino's pizza box shoved into her wastebasket and six empty Coke cans lined up on her desk. A half-empty bag of Nacho Cheese Doritos was filed under "N" in her file cabinet, and her keyboard was gummed up with chocolate crumbs from the pack of Oreos she was currently working her way through. Her brown hair was clipped back in a snarly mess, her white shirt had a small pizza sauce smudge on it, and her blue eyes were narrowed in concentration.

Cosmo Uno looked over the five-foot-high partition that separated his cubicle from Kate's. Cosmo was two years older than Kate, and two inches shorter. This meant he was thirty-three, 5' 4" tall, and had to stand on a box to snoop on her.

"Hey, Katie," Cosmo said, "what's shaking? What's doing? What's brewing?"

"I'm working," Kate said, her eyes glued to her screen, not indulging Cosmo by looking at him.

"You shouldn't be eating all those Oreos. They're going to make you fat. Maybe I should help you eat them."

Kate didn't move her head, but she cut her eyes in his direction. "You make a move on my Oreos and I'll shoot you."

"What are you working on? Are you still trying to find Nicolas Fox? Remember when you almost got him in St. Louis, but he disguised himself as a Hall of Fame guy and was doing color commentary in the announcer's booth at Busch Stadium the whole time you were looking for him? That was a good one. And then there was the time you were sure he was trying to steal a giant panda from the National Zoo, but Fox escaped through the Reptile Discovery Center. Ryerson was with you on that raid, right? I hear he ran out of the snake exhibit screaming like a little girl. I wouldn't have screamed. I like snakes. You should take me next time."

"No."

"Okay, I get it. You're a loner. You're the Lone Agent. Get it? *The Lone Agent.*" Cosmo gave a snort of laughter. "That's hilarious."

Kate slumped in her seat.

"I tell everyone I hit the cubicle jackpot on account of I'm next to you," Cosmo said. "Most of the agents on this floor are boring, but you always have something good going on with Fox. You know what I think? I think you're obsessed with him.

I bet you even think about him in the shower. I bet you think about him when you go to bed at night. I think you're hot for him."

Kate opened her top drawer, removed her Glock, and laid it on her desktop alongside her computer. Cosmo considered the gun for a beat, stepped off his box, and returned to his desk.

"Idiot," Kate murmured, stuffing another Oreo into her mouth.

For weeks Kate had been surfing newspaper websites and skimming crime reports from various law enforcement agencies. She was looking for big-money thefts and swindles that were audacious, creative, cocky, and self-indulgent, all trademarks of a Nicolas Fox scheme. It was tedious, laborious, utterly unglamorous work, but she hoped if she could get to the scene of Fox's next crime fast enough, while the tracks were still fresh, she'd have another shot at finally nailing him. She'd been chasing him for three years, and the chase had turned into a game for him, and Cosmo was right, it was an obsession for her. And okay, she thought the guy was kind of cute, and criminally brilliant, but that didn't mean she was hot for him, did it?

. . .

Nicolas Fox, currently posing as Merrill Stubing, wedding planner to the stars, held Caroline Boyett's hand as he led her out of her fiancé's Chicago penthouse living room and onto the rooftop garden. The wedding was set to take place on

Saturday, only five days away, and Nick was thinking about the placement of guests and principals. Placement was important because Nick's crew would begin moving through the penthouse relieving Caroline's fiancé, Milton Royce, of every valuable not bolted into the Carrara marble floors just as Milton's exhibitionist bride started her slow journey to the altar. Guests would be seated in the garden, positioned in such a way that they would be facing Lake Michigan, their backs to the interior of the penthouse. Only the officiating minister would be staring into the condo, and he was part of Nick's crew. Milton would also be facing the living room for a short amount of time, but thanks to his bride's kinky choice of wedding gown, Nick felt certain that Milton's eyes would be glued to her chest.

"This is so exciting," Caroline said. "In five days I'll be Mrs. Royce. Of course it won't be all fun and games. There'll be some work involved. I'll have to change over all my credit cards."

"So tedious," Nick said.

"Yes, and I'll have to be vigilant to make sure they're nothing less than platinum."

Caroline Boyett was going to be fifty-eight-year-old Milton's third and most expensive wife. He acquired her the same way he did his wealth—through a hostile takeover. When Milton met Caroline, she was the young trophy wife of the CEO of a Cleveland dog food company. Royce grabbed the dog food company on the cheap and sold it off for its underlying real estate value. Milton then seduced Caroline away from her husband with the promise of her being squired off to luncheons in his chauffeur-driven Rolls-Royce Phantom and waking up every day in his ten-thousand-square-foot $12.5 million penthouse. The penthouse was atop the Windsong Building, a twenty-story Beaux-Arts masterpiece on Chicago's Lake Shore Drive.

The problem for Milton was now that he'd wowed Caroline with his money, he couldn't put the brakes on her spending. Their wedding was going to cost more than Milton's first two combined, thanks to the grandiose notions of Merrill Stubing, the wedding planner Caroline called her "godsend." Stubing had earned the nickname three months ago when Caroline was standing in front of Neiman Marcus and he'd tackled her out of the way of a speeding Smart car. And as if that dramatic first meeting wasn't fateful enough, it had happened at the exact moment she was beginning to plan the wedding of her dreams. Caroline was envisioning herself on Milton's arm just as Stubing appeared out of nowhere and threw her to the sidewalk.

Truth is, the meeting between Caroline and Stubing wasn't attributable so much to fate as to meticulous planning. Nick and his crew had executed the Smart car stunt with practiced precision. And now Nick was taking the time to ensure that the wedding would unfold with practiced precision too, because the success of his heist depended on it. If Caroline rushed down the aisle, his carefully orchestrated plan would go out the window.

Nick paused in front of the open French doors, and he and Caroline faced Milton, who was standing on the far side of the garden on an X chalked onto the weathered granite tile floor imported from a pillaged Italian villa. Caroline was wearing skinny white jeans, gold strappy five-inch heels, and a magenta see-through blouse. Nick was wearing a form-fitting sheer black silk Armani sweater, tight designer jeans, and Hermès orange suede loafers. Milton was wearing the same thing he'd worn for the past thirty years: black slacks, black dress shoes, and a white shirt. He had a few strands of hair left on his head, a soft roll of fat around his middle, and a stent in one of his coronary arteries.

"In five days this rooftop will be a safety hazard," Nick said to Caroline and Milton. "The inferior steel girders that were used to cut costs will groan under the combined weight of your fat friends and relatives. I calculate there will be in the vicinity of twenty tons on the hoof, but do we care? No, we do not. We will be swept away by the beauty of the occasion. Lucky for you that you hired me. No other wedding planner would have the ability to take your mind off possible imminent death by the use of flowers and twinkle lights." He turned to Caroline. "And you, my dear, will be the ultimate distraction in your one-of-a-kind, shockingly flimsy wedding gown."

Caroline shivered in excited anticipation. "I'll be the talk of the town."

"Dumplink, you'll be the talk of the entire country," Nick said.

Caroline gave him an earnest look. "I want everything to be perfect."

"Perfection is my middle name," Nick told her. "If one of your guests choked on a meatball and died, if one of the millions of candles we'll be using set your living room on fire and everything went to cinders, I'd still make sure your wedding ended in perfection."

"I knew I could count on you," Caroline said.

Milton wistfully looked over the edge of the rooftop at the traffic below.

"If you jump it'll make a mess," Nick told him. "Your head will crack open like a cantaloupe, and they'll have to scrape your brains up with a spatula. And that would be such a shame, because you're a very attractive man when your head is intact."

Nick winked at Milton, and Milton grimaced.

"On the big day I'm going to escort Caroline out of the master suite to the French doors leading to the garden," Nick said. "She's going to stand there and let everyone ogle her. There's going to be a lot of *oohhh* and *ahhh*. And we might need to have some paramedics on hand in case any of the really old geezers has a heart attack when he sees her."

Caroline giggled and clapped her hands. "Yes," she said. "Yes, yes, yes."

Nick smiled. The human race never ceased to amaze him. Particularly, he was intrigued by the way people found each other. In an odd way, Caroline and Milton were a perfect match. They were both totally self-absorbed and ruthless and, by their own standards, very successful. Milton would tolerate Caroline until something new caught his eye, and Caroline would peck away at Milton until he was carrion.

And Nick knew that Milton wasn't the only male on the roof deck at risk of becoming roadkill. Nick was playing a dangerous game of cat and mouse with Kate O'Hare, taunting her with clues designed to annoy. Truth is, he was inexplicably attracted to her. She was a tantalizing mix of girl next door and junkyard dog.

"This is going to be so majestic," Caroline said. "When do I start walking down the aisle?"

"When you hear the band playing Burt Bacharach's 'The Look of Love,' that will be your cue to slowly glide down the aisle," Nick told her. "You will be a vision in white, and you will walk very slowly so you don't slip on the rose petals and break your back. Also if you walk too fast your breasts will bounce out of your bodice."

The slow walk down the aisle was important to Nick because he needed four minutes and eleven seconds of distraction to steal all of Milton's treasures, including his priceless collection of golden Chachapoyan tribal artifacts.

Caroline looked across the terrace to Milton. "Will Burt be here?"

"No, he will not," Milton said. "Burt was unavailable."

Not that Milton had bothered to check. The wedding was already going to be too expensive without flying in celebrities.

Caroline frowned. "It won't be the same without him."

Nick patted her shoulder. "I'll make sure you have the highest quality digital sound system money can buy."

Caroline continued to pout.

"What about Dionne Warwick?" Nick said. "Maybe Dionne is available. Wow, what a voice."

"Yes, Dionne!" Caroline said.

"She's not available either," Milton said, staring daggers at Nick, who pretended not to notice.

"What about her sister Celine?" Caroline asked.

Milton looked incredulously at his fiancée, and for a moment Nick feared he might cancel the wedding on the spot.

"Dionne Warwick doesn't have a sister Celine," Nick told Caroline. "You're thinking of Celine Dion."

"Yes," she said. "How about her?"

Milton looked like he was still contemplating jumping, and Nick saw his whole scheme slipping away.

"Not a good idea," Nick said. "If we had Burt or Dionne or Celine here, no one would notice them. Once you step out in your gown it will be all about you. You'll be the star of the show. Burt would get kicked to the curb. And you know how fragile some of those celebrity egos can be. We wouldn't want to be responsible for Burt's mental breakdown."

"I hadn't thought of that," Caroline said. "I'd never want to do anything to harm Burt."

"And you're the luckiest man in Chicago," Nick said to Milton. "All the other guys out there—well, at least the straight guys—are taking Viagra to get a good stiffy going. We're going to have to tranq you so you don't go animal on us and ravish Caroline on the spot when you see her in her wedding gown."

This got another giggle out of Caroline, and Milton finally smiled. He liked the idea that he might be able to go animal without pharmaceutical assistance.

"Every man on this rooftop is going to be wishing he was in your shoes," Nick said to Milton, "but she's all yours. Caroline will be your greatest, most enviable treasure."

Actually, Caroline and the four-carat diamond she had on her finger would be the *only* treasure left in Milton's penthouse.

The wedding would take place on the lake-facing end of the rooftop garden. The reception would be held in the living room, which had been cleared of its usual furniture and filled with tables and chairs. For the most part, the golden idols were displayed in Milton's study, bedroom, and dining room, areas that were on the city-facing side of the penthouse and would be off limits to the guests, allowing Nick and his crew almost unfettered access to the collection. Nick had already cataloged every item and assigned them to crew members by location.

Nick led Caroline across the garden to Milton. "When the song ends, you'll stand here together, under an obscenely expensive arch of flowers, and you'll speak your vows in the flattering glow of moonbeams and candlelight."

"I could cry just thinking about it," Caroline said.

"Me too," Milton said, contemplating the price of the flowers and candlelight, relieved that at least the moonbeams might be free.

Nick put his hand to his heart, showing that he was also overwhelmed with the wonderfulness of it all. "And here's the big finale, are you ready? I just love this part. When the minister declares you man and wife, the instant you kiss, the band will play a triumphant version of Neil Diamond's 'Sweet

Caroline' and the sky will erupt in fireworks from a barge on the lake."

"Will it be Neil?" Caroline asked.

"No, it will not," Milton said. "He doesn't do weddings."

"But he sang at the wedding in *Saving Silverman*," Caroline said.

"That was a movie," Milton said. "He doesn't do weddings in real life."

"He didn't in the movie either. They kidnapped him," Nick said.

Milton held his ground. "I am not kidnapping Neil Diamond."

"You would if you loved me," Caroline said.

"The band might drown Neil out, anyway," Nick said.

"You're right as always," Caroline said. "I'll settle for the band."

The way she put it, it seemed like Milton was getting off easy only having to pay for a band. So everyone was happy, especially Nick. Between the fireworks and the music, nobody would hear the bang when he blew open Milton's safe.

· · ·

Kate set a large coffee with cream and a small white bakery bag on her desk and booted up her computer.

Cosmo popped up and looked over the cubicle wall at her. "It's Friday, so you must have a cheese Danish in that bag."

"I don't get a cheese Danish every Friday."

"Yes, you do. Onion bagel on Monday, Tuesday, Wednesday, and Thursday. And a cheese Danish on Friday. Am I right, or am I right?"

"You're right. Don't you have work to do? Don't you have any pending files?"

"I was involved in the Ramos Green investigation, but Green died yesterday. He accidentally walked into a bullet. You live by the sword, and you die by the sword. What goes around comes around. Am I right, or am I right?"

Kate blew out a sigh. She tried hard to be a team player. And she wanted to like Cosmo. She really did. But jeez Louise, he was annoying. "You're right."

"So what about you?" Cosmo asked. "Are you making any progress with Fox? Are you closing in on him? Are you ready to pounce? You're going to pounce on him and nail him, right? *BAM!*"

Kate looked at Cosmo and wondered if he'd shut up if she punched him really hard in the face. Probably not. She would feel good, but it would be wasted effort. And then she'd feel guilty, and she'd have to buy him a bagel or something.

"So what are your plans for the weekend?" he asked.

Kate opened her coffee and took the cheese Danish out of its bag. "Nothing special."

"How did I know that? You're going to work, right? Not me. All work and no play makes Cosmo an unhappy boy. I have a smokin' date with a sizzling chick. Runner-up for Miss Lompoc. If they gave extra points for the biggest gazongas she would have won, if you know what I mean."

"Gee, I'd like to chat some more but I have stuff to do," Kate said.

"I bet you're wondering how a little guy like me can always get these hot dates."

"Actually, no."

"It's the size of my gun. Right off the bat, I show them my gun."

"I tried that once," Kate said, "but the guy I was talking to went to the men's room and didn't come back."

Three cups of coffee and a long morning of dead ends later, Kate stumbled onto a lead. "Holy Love Boat! Set a course for adventure!" she sang out. She did a happy dance while she waited for the article to print, ripped it out of the machine, and ran down the hall to her boss, Agent in Charge Carl Jessup.

Jessup had positioned his desk so that he faced the window and had his back to the door, a furniture arrangement he'd been told was horrible *feng shui* and was probably responsible for his chronic constipation, mild gingivitis, and the unusually high number of birds that flew into the bulletproof glass. But he didn't care. He liked to watch the traffic inching to and from the San Fernando Valley on the 405 freeway. He said it helped him think.

"I found Nick," Kate declared, waving the paper.

Jessup swiveled in his seat to look at her. He was in his fifties and had a face like a photograph that someone had crumpled up and tried to smooth out again.

"Congratulations. Where is he?"

"Chicago."

"How do you know?"

"It's a long story."

"I like long stories, particularly ones that end with big arrests."

"Four months ago Jerry Bodie, a guy who made his fortune selling timeshares to people who couldn't afford them, hired a high-end moving company to transport his classic car collection from Miami to his new home in Las Vegas. The cars never got there. The transport company was a fraud. It caught my attention because Bodie is just the kind of person Nick likes to swindle."

"Rich?"

"And crooked, ruthless, and greedy. The man Bodie hired to move his cars was Tod Stiles. That's the name of a character from the old TV series *Route 66.*"

"I loved that show. I don't remember the names of the heroes, but I'll never forget their car, a '61 Corvette. I wanted one just like it. Hell, I still do."

Kate tried out a mental image of Jessup in a '61 Corvette and came up short. She could better see him in a '54 Buick that was dragging a muffler and belching black exhaust.

"Yeah, well, anyway, I sent Bodie a photo of Nick and got a positive ID," she told Jessup. "Nick was Stiles. He probably had the cars sold before Bodie gave him the keys."

"How does a swindle that happened four months ago in Miami put Fox in Chicago today?"

"I checked out the passenger lists of every flight, train, boat, and bus out of Miami that left within twenty-four hours of

Bodie giving Nick his cars. I ran those lists against the index of characters in *The Complete Directory of Episodic Television Shows*. It's Fox's MO. He picks his aliases from old TV series."

"I knew that," Jessup said.

"Anyway I got one hit. Lewis Erskine flew to Chicago."

Jessup nodded. "Erskine was the hero of *The FBI*. Used to drive a new Ford around D.C. landmarks at the end of each episode."

"Are cars the only thing you watch TV shows for?"

"I like cars," Jessup said. "What else do you have?"

"Erskine never left Chicago. Mickey Mouse, Archie Bunker, Darrin Stephens never left. No television character left Chicago in that time frame."

"So in your mind this means Fox is in Chicago?"

Kate presented him with the computer printout. "This means he's in Chicago! For weeks I've sifted through Chicago papers for potential crimes, and I came up with zip, bupkis, nada, nothing. And then today while I was doing my usual fast scan I accidentally logged on to the Style section of one of the papers and this popped up on the first page."

"'Caroline Boyett to Wed Milton Royce'?"

"Look at the photo!"

"Lucky Milton," Jessup said.

Kate did an eye roll. "Look at the man with Boyett. It's Nick Fox."

Jessup squinted at the printout. "Are you sure? It says the guy is Merrill Stubing."

"Merrill Stubing was the captain on *The Love Boat*. The

article goes on to say how Merrill Stubing rescued Caroline from being hit by a car in front of Neiman's, and now he's her wedding planner."

"The guy looks poofie."

"It's Fox! He's a master of disguise."

"So I've been told."

Okay, so the picture was a little grainy, like it had been taken with a cell phone and not intended for newsprint, but Kate was still almost 50 percent sure it was Fox.

"Can you fact-check this a little before I fund a trip to Chicago?" Jessup asked.

"Yessir. Absolutely."

Kate rushed back to her cubicle and researched Milton Royce. The man had lots of money, two ex-wives, an extensive art collection, and what looked like the skimpiest combover in the history of hair. She could find no further information on the wedding planner. She returned to Jessup and asked him for a contact in the Chicago office.

Jessup scrawled a name and number on a scrap of paper. "Reginald Gunter," he said. "He's a good man. Don't drive him nuts."

"Fox is in Chicago," Kate said. "I feel it in my gut. I know he's there."

"Back in the day, when I was a special agent, I was convinced that a bank robber I was chasing was hiding out in Pittsburgh. I led a full-scale raid on a downtown hotel based on a pizza delivery order that I was sure he'd made. Meatballs, anchovies, and pineapple."

"Were your instincts right?"

"No. It was a major screwup that got my boss transferred to Sitka, Alaska." Jessup paused for effect. "I hate the cold, Kate."

Kate traipsed back to her cubby and called Gunter.

"I think Nicolas Fox is posing as the wedding planner for the Royce wedding," she told Gunter. "I need you to go to the Windsong Building and get an ID from the concierge. If you don't have a photo on file I can send one to you."

"I don't see Nicolas Fox as a wedding planner," Gunter said. "What's in it for him? He's a scammer."

"He's also a thief. What does Milton Royce have?"

"Lots of money. And a collection of golden idols."

"Then that's what he's after."

"Do you want me to approach Royce or his fiancée?"

"Negative," Kate said. "I don't want to take a chance on spooking Fox."

"It's going to be a zoo in that building," Gunter said. "The wedding is tomorrow night. We got an alert on it. It's going to be a media circus."

Kate paced for an hour and a half while she waited for Gunter to call back.

"You need to relax," Cosmo said, looking in on her. "You're leaking nervous energy, and it's giving me eczema. You want to know what I do to relax?"

"No! Do *not* tell me."

The phone rang, and Kate snatched it up.

"I couldn't get a positive ID," Gunter said. "The concierge wasn't sure. He said the wedding planner is flamboyant and has spiked-up blond hair, and the guy in the photo looks normal. Personally, though, I think you might be on to something. I couldn't find anything to verify Merrill Stubing or his business. I'll check around some more tomorrow."

• • •

At five A.M. Kate dragged herself out of bed, got dressed in the clothes she'd worn the day before, and shuffled into the kitchen to make coffee. She'd thrashed around all night, unable to get Fox out of her head.

"I hate him," she said to her Mr. Coffee machine. "He's totally corrupt. He has no regard for the law. He's arrogant. And he's *cute*."

Deep inside, Kate knew that Nick's cuteness was the single attribute that annoyed her the most. Criminals were not supposed to be attractive. At least, not as attractive as Fox. Fox was the physical embodiment of her dream man. How crapola was that? When she had time, she was going to have to reconstruct her dream man. Change his hair from brown to red. Give him a less than perfect body. And no more dreamy brown eyes. No more smiling, kissable mouth. Her dream man would have to have a mouth like a frog's, thanks to Nicolas Fox.

"Ugh," Kate said, grabbing the last yogurt out of the fridge. "Nicolas Fox is scum."

She took her coffee and yogurt to her laptop and pulled up Chicago news. She bypassed the night's killings and found a gossipy feature on the front page of the Style section.

People will be lining up along Lake Shore Drive tonight for a fireworks show courtesy of Milton Royce, the so-called "King of Hostile Takeovers." The fireworks, launched from a barge on Lake Michigan, are part of Royce's extravagant wedding ceremony, which is being held tonight at his twentieth-floor penthouse atop the famed Windsong Building. Controversy still surrounds the city's unprecedented decision to allow the fireworks over the strenuous objections of residents concerned about the increased noise and traffic.

The article went on to talk about accusations that city officials were too beholden to Royce, a big contributor to local political campaigns, and how the wedding, with its exclusive guest list, was considered *the* social event of the season.

"This has Nicolas Fox written all over it," Kate said to herself. "He's planning something big when the wedding is in full swing. I'm at least seventy percent sure."

She closed the Chicago news site and went to a travel site. Ten minutes later she was booked on a midmorning flight to Chicago and had a discounted room at the DoubleTree. It was Saturday, and she hadn't heard back from Jessup about funding an op, so she was on her own. She was going to Chicago on her own time and with her own money. She wasn't following protocol and it was probably a dumb thing to do, but she was doing it anyway. At the very least, she'd get to see some fireworks.

• • •

It was close to six o'clock when Kate checked in to her hotel. There'd been a delay at LAX that stretched the four-hour flight to five hours, there was a two-hour time difference between L.A. and Chicago, and the taxi ride into the city had been interminable.

She tossed her carry-on suitcase onto the bed and unpacked her Kevlar vest and FBI windbreaker. Not that she was planning on raiding Chicago's wedding of the year, but you never knew when a Kevlar vest would come in handy. And okay, there was a remote possibility that she might raid the wedding.

She realized she hadn't taken her phone off plane mode, changed her settings, and immediately got a message with photo from Gunter. The photo showed the wedding planner in tight jeans and a fitted silk shirt. His hair was blond and spiked. *Caught him helping with a flower delivery,* the message read. *What do you think?*

Kate called Gunter. "It's him," she said. She was almost 85 percent sure. "How quickly can you assemble a strike team and get them on scene?"

"Forty-five minutes to an hour. Assembling the team isn't the problem. The problem is disrupting a wedding on private property without cause and without appropriate authorization."

"Understood. I'm in Chicago. I just arrived. I'll go in alone, and I'll be discreet. All your men have to do is seal the building from the outside. How far is the DoubleTree from the Windsong?"

"Not far. It's a short walk."

"I'll meet you at the Windsong."

Kate jammed her vest and her windbreaker into a tote bag, shoved a couple extra ammo clips in, and grabbed a bag of chips from the minibar. She ducked into the bathroom and checked herself out. No mustard on her shirt from the ham and cheese sandwich she'd had for lunch. No sandwich bits stuck between her teeth. Her hair was no messier than usual. She swiped on some lip gloss and decided this was as good as she was going to get under the circumstances. Heck, it was pretty much as good as she got under *any* circumstances.

She reached the Windsong ahead of the team and hung in the lobby, watching guests arrive. The concierge gave her the fish eye, so she moved outside. While she waited, she called Jessup.

"I'm in Chicago," she said. "I'm visiting an old college friend, and I happened to run into Gunter, who happened to get a photo of the wedding planner. And I'm almost eighty-seven percent sure it's Fox."

"Eighty-seven percent?"

"Maybe it could go as high as ninety-two percent."

There was a vague noise on the other end of the line.

"Was that a groan, sir?" she asked. "Are you okay?"

"You're killing me."

"Just doing my job."

"And you're calling me *why*?"

"I was sort of thinking of inviting myself to the wedding. It's tonight, and I've got a strike team assembled."

"O'Hare, you can't just barge in on Milton Royce's wedding. Do you have cause?"

"He has a large collection of golden idols."

"I don't care if he has a large *dick* collection. You need a good reason to enter. For that matter you have at least eight percent doubt that it's Fox."

"My plan is to sneak in and see for myself before I call the team in. I'll be discreet."

"You're lots of things," Jessup said. "Discreet isn't one of them. I need permission for this. Hang tight while I make a phone call."

Kate disconnected and looked at her watch. She saw a van parking in a red zone at the end of the block and walked toward it. Gunter got out of the van and met her halfway.

"We're in a slowdown while we get permission," Kate said.

. . .

Caroline was wearing a tiny white lace thong, diamond drop earrings, and white satin kitten heels. The kitten heels were a concession to Milton so she wouldn't tower over him on their special day. She was in her dressing room with Nick, her arms outstretched, waiting for him to help her wriggle into her gown. Wedding guests were congregating on the other side of the oversize mahogany double doors that opened onto the master suite. Music and conversation drifted through the doors. Nick looked at Caroline and wondered how he was going to get her into the gown. He was very good at getting women *out* of their clothes but had little to no practice getting the clothes back on them.

"Be careful not to mess my hair," Caroline said. "It took *forever* for Maurice to get it to look like this."

Nick thought Maurice should have taken less time. Caroline looked like she was wearing the wedding cake on her head. Maurice had piled up the huge mass of platinum blond hair and decorated it with pink flowers and sparkle dust.

"We'll go up from the bottom," Nick said, hoping it was a good idea. "I'll hold the gown and you step into it."

He went down to one knee, and Caroline carefully stepped into the circle of silk, bringing her hoo-ha two inches from the tip of Nick's nose. Nick worked the material up to her ass, took a deep breath, and tugged. He was wearing a white tuxedo with a black tie and a pink handkerchief tucked into his breast pocket, and he'd sweated through his shirt from the exertion of remembering he was supposed to be gay. He slipped the gossamer-thin spaghetti straps over Caroline's shoulders, she arranged her double D's, and Nick zipped her up, thinking it would be a miracle if the straps held.

Caroline looked at herself in the ornate gold-framed full-length mirror. "Do you think I look fat in this gown?"

"Fat" wasn't the first adjective that came to Nick's mind. The first adjective was *YIKES!* And that was followed by *HOLY CRAP!!*

"You're not fat," Nick said. "You're stunning. No one will be able to take their eyes off you." And this was true because she was close to naked, with a scandalous amount of boobage showing. The gown was cut so low it was practically frontless and backless. The white satin material clung to her like plastic wrap, and the slit in the skirt was so high Nick was afraid the little man in the boat might jump out at any moment.

"This will be a night to remember," Nick said. "You stay here and think beautiful thoughts. I'll come get you when everything is in place."

He left Caroline in her suite, closing the doors behind him, and walked down the short hall to the living room. Guests were still hanging out, guzzling drinks and scarfing down hors d'oeuvres while his crew of a dozen uniformed caterers mingled among them with serving trays. He caught the eye of one of the servers, a pickpocket named Hoppy Hayward, and gave him a slight nod. It was the signal that it was time for the caterers to drift off to the kitchen and begin stuffing plastic trash bags with the Styrofoam packing pellets they'd stashed in the crates of linens and dishes.

Nick continued out to the rooftop garden, where Milton was knocking back his third martini of the hour. Milton was standing under a white gazebo that was sagging under a massive amount of floral color and twinkle lights. A band was blasting out Barbra Streisand songs, which were being sung by a Dean Martin impersonator. Paper lanterns swayed overhead, in imminent danger of catching fire from the hundreds of flaming candles set out on high-top tables and nestled in elaborate flower arrangements.

Nick approached Milton and gave him a wide smile. "Showtime! Are you ready?"

"Good God," Milton said, not looking all that happy.

"It's not too late," Nick said, nudging Milton with his

elbow. "You could walk away from all this and meet me at the bar on the corner. You know what they say: The only difference between a straight man and a gay man is a six-pack of beer."

"Get away from me," Milton said. "Stand on the other side of the room. The best part of this wedding is that I'll never have to see you again."

"I'll take that as a yes to my original question, so we're good to go." Nick said.

Nick returned to Caroline, ushering her out of the bedroom and through the living room. He signaled to the band and they went into "The Look of Love." Caroline and Nick paused at the French doors.

"This is it," Nick said. "Enjoy the moment."

Caroline nodded, gave Nick's hand a squeeze, and took a tiny step onto the rose-petal-strewn pink velvet carpet that led down the aisle. Everyone turned to look at her. There was a moment of stunned silence, then a collective gasp. Milton's jaw dropped and his eyes bulged. The lounge singer stumbled over a lyric. The wedding photographer couldn't snap pictures fast enough.

This is great, Nick thought. Everyone's happy. Caroline feels like a total sexpot. Milton is beside himself to be marrying a total sexpot. And the guests are on the edge of their seats, not sure where to look first, waiting for a nipple slip, hoping to catch a glimpse of the bride's wedding-day taco. And Nick was happy because all eyes would be glued to Caroline for the next four minutes and eleven seconds. He turned on his heel and

333

met his crew coming out of the kitchen with the trash bags stuffed with packing pellets.

"You have four minutes, starting now," Nick said, tapping his watch. "Go!"

The crew split, working room by room, grabbing idols, packing them safely into the bags, and carting them to the freight elevator off the kitchen and then down to the garage.

Nick went to Milton's office, removed a nineteenth-century painting from the wall behind Milton's desk, and exposed a wall safe. The theft of the golden idols would make splashy news, but the real moneymaker for Nick was a flash drive that Milton kept in his safe. The flash drive held all of the account numbers and passwords to Milton's offshore bank accounts. Nick took a handful of explosive Semtex putty out of his pocket and applied it to the surface of the safe.

• • •

Kate looked at her watch for the hundredth time. Why wasn't Jessup calling her? Did he realize time was ticking away? She could hear the band playing twenty floors above her, and half a block away she had two vans filled with agents playing craps and catching up on their Twitter accounts. She went inside the Windsong Building and approached the mountain of a man who was guarding the elevators. She flashed her badge and identified herself.

"I need to go up," she said.

"I bet."

"I'm serious."

"Nice try. Merrill Stubing, the wedding planner, warned me about you." The guard held up a photograph of Kate that had been lifted off her sister's Facebook page. "He said the paparazzi might show up pretending to be feds."

Kate looked past the guard and stared at the bank of monitors behind him. A uniformed female caterer was standing at a loading dock in the underground garage. The woman was handing bulging plastic bags to a guy who leaned out of the open rear end of a panel van that said YUMMY GOOD CATERING on the side. One of the bags split open, but the guy caught what was inside before it hit the floor. The object in his hands was a golden head about the size of a honeydew melon. On the monitor, two more caterers emerged from the service elevator and climbed into the van. The back doors of the van closed, and it pulled away. Another Yummy Good Catering van took its place from somewhere else in the garage.

"Robbery in progress," Kate said into her Bluetooth earpiece. She was 98 percent sure. "Seal all exits."

She turned and ran from the lobby and around the corner of the building to the back alley just as a van was heading for the street. Kate slipped into the garage before the roll-up door could drop down and seal the ramp. The van drove off. The door closed behind her.

She hurried down the ramp, slowing as she neared the first parking level. The woman was still on the loading dock and was now passing bags to a man in the second van.

Kate stepped forward, gun drawn. "Halt, FBI."

At that same instant the elevator doors opened. Four more caterers came out, saw Kate, and froze.

"Run!" someone yelled.

Everyone took off in different directions. Kate couldn't chase them all, and she couldn't lawfully shoot any of them, so she shot out the tires of the van instead to make sure it wouldn't be going anywhere. The Yummy Good Catering van slumped to the ground like a weary cow. The gunshots echoed through the garage.

Special Agent Gunter was in Kate's earpiece. "What's going on down there? I'm in the lobby, and I just saw you shoot a catering truck."

"They aren't caterers. They're thieves. They've scattered in the garage. Detain anyone who tries to leave."

Kate stepped into the service elevator and pressed the button for the penthouse.

• • •

Nick placed the blasting caps in the Semtex putty and emerged from Milton's office just as "The Look of Love" was ending and the last of the crew members slipped out the front door with their bags. He glanced at his watch. They'd pulled off the heist with eleven seconds to spare. He walked across the living room and checked on the progress of the wedding ceremony outside. Caroline was radiating sex at the altar, and Milton was beaming.

Nick felt his cell phone buzz with a text message from his crew leader. "The FBI is here! They're everywhere!"

Nick calmly went back to Milton's office, passed the safe rigged with plastic explosives, and strolled out onto the empty, city-facing side of the penthouse deck. He looked over the edge and saw the task force vehicles on the street. The building was surrounded.

· · ·

The elevator opened at the penthouse, and Kate stepped out into a short hallway. Two caterers rushed at her, knocking her out of the way. They jumped into the elevator, the doors closed, and the elevator descended. Kate walked through the living room and peeked out at the rooftop garden, where the ceremony was coming to an end. She scanned the crowd for Nick.

"Do you take this man to be your lawfully wedded husband?" a jowly, black-robed minister asked the bride's cleavage.

"I do," she said.

"By the power vested in me by the State of Illinois," the minister said, "I now pronounce you man and wife. You may kiss the bride."

The bride and groom kissed. The band and the singer belted out "Sweet Caroline." Fireworks erupted over Lake Michigan, and the penthouse shook.

Kate knew it wasn't fireworks that rocked the building. It

was a blast that came from the other side of the penthouse. She hurried across the living room, slipped on a splotch of spilled cocktail sauce, and clipped a tray of canapés that had been left on a serving table. Kate and the canapés went down to the floor in a clattering mess of tiny meatballs, avocado and spinach dip, smoked duck in soy sauce, and prosciutto cheese balls.

"Freaking fudge!" Kate said. "Damn. *Mother fornicator.*"

She scrambled to her feet and limped into the short hall that led to the master suite. Smoke was spilling out from under the closed and locked mahogany doors. Kate kicked the doors open, saw the scorched wall and the blown-open safe, and knew why Nick had planned a finale of fireworks. It was genius, Kate thought. You had to admire the man's style.

French doors opened off the master suite onto a balcony on which Kate could see Nick Fox facing her. He was sitting on the four-foot-high masonry balcony wall, his back to the city skyline. He smiled at Kate and gestured to her shirt.

"I see you tried the canapés," he said. "I made them myself."

Kate looked down at her splattered jacket and shirt, swiped up a glob of green and white goo and tasted it.

"Avocado and spinach dip," she said. "Needs salt."

"You'll have to let me cook you dinner sometime."

"I'll pass on that. I'm not crazy about prison ingredients."

"Neither am I." He glanced over his shoulder at the twenty-story drop to the ground.

Kate didn't like what the glance implied. "Don't do it, Nick."

"Would you miss me?"

"Yes!"

"How much would you miss me?" he asked her. "A lot?"

"Don't push it."

"Admit it, deep down inside you like me. You think I'm cute."

Kate narrowed her eyes. "Are you going to jump, or what?"

Nick smiled, sent her a little wave, swung his legs over the wall, and disappeared from view.

Kate felt her heart give a painful contraction. "No!" she shouted. "You idiot! I didn't really want you to jump!"

She crossed the balcony to the wall and peered over at Nick in time to see his customized handheld parachute open. She watched him for a minute as he glided toward the skyscraper canyons of downtown Chicago, ate a meatball that was stuck to her jacket, and then called Gunter. Next in line was a call to Jessup.

"I tried calling you," Jessup said, "but you weren't picking up."

Kate filled him in. "Gunter is coordinating a chase with cooperating local law enforcement," she said.

"If you need help with follow-up, I can send someone," Jessup said. "Cosmo, maybe."

"No! *Not Cosmo.*"

• • •

The FBI, the Chicago Police Department, and the Cook County Sheriff's Office all put choppers in the air, but they couldn't find any sign of Nick or his parachute. Kate led a search of the surrounding neighborhood, but she knew it was futile. There was too much ground to cover, and Nick had a head start. So she armed a bunch of agents with copies of *The Complete Directory of Episodic Television Shows* and sent them off to look for TV characters trying to leave town by planes, trains, or automobiles.

Somehow all of Nick's crew had managed to slip out of the building, but a third of the golden idols were left behind on the loading dock, so it wasn't a complete loss. And Kate had the satisfaction of knowing that her instincts had been 100 percent right.

She straggled back to her hotel just as the sun was coming up. She was exhausted, and done with smelling like cocktail meatballs. She wanted to shuck her food-stained clothes, take a hot shower, and wash the spinach dip out of her hair.

She unlocked her door, stepped into the room, and froze. There were Toblerone wrappers on the bed, room service dishes on the table, a bouquet of roses, and an unopened bottle of champagne chilling in a bucket of ice. Her first thought in her sleep-deprived state was that she'd walked into the wrong room. She was about to double-check the number on the door when she realized that a pink handkerchief was tied like a ribbon around the champagne bottle. She'd seen the handkerchief before . . . in the breast pocket of Nick's white tuxedo.

Un-freaking-believable, she thought. While she'd been dragging her butt all over town looking for him, the jerk had been in her room ordering room service and raiding her minibar. She had to give credit where credit was due. The man had Volkswagen-size cojones. Really big brass ones.

She drew her gun and looked under the bed, in the closet, and in the bathroom. No Nick. But he'd for sure been there. She sat on her bed and plucked a card off her pillow. In a masculine scrawl she'd come to recognize, Nick Fox had written *Looking forward to next time.*

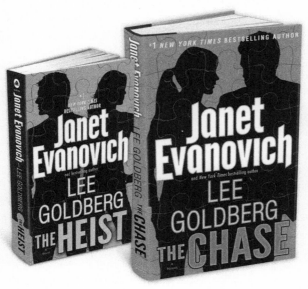

ABOUT THE AUTHOR

JANET EVANOVICH is the #1 *New York Times* best-selling author of the Stephanie Plum series, the Fox and O'Hare series with co-author Lee Goldberg, the Lizzy and Diesel series, twelve romance novels, the Alexandra Barnaby novels and Trouble Maker graphic novel, and *How I Write: Secrets of a Best-selling Author.*

www.evanovich.com
Facebook.com/JanetEvanovich
@JanetEvanovich